SECOND CHANCE WITH THE FIREFIGHTER

AMIE DENMAN

HEARTWARMING

If you purchased this book without a cover you should be aware that this book is stolen property. It was reported as "unsold and destroyed" to the publisher, and neither the author nor the publisher has received any payment for this "stripped book."

Recycling programs for this product may not exist in your area.

ISBN-13: 978-1-335-46048-6

Second Chance with the Firefighter

For questions and comments about the quality of this book, please contact us at CustomerService@Harlequin.com.

Harlequin Enterprises ULC
22 Adelaide St. West, 41st Floor
Toronto, Ontario M5H 4E3, Canada
www.Harlequin.com

HarperCollins Publishers
Macken House, 39/40 Mayor Street Upper,
Dublin 1, D01 C9W8, Ireland
www.HarperCollins.com

Printed in U.S.A.

“Thank you for inspiring Teddy...”

“It was fun.”

“He talked a lot about you—about the flower camp—last night and sang the ladybug song.”

Lauren’s smile lit up. “I hoped the kids would like that. I don’t have much experience with little kids, and it’s been a while since—”

Seth’s gaze locked on hers for a moment, and he felt the old tug of connection they’d always shared. This was getting dangerous.

He should walk away right now, but the scent of the earthy vegetables all around them took him back to summer days gardening or lying on the lawn. He’d missed those days so much, had let that bitter loss pile up with his other losses.

“Since we were kids,” he said, finishing her sentence.

“Yes,” she said. “But it’s nice to...be talking to you again.”

Seth swallowed. Lauren’s visit to his house had made it clear she wanted to make some sort of apology, but what would be the point? Encouraging her now was just asking for trouble.

Dear Reader,

Thank you for joining me on this Niagara Falls journey. *Second Chance with the Firefighter* is the fourth book in the Meet Me at Niagara Falls miniseries, and I hope you'll love this sweet story of childhood best friends rediscovering each other.

Niagara Falls is a beautiful place to visit, and not just for the world-famous waterfalls. The region has lovely parks, cities, trails and wineries. One of my favorite aspects of both the Canadian and American sides is the gardens—that's why one of the main characters in this book is a horticulturist! The Canadian side has gorgeous manicured gardens all along the bluff overlooking the falls. On the American side, the sprawling park has wonderful trees and perennials, and the many pathways invite visitors to wander. You can fall in love at Niagara Falls in more ways than one!

I hope you enjoy this romance.

Amie

Amie Denman is the author of over fifty contemporary romances. A devoted traveler, she loves reading and writing books you could take on vacation. Amie lives on the shores of Lake Erie with her husband, sons, extended family and numerous pets. She loves playing outside, running and paddleboarding. Her favorite indoor activities are reading and writing (of course!), sewing and crocheting, and playing her antique Steinway grand piano.

Books by Amie Denman

Harlequin Heartwarming

Meet Me at Niagara Falls

Falling for Her Fake Fiancé
Falling for Her Ranger
Christmas with the Single Dad

Return to Christmas Island

I'll Be Home for Christmas
Home for the Holidays
A Merry Little Christmas
Last Summer on Christmas Island
Under the Mistletoe

Cape Pursuit Firefighters

In Love with the Firefighter
The Firefighter's Vow
A Home for the Firefighter

Visit the Author Profile page
at Harlequin.com for more titles.

Writing a novel worth reading takes a team, and
I want to thank the wonderful people at Harlequin
for their creativity, attention to detail,
professionalism and encouragement.
Special thanks to my editor Dana Grimaldi,
who has been by my side for more than twenty books.
Her wisdom, talent and excellent advice have
made me a better writer with every chapter.

CHAPTER ONE

HOW LONG SHOULD a house sit in its quiet grief, coffee still in the pot, a book with a bookmark stuck forever at page seventy-five? Like a life stopped on that page. Lauren Benedict stood in her grandmother's kitchen barely eight hours after the sweet lady had—suddenly, it seemed—passed away. She'd come to make sure the windows were closed, doors locked, lights out. And, of course, to rescue Lord Henry.

Lauren gripped the back of the kitchen chair. The table was clean, not even a breakfast crumb to be brushed away. That was her grandmother. Even when her chest pain was bad enough for her to call 911 that morning, she'd probably put her coffee cup in the dishwasher first. Needing to do something, Lauren opened the dishwasher. Yes. A coffee cup, a toast dish, a butter knife. It had been a typical morning in the pretty kitchen with the yellow walls and the curtains with their polka dots like little bursts of sunshine.

Her grandmother had always been this way.

Friends were always welcome in this kitchen. The piercing pain in Lauren's heart stabbed a little deeper when she remembered those summer days, the breeze blowing the curtains over the herbs that grew on the windowsill. Even during the long winters in Niagara Falls, New York, right in the "snowbelt" with its duly earned reputation for heavy snow, Grandma Vera had houseplants blooming and a warm welcome at the ready.

It was June now and roses bloomed outside, sending their beautiful fragrance on the evening air. But her grandmother wouldn't be there to smell them.

Sobs erupted from her chest and Lauren pushed the dishwasher's door closed and put her head on the counter. This was where she'd learned to chop vegetables and prepare those windowsill herbs. Lauren had learned to love cooking and growing things right here in this kitchen. Had played hundreds of card games at the spotless table behind her—war, gin rummy, even poker, which had made her feel very grown-up one time when her grandmother was babysitting her and her sister.

Her sister, Maggie, a year older, had never let her win at cards, but her grandmother said that made Lauren a smarter player. She thought of her friend Seth playing cards with them. She knew he'd let her win more than once. He'd always been on her side.

Lauren pulled herself up, the childhood memory reminding her that she had to be strong. There was so much to do to prepare for the funeral. She'd been the one to take the call from the hospital and then make the sad call to her parents, who were, right now, on a flight from Florida. Her sister would drive home tomorrow, husband and kids in tow, from Indiana, where she'd lived for almost ten years. Maggie had gone off to college and never come back for any length of time.

Everyone knew why.

Right now, it was just Lauren, alone in her grandmother's house, feeling like she was a ghost, a silent visitor who suddenly didn't belong. She shoved off from the kitchen counter and grabbed a tissue from the box that always sat on the table just inside the back door. She blew her nose and tried to quell the storm of emotions the sight of her grandmother's gardening gloves stirred up. And her favorite rose trimmers. Her bright yellow garden clogs next to Lauren's purple ones that she always kept there, just in case she and Grandma Vera wanted to go outside right after the rain and smell the fresh, dewy roses. Lauren didn't have a garden at her apartment, so she and her grandmother shared the flowers in the large backyard that sloped down to the lake.

Lauren took a deep breath and let it out slowly, trying to stall the tears. She couldn't fall apart at every little thing. She was here to close windows and lock doors. Lauren went into the living room with its floral-patterned chairs and hand-crocheted afghans folded and checked the wide bay windows behind the couch. They were open "just a crack" as Grandma Vera liked them so she could get fresh air without risking the rain coming in.

"Oh," she said, dropping to her knees when she saw the ginger cat in his bed by the window. "Lord Henry, I didn't forget you."

Grandma Vera's cat had vast white patches mixed with dark orange—almost the color of the warm hardwood floors. Grandma always said the white patches kept her from tripping over the cat in the dark. Lord Henry stood on his hind legs and reached both white paws toward her, like a child asking to be picked up. Lauren picked him up and held him close as she knelt on the hardwood floor.

"Do you know?" she asked, her fresh tears dampening the cat's fur rubbing her cheek. She couldn't even finish the sentence. The cat knew. He was only four or five years old, and he'd been beloved by her grandmother that entire time, always on her lap or sleeping on her bed. He'd need a home now, and, of course, it would be with Lauren. Her grandmother had always insisted she wanted Lauren to take Lord Henry home if anything ever happened to her. She'd said so many times, especially in the last year as she'd struggled with heart disease. Lauren had checked on her daily, driven her to doctor's appointments and was her emergency contact.

She couldn't help her grandmother now, but she could love Lord Henry.

"We're going to be okay," she assured the cat. "You can come home with me tonight. I just need to check a few more rooms and then we'll gather up your things."

She put Lord Henry on the couch, but he jumped down and followed her. Lauren closed the bathroom window, turned off the closet light in the bedroom, poked her head into the spare room where she'd slept so many nights and then circled back to the pantry off the kitchen. A litter box was behind a little divider in the corner, and a nearby shelf held a bag of dry food and cans of wet food. There was a bag of treats, too. The cat pawed at her leg and Lauren took down the treat bag.

"Why not?" she asked. "I know you're sad, too."

She gave the cat a treat and then picked up the box of wet food cans.

And then she stopped cold.

Under the box holding a dozen cans was a white envelope with LAUREN written in bold letters. She put the box on the floor and picked up the envelope, hesitating before opening it. Knowing her grandmother, it was special instructions about caring for Lord Henry, probably the name and number of his vet—although that was also posted on the fridge—exactly how much he ate, where to shop for the best prices. She smiled. Probably some cash for cat supplies, just in case. Grandma Vera always thought ahead.

She turned the envelope over and broke the seal. Inside, there was a single sheet of paper with her grandmother's familiar handwriting in blue ink. It was a letter, so Lauren went into the kitchen and sat at the table where she could savor the last communication she was ever going to get from the woman who'd always been there for her.

Dear Lauren,

If you're reading this letter, I must be gone. Thank you for taking care of Lord Henry. He always liked you almost as much as he liked me.

Lauren smiled at her grandmother's gentle humor, even at a time like this.

I don't have to tell you how special you always were to me and how much I loved you. You already know. But I'll say it again anyway. Your sunshine has lit up every corner of my life, and I loved you from the moment you were born. Sharing my gardening passion with you and cooking in the kitchen where you're probably reading this letter was a joy.

Lauren stopped and wiped more tears. Her grandmother knew her so well.

I hope you'll think of me when you use my recipes and watch your flowers grow, but don't grieve too long for an old woman who had a wonderful life. Continue to be your beautiful self. Find joy and love. Put Lord Henry's cat tree in that sunny window by your bookcase for now. He'll love it there.

The cat jumped up on the table and Lauren paused to pet him. She wasn't kicking him off. Letting him on the table wasn't the worst thing that had happened that day. There were still a few paragraphs left, but Lauren hesitated to read them, wanting to hold on to the last words from her grandmother. Finally, she drew a deep breath and continued.

> *Your sister never cheated at cards, but she never let you win, either. She's strong and beautiful, and, of course, I loved her, too. But you were always a gentler version of Maggie, and I think you sometimes suffered for it. I know you never understood what happened with her and Seth,*

Lauren sucked in a breath. Why was her grandmother bringing up this painful memory in her final letter? Seth Jones had betrayed Maggie, destroyed his relationship with all of them and snapped the bonds of their friendship like he was breaking a branch over his knee. Lauren put her hand over the last paragraph, not wanting to read it, but desperate now to know. What had her grandmother been thinking?

She reached out and stroked the cat, who flicked his tail impatiently as if to tell her to get it over with.

"Fine," she said aloud and uncovered the last part of the letter.

> *and I've hoped for the last ten years that Maggie—or Seth—would tell you. It's their story to tell. My final request of you (aside from loving Lord Henry) is that you and*

your sister reclaim the closeness you had growing up and heal the sore spot from years ago.

Sore spot. That was a way to put it. As if she could go to the cabinet over the bathroom sink and take down the ointment her grandmother made from her own plants and apply it to that horrifying, inexplicable summer Lauren turned seventeen and her older sister got suddenly engaged and then un-engaged to Lauren's best friend.

She forced herself to power through the rest of the letter.

Talk to your sister and ask her for the truth about what happened. I'm sorry to lay this on you in a letter when I'm gone, but I hope you'll come to see that it's my final gift to you.

My sweet sunshiny Lauren, I hope life and love are good to you. You deserve all the happiness in the world.

Love always,
Grandma

"Ask Maggie what happened?" she asked aloud. She thought she knew what happened. Maggie and Seth were getting married, and then Seth called it off and broke her sister's heart.

Maggie had moved away not long after that so she wouldn't have to accidentally run into Seth. She'd gone to college out of state and never lived in Niagara Falls again. When she did come home to visit, everyone avoided bringing up Seth out of kindness for Maggie's feelings. Her entire family had taken Maggie's side, even Lauren, who sacrificed her friendship with Seth.

The truth was simple. Wasn't it?

It was a beautiful June evening, but Lauren shivered anyway. She wanted to sit at her grandmother's kitchen table, quietly, with her feelings. But the letter inserted itself into her grief like an unwanted guest at a funeral.

She folded the letter, put it in the envelope and tucked it in her purse. She wasn't showing it to anyone. Not yet anyway.

"Ready?" she asked Lord Henry. She went down into the basement and found his cat carrier, and then she bundled the cat and his belongings to her car.

"I have nice windows," she told him when he yowled at her from the passenger seat. "You'll be happy."

CAPTAIN SETH JONES stared down at the dog curled at the bottom of his equipment locker, wedged in next to his fire boots. He picked it up and cradled it, scratching behind its little ears.

"You're so ugly," he whispered. "And you smell."

The dog licked his face, and Seth resisted the urge to wipe off his cheek. He didn't want to offend the poor animal.

Chief Bearett Center, known affectionately as Bear to everyone because of his size, leaned on the cabinet next to Seth's locker.

"He's all yours," Bear said.

"Oh, no," Seth said. "No, thank you." He put the dog on the concrete floor of the fire station, and the dog immediately relieved himself on the tire of a nearby fire truck.

"See?" Bear said. "He could have done that in your locker, but he didn't. The dog loves you. I think he chose you."

Seth shook his head. "He chose this fire station, and you were supposed to find his owner."

"No joy, I'm afraid. Vet says he doesn't have a chip, we've put up signs all over Niagara Falls and it's on our social media."

"It's only been two weeks. We can't give up," Seth insisted.

Bear laughed. "You're the king of lost causes, you know that?"

"I am not." Seth pulled his gloves from his locker and inspected them for holes. Yesterday's house fire—a total loss, but thank goodness there were no injuries—had been a tough one. The smell of smoke still emanated from his turnout gear.

Bear laughed. "Remember last winter when it snowed two feet and you were out shoveling around fire hydrants even though I told you it was useless because it was just going to snow another two feet before it was over?"

Seth checked the batteries in his flashlight, ignoring his boss.

"And when Jeremy backed over the new landscaping with the tanker, you didn't give up on that magnolia and nursed it back to health," Bear added, gesturing out front where, through the open doors of the fire station, they could see the small but vibrant tree. Seth gave it a quick glance and went back to inspecting his gear.

"It goes against the grain, but we have to give up," Bear said. "No one wants Sparky."

The dog trotted over and sat at Seth's feet.

"You named him?" Seth asked.

Chief Bearett shrugged. "Used to have a firehouse Dalmatian named Sparky. I thought this little guy could take up the torch."

Seth stared at Bear. "A firehouse Chihuahua," he said. "You can't be serious."

"He won't live here all the time. He'll go home with you."

"I'm not adopting a homely, homeless Chihuahua," Seth said, speaking low and shielding his mouth with one hand so the dog wouldn't hear.

"You can't turn him down now that he has a name," Bear said.

"No."

"Your son will love him," the chief said.

"And now we're at a definite no," Seth said. "Having Teddy with me for the summer is enough of a juggling challenge. I'm not adding a dog."

"But—"

The chief was interrupted by the blare of the overhead speaker announcing a dumpster fire behind one of the hotels near the falls. Four men burst from a nearby door that led to day quarters and began grabbing gear and starting trucks. Seth jammed his feet into his boots and pulled up his turnout pants, which were stored for quick dressing. He grabbed his coat and helmet and started for the driver's seat, almost tripping over the dog on his way. He paused just long enough to scoop up the animal and set him in the bottom of his empty locker.

"Stay there for a minute. Do not get run over."

The dog nodded his tiny Chihuahua head, and that was the image in Seth's mind as he pulled out of the station and drove the fire truck through the downtown streets, siren wailing.

The chief, in the passenger seat, blew the air

horn as they approached an intersection and Seth slowed down and made eye contact with drivers before he continued through the red light. Some of the firefighters were adrenaline junkies, especially the younger ones, but twenty-eight years on the planet had taught Seth to slow down and be aware of his surroundings at all times.

King of lost causes, he thought. Ridiculous. It wasn't even true—he *did* give up on lost causes, whether he wanted to or not. His marriage had been a lost cause he'd tried to rescue until his wife took it out of his hands by filing for divorce. He'd fought for shared custody and won, though. Teddy was all his for the summer before kindergarten started.

"Shame about Vera Benedict," the chief said. "I know you were friends with her family."

Seth absolutely did not want to talk about this, especially when his mind needed to be on driving the massive fire truck through streets crowded with summer tourists.

"I was."

Nanna Vera. The sweet lady who'd been like a grandmother to him. She'd told him to just call her Grandma since he was at her house all the time as a kid, but he didn't think that was right. Lauren and Maggie had the right to call her Grandma; he was just Lauren's friend who appreciated a nice yard with a swing set and a kitchen table with good food. So they'd settled on Nanna Vera. Her home had been a refuge from his turbulent house, where his mom was gone and his dad drank too much.

"Hate it when we can't save them," the chief said. "I can't believe she managed to make the 911 call but then her heart had to go and give out before we got there. You always hope when you bring them in the ER can pull off a miracle... Not this time."

"There's a fire department connection on the back of this hotel for water," Seth said. Not only did he not want to talk about that morning's call to a very familiar address, he also needed to keep his mind on his job. He'd taken an oath to serve the people of Niagara Falls, protecting lives and property. He also needed to protect his own life. His son depended on him. "I'm going to pull up on the south side by the connection."

"Hang on, it'll depend on where the dumpster is," Bear said. He got on the radio and asked dispatch if the person who reported the fire could give an exact location of the fire.

Some of the downtown hotels were small, but this was a big one with an underground parking garage, multiple entrances and fifteen stories of rooms. Seth, along with the rest of the department, knew the buildings of Niagara Falls well—especially the hotels, where occupants could be asleep or fail to familiarize themselves with the location of the stairs and fire exits. People got vacation brain and got lulled into a false sense of security. He'd seen it plenty of times, and it was his job to keep them safe even when they were distracted by everything the tourist area had to offer.

"Southeast corner," the dispatcher said over the radio.

"Copy," Bear said. He put down the radio. "Your plan to hook the connection on the south side is good. We won't need to pull much hose to knock this one down."

"As long as it hasn't spread to the building."

"Fingers crossed," the chief said.

Seth passed the funeral home three streets back from the tourist area. The white building with its green awning always took him back to his mother's funeral when he was only eight. His father had gripped his hand so hard it hurt. It was only a little while later that his dad turned to alcohol instead of clinging to his only child to cope. And now, Nanna Vera's funeral would be there. Maggie would be there. And Lauren would be there.

He should go and pay his respects, but they wouldn't want him there. Maggie hadn't been back in town for years that he knew of, but he still saw Lauren around. It was hard to avoid someone in the relatively small town, especially when he had a very public job and she was outside all day long as a horticulturist with the park system. And Lauren still carried her family's anger toward him.

They'd avoided each other, which probably saved him a lot of pain. When you let someone pull you in and love you, you're giving them access to your heart—and inviting a deep scar when it's over and that love is no longer available to you.

He'd avoid the funeral, even though Nanna Vera deserved his final respects.

The light was green, but the chief laid on the siren anyway as Seth steered the truck through the intersection, made a right-hand turn and came up behind the hotel exactly where the water hookup was located. He knew where it would be. Niagara Falls was his hometown, and he'd been a firefighter in here for a decade, climbing up to the rank of captain.

He'd spent ten years putting out fires, but some things from his past still burned.

CHAPTER TWO

LAUREN SELECTED PINK and yellow roses from her grandmother's garden and tucked their stems into a clear glass vase. She'd already tied a cheerful ribbon around the vase's neck. Next, she cut some greenery from a bush and tucked it among the roses in the arrangement. She knew her grandmother would prefer having her own flowers at her funeral instead of a hothouse arrangement from a florist—especially since the roses in Vera's sunny backyard wouldn't be seen by anyone now.

Except Lauren. She would come every day and take care of them when she checked on the house. And it would be Lauren's job to clean out the house and figure out what to do with it. Her parents were executors of the will, of course, but they'd moved to Florida after an early retirement for the weather. Her sister, Maggie, lived several states away and was too busy with her young family.

So the cleanup was on Lauren. She didn't

mind sorting her grandmother's sweaters and donating them, going through her books and cookware or cleaning out the fridge. She was happy to do that. It was the emotional cleanup Lauren was dreading, and a funeral was either the best or the worst time in the world for her to ask her sister what their grandmother meant about the truth involving Maggie and Seth.

Seth. The man she'd blamed for years and given the cold shoulder to, out of loyalty to her sister.

A thorn hooked her little finger as she picked up the vase and walked out to the driveway, where her car was parked. She'd already loaded her pockets with tissues, and she pulled one out to stop the bleeding.

If only that thorn would be the hardest part of the day. Satisfied that her finger wouldn't bleed on her dress, she put the vase on the floor of the passenger side and packed things around it so it wouldn't spill.

Her sister greeted her at the door of the funeral home with a hug. "Are you okay?" Maggie asked. "You were so quiet last night."

"I'm okay," Lauren said. Dinner with their parents last night had certainly felt strained. She held out the vase so the roses wouldn't snag on her sister's outfit. "Your dress is really pretty." Maggie herself was really pretty. Her hair was a vibrant auburn and, at twenty-eight, she was more beautiful than ever. And she looked happy.

"Thank you," Maggie said. "You look good, too."

Lauren doubted that. She'd always considered herself average. Average height, brown hair with a hint of red, but not the richness of her sister's. Hazel eyes. Nothing spectacular. People told her she had a great smile, but she assumed it was because she had so much practice using it. She always had plenty to smile about, doing horticulture work she loved in her hometown, which she also loved.

Lauren reached into her well of happy thoughts. The smell of the falls, mist rising off them in early mornings. Rainbows. Tourists in wet raincoats laughing as they got off the *Maid of the Mist* or finished their trek through the Cave of the Winds. Flowers blooming and butterflies and huge arching branches of oak trees. Canada geese waddling along with baby geese in the springtime.

The happy thoughts helped, but her eyes still burned.

"We'll get through today," Maggie said, big-sister-ness in her tone. "And then we should get caught up. I can leave Jerry and the kids at the hotel."

Get through today. Get through her beloved

grandmother's funeral as if it was something to check off and then return to her regular life. Maggie hadn't been as close to Grandma Vera as Lauren had. She'd moved away, married and had two kids.

"Sure," Lauren said, forcing a smile. "We could go for a walk along the falls. I'll show you the flower beds I planned and the trees we're cultivating. This is such a beautiful time of year and everything is blooming. Grandma loved walking along the falls."

She felt herself tearing up again, but Maggie put an arm around her and steered her through the door. "Do you think there will be a lot of people here for the funeral?" Maggie asked.

"Grandma had a lot of friends in the community. You know how generous she was, and everyone loved her."

Maggie nodded, and Lauren wondered if she was worried Seth might show up. Now that there was a seed of doubt in Lauren's mind about what had happened between Maggie and Seth, Lauren couldn't help thinking about it. She should be thinking about her grandmother's funeral… But hadn't Grandma Vera said herself that the letter was a final gift to Lauren? Having something to dwell on was, perhaps, a distraction from her grief.

"You're so much like her," Maggie said. "And

not just because you love plants and you're a great cook."

"Thank you." Lauren smiled at her older sister and resolved to tread very carefully later on their walk. There may be more to the story of Maggie and Seth, but she wasn't going to risk hurting her sister to find out. She wanted to leave all the hurt in the past, and she'd always thought she had.

Inside, Lauren took heart from all the beautiful flowers surrounding her grandmother's casket—even though she knew Grandma Vera would appreciate the simple roses from her own garden the most. As mourners came through the receiving line, many of them shared sweet stories about Vera, and Lauren felt peace mixed with sorrow as she stood with her parents and sister accepting condolences.

It was only after the formal service had ended and she'd gotten back into her car for the procession to the cemetery that she breathed a sigh of relief. Seth hadn't come to the funeral. She didn't want to face him, not with her sister and parents right there and especially not under these circumstances. She hadn't told anyone about the letter, but if she wanted answers, she couldn't keep the secret forever. She was going to have to risk asking before her sister returned to her home in Indiana tomorrow.

As Lauren laid a wreath at the cemetery, she

made two resolutions. She would ask Maggie about Seth as gently as possible, and she would come back and plant a beautiful rosebush at her grandmother's grave. Flowers made everything better, and sweet Grandma Vera deserved a beautiful reminder.

SETH HAD SAID no in every way possible, but who could reject a dog whose trusting eyes were boring into yours. Seth held the creature under one arm like a football while he waited just inside the door at day care. The teacher greeted him and went outside to find Teddy on the playground.

Seth had walked, but his assumption that the dog would enjoy a walk was off the mark by two blocks.

"Good thing you only weigh about fifteen pounds," he told Sparky.

He still wore his firefighter uniform—navy-blue pants and shirt with the department's insignia—because the day care was located on a street halfway between his house and the fire station. His son was accustomed to being picked up on foot on nice days. Sometimes he smelled like smoke or sweat, depending on the day, but Teddy never seemed to mind.

The teacher came back holding Teddy by the hand, and the boy zeroed in on the dog in his dad's arms. Teddy's eyes opened wide, and he stopped in front of his dad and stared at the dog in wonder.

"Dog," he said, his tone implying a whole sentence. Seth hadn't allowed himself to get his hopes up, or so he'd thought. But he realized he had still hoped the dog would inspire his son to unleash a whole dialogue. The speech therapist was always telling him to give his boy time. Teddy *could* speak and use whole sentences, and Seth had to be patient. It would come.

Seth knelt down so the Chihuahua—still smelly—was eye level with Teddy. "This is Sparky and he's going home with us tonight."

He didn't want to make big promises. The dog's true owner could still be found, even though it wasn't likely.

"Just tonight?" Teddy asked.

"Maybe longer. We'll see." The dog struggled to get free, and Seth steered his son outside, not wanting to cause a scene at day care if all the other kids saw this dog that *some* people found adorable.

Outside, Seth put Sparky on the sidewalk and held the leash while Teddy got down on the ground and played with him. The dog rolled over and offered his belly, wagging his tail wildly. Teddy giggled and ran his hand over Sparky's belly.

"Walk?" Teddy asked, gesturing toward the leash in his dad's hand.

Again, an entire sentence, *Can I walk him?* was implied. Seth wanted to correct Teddy and suggest a complete sentence, but now was not the time. He didn't want anything to dim the smile on his son's face.

"I'll help," Seth said. "We can both hold the leash at first, just to make sure Sparky is going to be a good walker."

"Park?" Teddy asked.

"I'd love to go to the park," Seth said, modeling a complete sentence. He scooped up Teddy's backpack and shouldered it. Seth held on to the loop at the end of the leash, and Teddy gripped a section partway down. Sparky hopped around in front of them on the sidewalk, weaving back and forth as if he'd never had even five minutes of leash training. At this rate, it was going to be a long walk to the entrance of the state park, but it was a beautiful June evening, and Seth could use the decompression time.

The past few days had been tough. A house fire, an unsuccessful attempt to save Nanna Vera, a dumpster fire and tourists tangling with other tourists in their cars, which was typical for summer in a town that saw a lot of activity during tourist season.

It was the call to Nanna Vera's that weighed

on him, but not entirely because they hadn't been able to save her. They'd done everything they were trained to do, and all the first responders had experience handling hard situations—not that it got easier.

For Seth, being back in that house dredged up the past for him. He'd had a choice about what happened a decade ago. No matter how much he suffered because of it, he wasn't a victim. But losing Lauren's friendship—losing *Lauren*—had been like turning off a light, and that light had remained dark since he was eighteen. He'd had a lot of practice forgetting about it and focusing on the here and now.

He held his son's hand and the leash as they walked through the entrance gates of the Niagara Falls State Park. The large visitor center here had been newly renovated, and dozens of tourists were around the plaza taking pictures. Seth breathed deeply and inhaled the aroma of the falls mixed with flowers in bloom all around them.

"Water," Teddy said.

Seth nodded, assuming his son was talking about the mist rising off the falls. Teddy tugged at his hand and pointed to a drinking fountain with a spigot close to the ground. Another dog, a beautiful German shepherd who dwarfed Sparky, was currently drinking from it.

"Oh," Seth said. "Good idea. That was a long walk for a dog with legs the length of my finger."

Teddy giggled.

They waited their turn and then Seth held the spigot on while Sparky lapped the water. Teddy watched for a minute and then started to shift around and fidget.

"Do you need to go to the bathroom?" Seth asked.

Teddy nodded. "Bad."

Seth scooped up the dog in one arm and his son in the other and headed for the bathroom by the visitor center. He was walking fast and nearly collided with two women coming toward him.

"Sorry," he said automatically, not taking his eyes off the restrooms as he moved swiftly.

"Seth."

His name stopped him in his tracks, and he turned. Maggie and Lauren Benedict faced him with nearly identical expressions of surprise, and he wasn't sure which of them had spoken. The sisters still looked alike, although he'd always found Lauren to be a softer, prettier version of her older sister. He knew Maggie was married and had kids now. And, of course, she was in town for her grandmother's funeral—the one he had chosen not to attend earlier in the day because he didn't think they'd want to see him.

And now here they were like two ghosts from his past.

"Daddy," Teddy urged.

He was speechless, facing Lauren and Maggie, and there was no time to think about what to say. Instead of risking a bathroom accident, Seth did the only thing he could. He turned swiftly and made a beeline to the bathroom, still juggling his son and his dog. He paused at the entrance to the bathroom. Could he manage the dog in there and help Teddy if he needed it?

"I'll take your dog while you go in."

He couldn't believe it. He knew the voice this time, but he hadn't had a conversation with her in a decade. He'd seen her around town, of course, but they'd steered away from each other as if they were avoiding a collision. What had changed? It didn't matter. He had no time to consider the question.

"Thanks," he said. He handed the leash to Lauren Benedict despite how surreal it felt. In the split second he looked at her, he saw tear streaks on her face but also the glimmer of a smile.

"You're the flower lady," Teddy said out of nowhere.

Seth's attention snapped back to his son, who had just used a complete sentence for the first time that day *and* talked to a stranger. She *was* a stranger to Teddy, wasn't she? Of course, Seth knew Lauren worked in horticulture in the parks system, but how did his son know that?

"Hi," Lauren said, turning her smile on Teddy.

Seth didn't know what to say, so he hurried his son into the bathroom, glad to have a reason to close the door. With the emergency handled and Teddy's hands thoroughly washed, Seth guided his son outside where Lauren knelt on the ground, rubbing Sparky's tiny ears. Maggie sat on a bench across the courtyard. Maybe she wasn't a dog person. He'd technically been engaged to her for almost a month, but he didn't know if she liked dogs, cats or some other kind of pet. He'd never known Maggie as well as he'd known Lauren.

"Thank you," Seth said. "This is Teddy."

Lauren said hello, and the boy sat on the ground next to her.

"I knew you had a son," Lauren said. "Grandma told me." Her smile faded and Seth was afraid she was about to cry, but then she collected herself. "I didn't know you had a dog, though."

Seth had assumed that if he and Lauren ever had a conversation, he'd feel incredible tension between them. In fact, the last time they'd had any kind of verbal exchange, it had been her telling him off after she found out about the broken engagement. He'd lost her friendship, but he'd felt as if he'd lost his entire childhood with its memories wrapped up in the cozy blanket of the Benedict family's love.

But ten years had passed and he'd gotten over it. They had no power to hurt him now. And the tension wasn't there anymore.

"Sparky wandered into the fire station and moved into my locker," he said, sticking to facts. "Recently."

"Oh."

Seth's glance flicked over to Maggie, who still sat on the bench.

"I'm sorry about Nan—your grandmother," he said.

Lauren nodded. "The funeral was today."

"I know," Seth said softly. "I was there when…it happened." He could practically feel her sorrow—maybe because he shared it and maybe also because as kids they'd known each other so well. If things had turned out differently back then…

"You were on the call," Lauren said quietly.

"I was. We did everything we could."

Lauren swiped away a tear, got up and dusted off her pants as if she was cleaning away old cobwebs. "The red roses are about to bloom," she told Teddy. "Maybe your teacher will bring you back to see them this week."

"Okay," Teddy said. He looked up from his job petting Sparky. "Bye, flower lady."

"Bye," she echoed. She looked at Seth for a moment as if she wanted to say something more, and then she turned and walked back to her sister, who jumped up when she approached, took Lauren by the arm and turned in the other direction.

CHAPTER THREE

"YOU COULD HAVE said hello to Seth," Lauren told her sister as they took the path along the falls and the sound of the rushing water filled her ears. Her head was already buzzing with what her sister had revealed, and now her nerves were on edge. Running into Seth tonight was the worst timing in the world, and even though she'd just chided her sister for giving him the cold shoulder, Lauren had to admit to herself she would have done the same thing yesterday.

She hadn't known the truth yesterday, but Maggie had always known.

"I didn't think he'd want to see me. He didn't come over to me, either," Maggie said.

"That's cowardly." Lauren wanted to be generous to her sister, but Maggie sounded so petty and childish.

Maggie's lip trembled. "I know."

"I'm sorry, but I'm still just really shocked," Lauren said. She and her sister had been talking for almost an hour when they ran into Seth, but it was going to take a lot longer than that for Lauren to truly process what she'd learned. Maggie's admission had shattered her entire understanding of the past ten years. She couldn't believe it had taken her grandmother's death and a letter to finally bring out the truth. Even her parents didn't know—yet.

"When are you telling Mom and Dad?" Lauren asked. She deliberately phrased it as "when" instead of asking "if." Too much damage had already been done by this secret.

Maggie sighed. "I know you think I'm a villain, but I was eighteen and scared and I took the easy way out."

"Confiding in your own family might have been the easy way out," Lauren said. "We would have supported you."

"You were just a kid."

"I was seventeen, almost as old as you were."

"I know," Maggie admitted, her voice low. "But I can't go back and change anything."

Lauren felt sick just thinking about the last ten years of silence between her family and Seth. Why had he never told her what had really happened? They'd told each other everything when they were younger. She'd once thought they always would.

Had anyone asked him for his side of the story?

Her family all blamed Seth.

Lauren had blamed Seth.

All the water rushing past and dropping over the falls couldn't wash away her guilt at the way they'd all treated him. The way she'd treated him, especially because she was devastated that he'd thrown away her friendship—more than friendship. She'd loved him, but she'd never told him that.

"This is why Grandma continued to be nice to him and kept in touch with him all these years," Lauren said. "I always thought she pitied him because of his parents, but I still couldn't understand it. How did Grandma know?"

"I told her," Maggie said. "She didn't buy the engagement story at all, and she confronted me about it. I begged her not to tell Mom and Dad or you, and she said she wouldn't. She never did until she wrote you that letter."

"I talked to her every day," Lauren said. "She could have told me a thousand different times. I can't understand why she didn't." She also could not understand why her grandmother had called this information a gift for Lauren. It felt more like a grenade.

Maggie sat on a boulder and looked at her hands, and Lauren sat next to her, not quite touching her. "I made a huge mistake," Maggie said, her voice cracking. "I was wrong. No one likes to admit those things about themselves, even if they're true."

Lauren watched a young family stroll past. The mom gave her and her sister a curious look, obviously wondering why they both had teary eyes. Lauren gave the woman a reassuring smile, even though today had been one of the toughest days of her life. The other toughest day had been finding out at seventeen that Seth—her Seth—was engaged to her sister.

She put a hand on Maggie's leg. This conversation was far from over, but she needed to find something healing before they both broke any more. "Let me show you my favorite flower bed before the light fades too much."

Maggie raised her head and gave Lauren an anguished look. "I'm sorry."

Lauren nodded. "I know."

"Are you going to…say anything to Seth? You probably see him around town."

"I don't know," Lauren said. "I have to think about it. We've avoided each other all these years, and anyway, he probably doesn't want to talk to any of us. He didn't come to the funeral."

"He didn't," Maggie said quietly. "But Grandma would have blamed me more for that than him."

Lauren stood and tugged her sister up by the hand. "Enough blame for one night. It's been a hard day and we're going to go smell the flowers. It's the only way to feel better right now."

That's what she told her sister, but Lauren already knew she wasn't going to feel better until she found a way to repair the damage her family—Lauren included—had done to Seth Jones.

"TEDDY," SETH SAID, keeping his voice low and even despite the turmoil in his chest. "Have you met the flower lady before?"

They were walking on the path along the falls, going the opposite direction of Lauren and Maggie. One encounter had been enough for Seth, and he very much felt as if there was something going on he didn't understand.

The boy nodded as he carefully avoided stepping on a bug.

"Did you meet her here at the park?" Seth asked.

Another nod.

"When your day care group came here for a walk?"

One more nod.

Seth swallowed. Some of the other firefighters had little kids, and they complained about the constant questions and singing and more questions they endured at home. Seth loved Teddy more than the whole world, but he would give a large chunk of that world to have the problem of too much communication from his five-year-old. How was Teddy going to manage kindergarten if he didn't learn to express himself?

Not learn, he reminded himself. His son knew how. He just…didn't.

"I love hearing about your adventures while I'm at work," Seth said.

"Adventures," Teddy said.

Seth's heart lifted. Maybe that word appealed to Teddy and he could build on this. Hadn't Seth loved adventures as a child? He'd considered escaping from his toxic house an adventure, although he didn't understand it as such until he was older and could look back on it all. Sometimes he was a pirate, searching for lost treasure. The Benedict family had a rowboat on the lake behind their house. Lauren always wanted to steer while he did the rowing. They'd be gone for hours and there was always food waiting for them in Nanna Vera's kitchen. He felt a lump in his throat when he thought of Nanna Vera, the one Benedict who hadn't cut him off.

Had she known what really happened with Maggie? It didn't matter. Even if she had known, the truth had died with her. He drew a deep breath and pulled Sparky closer as a man with a Dalmatian walked by. He sighed. *That* was a fire station dog. And he was stuck with a shaggy Chihuahua.

"Did you have adventures today?" he asked his son.

Teddy shook his head.

"We could go on adventures," Seth suggested. "What would you like to do?"

"With Sparky?"

"Sure," Seth said, although that definitely depended on what kind of adventures. They paused on a walking bridge and watched the water rushing underneath. Some large slabs of rock caught tree branches in the rapids. It was mesmerizing, watching the water that was about ten seconds away from going over the falls. The bridge had a solid railing, but Seth kept an arm around Teddy anyway.

Sparky yipped and danced.

"Can't see," Teddy said, apparently advocating for the dog.

Seth picked Sparky up and held him securely under his free arm, and the three of them watched the water together. Water under the bridge, the Benedict family. They'd felt like his family when he was young. They'd held him together. Loved him. Provided a safe haven. Which was why he did what he did, never realizing he was risking everything until it was too late.

"Flower lady," Teddy said, pointing.

Seth followed Teddy's gaze and saw Lauren and Maggie in the distance, walking the path along the water. If he stood there long enough, they would cross the bridge he was on. He had no desire to pour salt in that wound again.

"Are we ready to go home and get Sparky settled in?" he asked. "I think he might be hungry, too."

"Hungry," Teddy agreed.

"He ate at the station, but we're going to need supplies. Let's stop by home and then go on a pet shopping adventure. We can get a bed and food, and you can be in charge of picking out toys for him."

Teddy's face lit up as he turned his attention from the flower lady and gave Sparky a look of devotion.

"You need a ball," he said to the dog.

Seth laughed, delighted by the full sentence and by the happiness on Teddy's face. He had a whole summer with his son. It was part of the shared custody agreement. His ex-wife was traveling for work but would be back right before kindergarten started. Then, they'd continue the carefully scripted back-and-forth, poor Teddy being the seesaw. Sometimes he wondered why Hannah insisted on having her half when her parenting seemed half-hearted. Did she ever sing the alphabet with Teddy or try to spur him into conversation? Seth hadn't made a formal accusation, but he suspected part of Teddy's communication issues stemmed from his ex-wife's personality. She hadn't communicated with Seth, either, until it was too late.

He was taking full advantage of his bonus summer with Teddy, and he would never let his son down or make him feel as if he needed to go on a pirate adventure to escape his home.

"Do you think the ball should be a squeaky one?" Seth asked.

Teddy laughed, and it sounded like music to Seth.

"Red," Teddy said.

"Let's go buy a red squeaky ball, dog food and a comfy bed," Seth said, again modeling complete thoughts in sentences as the speech therapist had suggested. He was tired and wanted to shower and get out of his work uniform, but he reminded himself to be grateful and embrace the moment.

He held his son's hand and the leash in the other as they took an alternate route toward the park's entrance so he wouldn't run into the ghosts of his childhood.

CHAPTER FOUR

LAUREN DROVE HER parents to the airport in Buffalo for their early morning flight back to Florida. It seemed to her that there was so much to say despite having spent the last five days with them. There was never enough time with people you loved.

Her dad picked a clump of cat fur off his pants and rolled down the passenger side window to let it go on a gust of summer air.

"I was saving that to make a blanket," Lauren said.

She heard her mother laugh in the back seat. "Lord Henry has already transformed your couch into an abstract painting of himself with all his shedding. I wonder if it's stress."

"Could be," Lauren said. "But I'll give him lots of love and assure him he's not alone, and pretty soon he'll be cheerfully knocking plants off the windowsill."

She felt her mother's hand on her shoulder. "You have the best attitude about everything."

Lauren sighed as she merged onto the road to the airport. "Not always. I was a bit brutal to Maggie when she finally fessed up. It hurt that she never trusted us with the truth."

"It does hurt," her dad said. "Grandma didn't tell us, either."

Lauren nodded. She and her parents had had a serious talk with Maggie before she went home with her husband and kids, but it felt like being on a long road that had suddenly ended. The truth was out. Roll credits. Nowhere to go from there. It stung that Lauren and her mom and dad had been in the dark when Grandma Vera wasn't, and it added a layer to their grief at her passing. Not anger, not even a sense of betrayal. Just a feeling that there was a missed opportunity to come to peace with something they should have resolved a long time ago.

"I feel awful," her mother said. "About Maggie, of course. But also Seth. I don't know what to do about any of it. I wish I could go back in time. For everyone's sake. Yours, too, Lauren." Her mother sighed. "You and Seth were…well, inseparable."

"We were," Lauren said. The trees along the road had new thick green leaves and summer flowers were unfurling colorful petals. It was June, too lovely a month in the Niagara region for regrets. A knot of remorse ten years in the making prevented Lauren from taking a deep breath.

"Has anyone talked to him about it?" her dad asked. "I mean…now that we know."

Lauren shook her head.

Seth had no way of knowing about the letter from Grandma Vera, and he probably believed his only remaining link to the Benedict family was lying under a blanket of flowers at the city cemetery. Was he lonely? How did he feel about the Benedict family…and Lauren herself? She hadn't allowed herself to miss him all these years. Lauren had told herself he'd discarded their childhood friendship and all the good memories when he backed out of his engagement with her sister.

Except that he hadn't.

After Lauren hugged her parents goodbye in the airport departure lane and got back in her car by herself, her own sense of loneliness weighed on her. She had Lord Henry waiting at home, and he was very snuggly. Excellent company. But Lauren needed to get back to reality, a place of healing. She was going back to work. She already had on her Niagara Parks uniform of green pants and a white long-sleeved shirt. Her gloves, lunch and water bottle were in the back seat, and she couldn't wait to visit her beloved rose garden.

She'd seen the roses on the walk with her sister, and her fingers had itched to prune off spent blossoms, but it hadn't been the time. Today, she was ready to take a fresh look at everything. She still didn't view her grandmother's letter as a gift, but it did feel as if she'd shed a layer and now she had the chance to see what was underneath. Pruning was good for plants and trees, and removing old growth helped things grow. Lauren tried to apply that same philosophy to herself.

"Hey," her friend Marlin said when Lauren arrived at work partway through the morning. "Hug?"

Lauren accepted a long hug.

"It's so hard to lose someone you love," Marlin said. "Do you want to talk?"

Lauren wanted to tell her about everything, including the letter and the nagging feeling that she needed to do something to atone for her family's treatment of Seth. Marlin was a heart-on-her-sleeve person and she'd probably shed sympathetic tears if Lauren got into it with her. But Lauren didn't feel strong enough to hold out against tears. Not yet.

"I think I need flower time," Lauren said. "A morning of pruning roses and then I believe weeding the annual beds is on my afternoon list. It's going to be hot, but maybe I'll catch some mist off the falls."

"My hair is at full-frizz already, and heat and mist are only going to make it worse," Marlin said. "And I'm sorry to tell you this, but the rose pruning may not be as peaceful as you're hoping. We've got the day care visiting again."

Although Lauren knew her friend had reservations about the large group of chatty kids, Lauren loved their innocence and questions. Sure they tended to run along the garden paths, squealing with the joy of making noise and being outside in the sunshine, but wasn't that what garden paths were for? It was the authenticity of kids that Lauren appreciated. The young ones said exactly what they meant, even if it wasn't flattering.

Lauren smiled. "That will make it more interesting."

Marlin sighed. "I'm still feeling self-conscious about my uniform after that little girl said I dressed like the man who mowed the lawn at her house."

Marlin's knees were already dusty and she had a streak of dirt on her cheekbone. Before lunchtime, Lauren would look the same way. She hosed off her boots every day after work, wiped down her gardening tools and washed her gloves. It was a rewarding but dirty job. She reached into the Gator she usually drove and found her hat right where she'd left it almost a week ago when she'd gotten the call from the hospital and dropped everything.

It felt like a month since she'd been at work, and putting on her uniform had been soothing, like visiting an old friend.

"It's a similar line of work. An honest comparison," Lauren said.

"I prefer trees and plants to most people I know—except you, of course," Marlin said. "But some of the kids are cute when they're not yelling."

Lauren shrugged. "Yelling is part of childhood. When I was a kid, we used to take a rowboat onto the lake behind my grandmother's house, and there was this one part where there was a terrific echo if we were loud enough."

The memory had been buried a long time, along with a lot of her memories of fun things she did with Seth as a kid. A lump rose in her throat and her eyes stung.

Marlin put an arm around her. "I know you'll miss your grandmother."

Lauren nodded. She would miss her grandmother immensely. But it was the loss of something else that had her tearing up at the moment. It had been happening the last few days, childhood memories involving Seth cropping up. The gates of those recollections were open thanks to her grandmother's letter, and Lauren wasn't sure how to handle it. She'd tried shutting them again and ignoring the flashes of memories that streaked like sunshine into her thoughts. She'd been successful at it for years because she believed she had to be.

But she'd been misled.

"A lot has changed," she acknowledged. "But I'll be okay."

"I know you will," her friend said. "But you have to give yourself time. Are you sure you're ready to come back to work?"

"Yes," Lauren said. "I want to be here." She smiled. "Although Lord Henry might disagree. When I put my lunch bag on the kitchen table so I could pack it, he jumped up next to it and swiped it right off."

Marlin laughed. "Cats."

"He's a classic cat. Loves sunshine and naps, stares at me while I'm sleeping and can't stand a closed door. Luckily, being a cat, he's probably not missing me at all right now and is happy to have the house to himself."

"Much lower maintenance than a dog," Marlin said.

"True. But I like dogs, too." Lauren thought about the adorable Chihuahua tucked under Seth's arm as he dashed with his son toward the bathroom. There was so much she didn't know about Seth's life since her family had cut him off. She knew the bare facts—that he'd married and divorced, had a son and now a dog, and was a firefighter in town. But he was practically a stranger to her.

Still, she wondered if he still loved strawberries and chocolate milk and if anyone had made him a birthday cake—white with chocolate icing, his favorite—all these years later.

"Here they come," Marlin said.

Lauren glanced over and saw a line of children from the Rainbow Clubhouse with an adult at the front and back of the line. It was almost ten o'clock and high time she got busy doing her job, even if she was only putting in a partial day. But she didn't get in her Gator and take off for the rose garden she intended to prune. Instead, she waited for the line of kids to approach so she could wave to them as they went by.

Adorable, every one of them. One of the girls wore a pink T-shirt with frilly sleeves and a flower printed on the front. Another girl had a Niagara Falls T-shirt with a big rainbow. A boy near the front of the line wore a T-shirt with a fire truck on the front—Teddy, of course. The day care class had visited several times, and one of those days Lauren's boss had asked her to give a short lesson on the wildflowers blooming along the path. She didn't know at the time who he was, but she did remember that Teddy was really interested and even asked a question—something about animals eating the flowers.

"Good morning," Lauren said to the group as the lead teacher approached. "Welcome to the park!"

"Hi, flower lady," Teddy said.

"Hi, Chihuahua owner." Lauren gave Teddy a big smile and a little wave.

"Wow-a," he said.

The teacher at the back of the line paused to chat with Lauren and Marlin. "We were talking over at the center and we were wondering if we could make a formal arrangement to bring a group here a few days a week and maybe have a mini-lesson like the one you did before."

"I'd love that," Lauren said. "But you'll have to clear it with my boss Barb at the parks office first."

"I'll call," the teacher said. "Thanks. The kids have been talking about it a lot and we hate passing up any opportunity for learning."

She hurried off to reclaim her place at the end of the line.

"Better you than me," Marlin said.

"It'll be fun. And who says you're not going to get roped into helping?"

Marlin shook her head. "I have a very important poison ivy removal near some willow trees I've been neglecting. I'll be much too busy."

Lauren laughed. "Don't forget your long gloves."

"Don't forget your earplugs," Marlin said with a grin as she took up the handles of the wheelbarrow she'd parked when she stopped to talk with Lauren.

Lauren watched the line of children toddle off toward the bridge leading to the Bridal Veil Falls. They were so cute and innocent, probably imagining adventure at every turn of the path and turning a walk in the park into a grand quest filled with danger and magic and joy.

She couldn't help but remember that she and Seth had been like that when they were young, too.

SETH SERVED UP the chicken and dumplings he'd put in the slow cooker before work. As a firefighter, he didn't love leaving the appliance running all day when he wasn't home—not that he'd ever use one with a frayed cord or sitting on a cluttered counter—but as a single dad, he did love coming home to a waiting dinner.

"Did you wash your hands?" he asked.

Without a word, Teddy got up and stood on the stepstool by the kitchen sink, where he silently scrubbed his hands. Sparky sniffed the air and observed the handwashing ritual, wagging his short tail.

"One of the other firefighters said his daughter sings the alphabet while she washes her hands just to make sure she does it long enough to get off all the germs. Do you want to try that?" Seth asked.

Teddy nodded, so Seth began singing. He made it all the way to *Y* before Teddy joined in for the last two letters, but it was something. Maybe next time Teddy would jump in earlier.

Seth sat across from his son at the small kitchen table, and Sparky took up position by Teddy's chair. "We had a car fire today," he said. He paused, hoping for a question. "It was an electric car, the kind that runs on big batteries. The fire probably started there, but it was outside so no one got hurt."

Teddy chewed his food and swallowed. "What color?"

"It used to be silver, but not anymore. I think that lady needs a new car."

Teddy ate in silence.

"Getting a new car can be fun, though," Seth said. "Going to the car lot and looking at all the choices. Sometimes I think about getting a new truck. We could go look together if you want."

"Okay," Teddy said. He reached down and

petted Sparky, who gazed up at the table, nose twitching.

"No people food for Sparky. It's not good for him."

"Okay," Teddy said, turning reluctantly away from the little brown-and-black dog with the big soulful eyes.

"Did you do anything fun at day care today?" Seth asked.

Teddy shook his head, and Seth reminded himself to ask specific questions instead of vague open-ended ones. Both Teddy's speech therapist and his day care teacher suggested that strategy. Seth wondered if he'd talked much at Teddy's age, but there was no one to ask. Had he talked with his mom at the table about his day? He wished he could remember even a scrap of conversation with her. Would she have loved being a grandmother?

"It was sunny," Seth said, pushing those sad thoughts aside. There was nothing he could do about the past. "Did you go outside and play?"

"Yes."

"At day care or somewhere else?"

"Else."

Teddy scooped up some chicken and vegetables. Seth was happy to see his son eating heartily. Whatever he'd done at day care, he did have a good appetite.

"Did you go to the park by the falls?" Seth asked, hoping he was guessing correctly at the "else."

"I saw the flower lady and my teacher stopped to talk to her," Teddy said.

Wow, was that a lot of words. Seth's food stuck in his throat. He knew now who the flower lady was, but even a mention of a Benedict took him back to one of the most painful times in his life. Losing his mother and then being neglected by his dad had been agony, but losing the family that had helped him heal had almost been worse.

"That's nice," he said.

"She had a green hat and pants and a little green truck," Teddy said.

Just his luck, the only subject he could get Teddy to discuss was Lauren Benedict. What was so fascinating about her that she'd inspired his son like this? Seth had a flash of memory, riding his bike alongside Lauren on a hot day, racing her up a hill, laughing. She'd been like sunshine to him, filling a deep hole carved by his own family. He'd grown up in the warmth of the Benedict home. And Lauren's warmth.

"Do you know what those little trucks are called?" Seth asked. He'd seen the park service employees driving them and had been in one a few times when they had emergency calls at the state park or did joint training with the park rangers. With the many trails winding along the falls and the constant mist, tourists and even locals had accidents. Unfortunately, sometimes people did intentionally foolish things too close to rapidly moving water, so rescue training was a regular occurrence.

Teddy shook his head and didn't say anything, but he looked interested.

"Some people call them a side-by-side and some people call them a UTV."

"Can we get one?"

Seth laughed. "It would be fun, but we'll have to stick to riding our bikes." There was a red-and-blue superhero-themed bike in Seth's garage, and one of his summer goals for his son was to take the training wheels off. "We could ride bikes this evening after dinner."

Teddy chewed and appeared to consider Seth's suggestion. "I said hi flower lady and she said hi wow-a owner."

Okay, we're still talking about Lauren Benedict. Seth fought to keep a pleasantly neutral expression. His past pain was not his son's, and he'd tolerate almost anything for Teddy's happiness. "Chihuahua," Seth corrected. He repeated it slowly and counted the syllables on his fingers, tapping them on the table.

"Yes," his son agreed.

Seth reminded himself to be patient. Everything worth doing takes time, and even tiny steps are still movement.

After dinner, Seth and Teddy worked together to clean up the kitchen—Teddy getting the important job of putting the plates, cups and silverware on the counter above the dishwasher—and then they played with Sparky in the backyard until the dog burned off enough Chihuahua energy to go inside and curl up by the couch.

Seth wanted to stretch out on that couch, but instead he put on his helmet and adjusted Teddy's helmet, and they walked their bikes to an empty church parking lot down the street where they could practice riding without dodging cars. Teddy pedaled enthusiastically around the lot for thirty minutes but shook his head when Seth suggested raising the training wheels.

Seth didn't push the issue and instead coaxed his son back home for bath and bedtime. It was only after Teddy was in bed that Seth took his son's backpack off its hook to make sure there wasn't leftover food inside. That was when he found a parent survey from day care asking for input and suggestions for enrichment activities. Some of the suggested ideas were the children's museum, the aquarium and possibly an extended camp experience with the state park's horticulture department.

He sat at the kitchen table, Sparky in his lap,

considering the survey. Teddy hadn't mentioned the letter in his backpack, so the day care staff must have decided to ask parents first before letting the kids get excited about any specific plan. Clearly, Teddy would be eager to see Lauren if the horticulture camp happened. Did he want his son spending time with her?

His pen hovered over the survey. He checked off the aquarium and the museum, but not the horticulture camp.

CHAPTER FIVE

THEY WERE MOVING fast from the initial idea of having flower camp to actually planning it, Lauren thought. And she welcomed the distraction. Her grandmother's funeral was almost two weeks in the past, and each June day seemed to open her heart to the sunshine a little more. Her grandmother would have wanted it this way, and Lauren told herself it was okay to let go of the grief a little at a time and allow the petals of it to unfurl. There was still beauty. Lord Henry's fur shonc in the morning sunlight in her apartment. Her grandmother's garden bloomed as if nothing had changed. She'd piled most of her grandmother's clothing into her car and donated it to a local charity where it would find a new life with someone else.

Still, she was glad to be busy planning activities for the camp, which was scheduled to start in another week. Jill, one of the teachers at the day care, had met with Lauren and her boss, Barb, and they'd agreed on ninety-minute sessions three days a week for six weeks. Amber from the park's educational outreach office would also be involved. Weather permitting, the children would walk over and be outdoors in various locations throughout the state park. On rainy days, the day care had a bus and there were indoor venues at the park they could use.

Lauren hoped for sunny days, every day, even though she knew her beloved plants needed the rainy days, too.

"Here's the list so far," Jill said at their meeting. "Nine children. We're still waiting to hear from a few of the parents."

Lauren leaned across the desk, looking for one particular name on the list. No Teddy Jones. The happiness of sunshine and roses dimmed as if someone had switched off a light. Half the joy of growing and nurturing plants—more than half, really—was sharing their beauty with others. Her grandmother had taught her that. After the recent revelation about Seth and Maggie, Lauren's heart was heavy with the weight of missed opportunities.

She told herself it wasn't her fault that Seth got cut off. She hadn't known the truth. It was Maggie's fault, yet she didn't actually blame her sister. People make mistakes when they're feeling desperate and vulnerable. Maggie could have corrected it years ago, though, but the damage had already been done. There was no going back, right? That was the question that haunted Lauren. Was there a way to recapture her friendship with Seth? And why was that so important to her? If he'd wanted to, he could have sought her out and told her the truth anytime during the past decade. But he'd remained silent.

"I hope a few more will join," Barb said, "but we have plenty to get started and sometimes a small group has its benefits."

Lauren nodded and smiled and participated in the rest of the planning session, which involved discussing regulations involving the children's health and safety as well as activities and curriculum. All the while, though, she was thinking how much Teddy would love the flower camp and feeling guilty knowing that she was probably the reason he wasn't enrolled. Seth didn't want any interaction with her.

The feeling made her feel like something inside her was shriveling, like withering leaves. She thought about it all day long, and it distracted her from enjoying the spicy scent of mosquito-repellent marigolds in pots outside the visitor center. She couldn't concentrate on mixing the organic flower food for the petunias, which were already sending out long, lush vines with huge purple flowers. She was mad at herself. How could she have let her friendship with

Seth go dormant? She tried to remember back to the ended engagement, her sister's tears and obvious broken heart. Maggie had been hurt, but not in the way she said she was.

Lauren should have asked more questions at the time, but it would have been cruel to press Maggie for information, and Lauren herself had been barely seventeen and still reeling from losing her best friend. She would never understand why Grandma Vera had waited until her death to reveal the truth. Maybe the older woman had intended to let things settle and hearts heal…but then time got away from her and, after a while, it had seemed cruel to reopen the wound.

But that wound never closed anyway.

Lauren put away the fertilizer before her distraction caused her to make a big mistake and then she peeled off her gloves. The afternoon sun had faded to a hot but mellow light, and it was time to go home where Lord Henry would need a dish of salmon and some love. She had ridden her bike to work, which she did every day that rain wasn't forecasted. There were several different routes she could bike home, but she chose the one that went right by Seth's house.

His truck was in the driveway, which didn't necessarily mean he was home. She knew he walked to work on nice days. She'd seen him. Biked past him dozens of times. She'd always felt justified in ignoring him, safe in the knowledge that blood was thicker than water and she was staying in line with her family by taking Maggie's side.

Those battle lines seemed so unnecessary now. And wrong. She slowed in front of his house. His garage door was up. That meant he had to be home, right? She could see two bikes inside, one adult and one child size.

Lauren stopped in front of his house, heart pounding. She had no plan and no idea what to say. She walked her bike up Seth's front sidewalk and dismounted. If he happened to look out the front window, he'd see her lurking just feet from his front door. And assuming he was home and willing to talk to her, she still wasn't sure what she would say.

She should leave. It wasn't too late to ride away unnoticed. Maybe she could come back another day when she'd thought this through.

Or she'd chicken out. Ghosts lying silent for a decade had perhaps better be left—

Loud, yipping, insistent barking emanated from the house and she saw the front curtain move. Caught. Lauren froze. She could hop on her bike and pedal furiously away, or she could stand and face the damage her family had done and try to atone for it.

She climbed the three steps onto Seth's front

porch and rang the doorbell. Even if Seth was already aware of her, this would prove—perhaps just to herself—that she was operating with intention.

The barking continued and grew in volume, but the door didn't open. Lauren rang again. Now that she was here, she wasn't giving up. More barking and then a muffled voice and then the dog settled down. Seth *was* in there.

Lauren knocked on the front door, her fingers rattling the screen door. She counted to five, and her determination faded. Seth didn't want to see her. Her shoulders sank. She was at his home, uninvited. The man had a right to privacy and peace, especially after he'd suffered for a long time.

She turned and left the porch.

"YOU DIDN'T DO me any favors, Sparky," Seth said. "But you're not the worst guard dog."

The Chihuahua hopped and wiggled, clearly believing he'd pleased Seth.

Lauren had ridden past the fire station dozens of times. Had biked past his house. Their paths had crossed. So many times he would have given anything to have her back in his life, but those times were long past. And now she was on his front stoop. Seth put a hand flat on the inside of his front door as if he was holding it shut… Or was he trying to balance himself? All he had to do was open it.

Sparky had stopped barking. Lauren could ride away, perhaps thinking no one was home. Seth could go back to the hour of peace and quiet he had until he picked Teddy up from a friend's birthday party.

But he wouldn't have peace. He knew that.

Seth turned the knob and opened the door. The slight creak of the hinges arrested Lauren's movement, her leg frozen midair as she was swinging it over her bicycle. She lost her balance and tipped the bicycle, trapping her other leg underneath it and falling back on her elbows.

Seth dived through the door and raced down the steps, but Lauren was already extricating herself from the bike and getting up, rubbing her elbow.

"Are you okay?" he asked, reaching out but stopping just short of touching her.

She nodded, and he picked up her bike and put down its kickstand.

"Are you sure? Let me see your arm."

Lauren bent her elbow so he could look at it. There was a bright pink scrape from contacting the concrete sidewalk. It probably stung like crazy, but they'd had far worse scrapes when they were kids. Neither of them had shied away from climbing trees or racing their bikes or jumping off the dock.

"I could…put something on that for you," he offered. "It looks like it hurts."

Lauren dusted off her work pants. "It's okay."

They stared at each other. Seth didn't know what to say, but he wasn't the one whose turn it was to speak. Lauren had stopped by his house, her visit unannounced and unprecedented. She was there for a reason.

He waited. In the silence, he heard tapping on the screen door behind him and glanced back. Sparky was standing on his hind feet, trying to see out.

"Your dog is adorable," Lauren said. "I…have a cat now, my grandmother's."

Seth had wondered what would become of the cat he'd seen at Nanna Vera's. The poor thing had peered through the kitchen doorway as he and the other paramedic had tried to resuscitate Nanna Vera. It was always sad, seeing pets lose their owners, and sometimes the first responders felt a responsibility for locating temporary pet care. In this case, he'd known Lauren was local and would handle things at the cute little house where he'd spent so much of his childhood.

"I'm glad he found a home," Seth said.

Lauren nodded. "Grandma named him Lord Henry, and he does like being treated like a member of royalty. He's the king of my couch and is picky about food."

"I'm glad my dog isn't named Sir Sparky. It would give him ideas."

Lauren smiled at him and, for a moment, he felt like a kid again, the two of them sharing a joke, sitting around a firepit in the shared yard between her parents' and her grandma's houses. The warmth that filled him was almost painful.

"What did you… Why are you here?" he asked, his words sounding gruff as he battled his emotions.

"I wanted to talk. Can we…just talk? For a minute?"

Seth glanced at his watch, mostly to buy himself a few seconds but also to imply he didn't have much time. "I have to pick Teddy up in a few minutes," he said, though the few minutes was closer to sixty minutes.

"I'll be quick," Lauren said. "Please." She hadn't been flustered by falling off her bike and scraping her arm, but her cheeks flushed pink now. "I wanted to say something I wish I'd said a long time ago, but I didn't know until Grandma died, and now I'm afraid it's too late."

Her words rushed out and Seth's brain hurried to keep up and process.

"I'm sorry," she said, looking at him with tears in her eyes. "All these years, I thought you had misled Maggie and then broken her heart. She let us all believe that, and we thought you betrayed our family's love for you." She looked down and took a deep shuddering breath.

Seth took one of his own. He hated seeing anyone suffer, and Lauren was suffering right now. But then he remembered his own misery, being eighteen with no safe haven anymore. No more Benedict family where there was always a light on and something to eat. No more Lauren, who understood him without even asking questions.

She hadn't asked questions before turning her back on him alongside her parents and sister.

She looked up again. "I thought you betrayed me." The tears fell freely on her cheeks and he almost broke and reached for her. He clasped his hands behind his back, his grip almost painful. He waited. Those words were going to haunt him, and he was tired of being haunted by the Benedicts.

Lauren pulled herself together and dried her tears with the sleeve of her uniform shirt. Seth felt exposed. The afternoon sun beat down on him. They were standing in his front yard where neighbors or anyone passing by could see them, him standing like a statue, a beautiful woman crying in front of him. Worse than anything was the raw nerve endings she'd exposed. He felt as if they were in flames. This was a fire he couldn't fight.

"Grandma left me a letter telling me to ask Maggie what really happened between you two."

Seth sucked in a breath. Nanna Vera had made a legacy request. His knees felt weak and he unclasped his hands, needing them at his sides for balance.

"So I did," Lauren said, her voice so low he could hardly hear it. He resisted the urge to sway toward her so he wouldn't miss a word.

"What did she tell you?" he asked, feeling as if he was in a fast-moving current of water rushing toward the falls. Was the truth finally out?

"That summer when I was seventeen and you were eighteen…"

Their eyes met, and Seth remembered every summer evening with Lauren. Fireflies lighting the dusk. He'd taken her hand once, helping her into the rowboat. And he'd held it long enough to know their friendship was turning into something more. He'd believed she knew it, too.

Lauren swallowed. "Maggie told me about the pregnancy."

Seth let out a breath. He couldn't believe this was happening.

"My parents didn't like that guy she was dating. At all. They didn't trust him, and they had warned her not to get involved with him. I'm sure they were relieved when she suddenly ended up—" Lauren's voice shook and she paused. "Engaged to you instead." A tear slid down Lauren's cheek. "It wasn't even your baby, and you tried to rescue her by marrying her."

"Lauren, there's no point in rehashing what happened." Remembering the pain from that time in his life made the walls of his chest constrict, and he could hardly breathe. He'd been young. He'd been loyal and grateful to the family that showed him love. He'd believed he could rescue Maggie. It was the first time he learned a painful lesson that you can't always save people, and even if you do, there's always collateral damage.

He'd absorbed that damage and sacrificed his feelings for Lauren in one big, well-intended gesture. He wanted to go back into his house and close the door on all of it, but Lauren had her shoulders squared now and looked determined to keep going.

"She told me about that summer night she was crying on the dock and you came along. That she told you she was pregnant and you offered to marry her."

He remembered that night so vividly. Had relived it over and over.

"I can't believe you did that," Lauren said. "You're such a good guy, and you thought you could save her from facing the consequences of her pregnancy."

Seth took a step backward. "You think I'm a good guy now?" He couldn't keep the bitterness out of his words. When Maggie had suffered a miscarriage just a month after their engagement, she'd told him she was calling the whole thing off. She was devastated, so he'd offered to take the blame for ending things. The Benedict family had treated him like a criminal.

"I do," Lauren said.

She held out a hand as if she was making a peace offering. "I came to say thank you. I never knew what you tried to do, that you wanted to rescue Maggie. My parents never knew. We treated you like you were the bad guy, but now we know you weren't. Not at all." She sucked in another deep breath and her outstretched hand shook. "So I came to say thank you for what you did, and I'm sorry. I'm so sorry for the way we—I—treated you afterward."

Seth's knees still felt as if they were made of pudding, but he held his ground and didn't take her hand. This was an apology he would have relished years ago. It would have been the balm he needed, the hope he craved. But so much time had gone by. It felt like rolling up to a burning house with the fire truck when the whole place was already ashes.

"You really didn't know," he said.

Lauren shook her head and finally dropped her hand. "Not until the evening of Grandma's funeral. When you saw me and Maggie walking in the park. You were with Teddy."

The mention of his son made him stiffen. His son was his future. Lauren was his past and she didn't deserve his emotional energy. She'd forfeited it. He'd moved on. He shook his head, still keeping his hands at his sides. "It doesn't matter anymore."

"It does," Lauren insisted.

"Why?" he asked. "Do you think an apology now erases what happened? It was a long time ago. You should let it go." He crossed his arms and willed himself to be strong. He was not going to be drawn into the past. It had taken far too long to recover the last time.

"But I want—"

"What? What do you want, Lauren?" His words came out bitter. Sparky scratched at the door behind him and whined. Seth wanted to retreat inside his house and sink down onto his couch with the little dog, process everything Lauren had told him in private. He needed time to pull himself together before he had to pick up Teddy.

She swallowed, and Seth could see that Lauren either wasn't sure what she wanted or didn't know how to ask for it. He could rescue her by telling her all was forgiven. But no one had come to his rescue.

"Why didn't you tell me the truth?" she asked.

The direct question hit a nerve because it was one he'd wrestled with a lot, especially at first. Poor Maggie had been emotionally destroyed at the time by her boyfriend's betrayal and then the miscarriage. Seth had offered to take the fall, to tell everyone he'd made promises and broken them, broken her heart.

Some part of him hadn't thought the Benedict family would believe the story he and Maggie had concocted. Didn't they know him better than that? Didn't Lauren know him better than that? But they'd accepted it, defended Maggie and shut him out.

"I made a promise to Maggie," he said.

Lauren's shoulders sagged. "I get why you kept that promise at first, but wasn't there a single point in time over the last ten years that you might have thought of revealing the truth?"

"Did she?" he asked.

Lauren looked down. "No."

He knew he shouldn't say it. He was hurting himself by voicing it as much as he was hurting Lauren. But the question had been on his heart for a long time. "Wasn't there a single point in time over the last ten years that *you* might have asked me what happened?"

Lauren's tears started afresh. "I thought I knew what happened. Can you blame me for taking my sister's word?"

The fight went out of him. "No. I can't blame you for siding with your own family instead of the scruffy neighbor kid who'd already taken advantage of you all enough."

A small sob escaped Lauren. "That's not true. You weren't taking advantage. You were my best friend."

You were my best friend, too. Until she was suddenly gone. She couldn't swoop in now and try to make amends or rekindle that friendship—if that was even what she was trying to do.

Seth crossed his arms. He had to end this conversation now before it got any more personal. He needed to escape before he let himself get destroyed. Again.

"You survived just fine without me," he said coldly. He turned and vaulted up his steps, leaving Lauren sobbing in his front yard. He closed the door and turned the lock, and then he sat on his couch, Sparky on his lap, and rested his head against the cushions. He had to compose himself before picking up Teddy. His own father had allowed losing his wife to damage his parenting, leaving Seth to grow up lonely and turn to a neighboring family for love. His father had died a hopeless drunk a few years ago without ever knowing his grandson. Seth would never allow his personal losses or pain to interfere with giving Teddy the happiest, most stable childhood possible.

He didn't want Teddy to ever depend on someone else who could turn their backs on him.

CHAPTER SIX

LAUREN OPENED ONE eye and stared at Lord Henry, who was asleep on her chest. He had politely avoided her bed for the first week but then had slowly crept right into every crevice of her life, bed included. He followed her into the bathroom, gave her unblinking stares as she watered her house plants and had become a relentless lap cat, never taking no for an answer.

"You're needy," she said. Not that she was complaining. Her miserable encounter with Seth a few days ago had left her doubting her memories, her feelings and her motives for trying to right a wrong.

Lord Henry tilted his head and gave her an expression that seemed to be cat-judgment. "Okay, I'm needy, too," she admitted. She accepted his nudging, enjoying the feel of his soft fur on her face. The unconditional love erased some of the pain of Grandma Vera's loss. But she wished she could have just five more minutes with her grandmother so she could ask one big burning question: Why had she never told Lauren the truth about Seth? Her grandmother could have saved Lauren years of heartache.

And also…maybe… Seth could have been saved some heartache, too. He *had* missed her… Hadn't he? Was he as devastated as she had been to lose their friendship? She may never know. He clearly didn't want to talk to her or revisit any of it. He was angry. She'd opened the door and her feelings were out in the wild where they were in great danger of being trampled.

Seth had pointedly closed his door, practically in her face.

Lauren sat up and Lord Henry jumped off the bed and headed for his food bowl in the kitchen. With rain in the forecast later in the morning, she wanted to get to work early and knock some of her outdoor projects off her list, just in case she ended up taking refuge in the greenhouse later. She brushed her teeth, pulled back her long auburn hair, which had dried into waves overnight, and buttoned up a clean uniform shirt. Lord Henry was waiting in the kitchen, and he enjoyed his breakfast while she ate hers and packed her lunch.

"Enjoy the sunshine on the couch this morning," she advised the cat.

At work, Lauren filled the gas tank of her UTV and loaded it with her favorite gardening tools. There was a blooming bush—a weigela—that needed to be pruned back now that the blossoms had faded. The weigela was right along a busy pathway, and she drove straight to it to get it done early before she'd be in the way of tourists. The bush was huge, almost obstructing one of the paths, but she hadn't wanted to cut it back before it bloomed. The long pink and white sprays were so pretty. Now that the bloom was past its peak, she could trim the big branches without affecting next year's bloom.

Lauren smiled and nodded to a few early morning walkers and joggers. *Good for them, getting here before the crowds and the rain.* She hummed a little as she shaped the bush, carefully reaching into the thick growth to find the right place to cut the branches. She didn't feel like singing this morning. Not with her soul-searching over the past two days after she'd tried talking to Seth. Her heart was tender, as if it was bruised and someone had poked it again in the same sore spot.

But she hummed anyway to cheer herself up. After a moment, though, she realized the humming wasn't coming entirely from her. It took her a moment to recognize that it was actually buzzing. Deep buzzing that could only come from a multitude of insects.

And that was when she saw the hornet's nest

built deep under the overgrown bush. She didn't have time to react. They came at her in a drove and she felt fire on her neck and arms. Lauren dropped her clippers and ran the few feet to her UTV. To her horror, she saw a woman jogging along the path, coming up behind the bush. "Run," she shouted, but the woman just looked at her in confusion. "The other way," Lauren shouted.

But it was too late.

The hornets were furious, and they attacked the jogger, too.

"Get in!" Lauren shouted from the driver's seat. The woman dived into the cart and Lauren sped down the path, trying to outrun the hornets. She got on her radio and called the office to send someone right away to close the path and deal with the hornets. Her neck and arms were on fire and Lauren didn't stop the cart until she got close to the visitor center.

"Are you okay?" she said, turning to the woman.

The woman stared at her, her eyes huge. The woman was definitely not okay. She had a hand on her chest and seemed to be struggling to breathe. Was it just because she'd been jogging and then had a huge shock?

"Did you get stung?" Lauren asked. As a horticulturist, she'd been stung dozens of times. It was never pleasant, but she knew the pain would fade.

Instead of answering her, the woman pointed to a bracelet on her wrist with a medical symbol. Lauren grabbed her wrist and read the words that turned her blood to ice. She grabbed her radio. "911," she told the parks dispatcher after she identified herself. "Hornet attack. Beesting allergy by the visitor center. Help!"

The woman was very fair-skinned with blond hair, and the red welts from the stings were already appearing on her skin. Lauren's neck and arms were on fire from her own hornet stings, and the cramped quarters of her UTV made her feel constricted, breathless. There was a bench nearby. Lauren scrambled out of the vehicle and took the jogger by the arm, urging her toward the bench. Maybe she could breathe better there with the fresh air coming off the falls. How far away was help? The bench was only a few feet from the UTV, but the woman's knees buckled and Lauren held on to her, easing her down onto the grass.

EpiPen! That was what she needed right now. The parks staff did training every year on basic first aid, which included the use of the auto-injectors. There was one in the first aid kit on her UTV… Wasn't there? She tried to remember, her mind racing. Lauren wanted to run back to her UTV but she'd have to leave the woman alone for a minute.

It was barely seven in the morning, too early for most tourists, especially with rain in the forecast.

Lauren started to get up, but the jogger grabbed her arm, her fingers clawing into Lauren's skin. The woman breathed rapidly as she pointed to the fanny pack she wore around her waist, and everything clicked in Lauren's brain despite the burning agony of her own multiple stings and the rising panic in her chest.

Lauren unzipped the pack, found an EpiPen and held it up for the woman to see. She hoped it would reassure her that help was imminent. Lauren took ten seconds to read the instructions. She had to get this right and only had one shot at it. The auto-injector wasn't exactly like the one they practiced with at first aid training, but the directions were clear. She removed the cap and looked to the jogger, who nodded furiously. Lauren pressed the pen firmly against the woman's thigh, flinching a little at the zing it made, and then she checked her watch. 7:02. The first responders would want to know what time she administered the shot.

She was never grumbling about attending the mandatory safety training again.

Lauren knelt behind the woman and let her lean against her. "You're going to be okay. The shot will work. Any second now you'll feel the relief. It'll be okay. You'll be okay." Lauren repeated the reassurances over and over, as much for herself as for the suffering jogger. She checked her watch again. 7:03. Only a minute had passed, but it felt like a year. What if the shot didn't work? Finally, she heard sirens getting louder and closer and her own breathing eased.

HE WAS TEN minutes early for his seven-o'clock shift and had just walked into the fire station when he heard the call out. It was up to the officer on duty, but generally if there was a call at shift change, the shift coming on took it. Seth cocked an ear, listening to the dispatcher, already mentally preparing himself to grab whatever gear necessary and be ready to roll.

"Medical emergency near visitor center state park," the dispatcher's voice said. "Report of park employee attacked by hornets, possible anaphylaxis, victim has difficulty breathing."

There were emergencies and there were Emergencies. This was a big one and seconds mattered. Seth rolled up the overhead door and started the ambulance. The chief jumped in with him. "Go!"

Seth headed out first with the ambulance, and he heard one of the other trucks right behind him. He was already mentally reviewing the park entrance and quickest route to the visitor center. Local first responders knew the vast state park well, including the roads and entrances that were foot-traffic-only except for emergency vehicles. The state park had its own rangers who were often first on the scene and were helpful in directing the fire department. People with emergencies tended to panic and move around. Whoever was attacked by hornets could be inside or outside, on the near side or far side of the visitor center. Seth's best hope was that someone would be greeting them and waving their arms.

Park employee attacked by hornets. A name and a face popped into his brain. Lauren was a park employee and doing the kind of work that would expose her to a hornet's nest. Difficulty breathing. The thought gripped him, and a rush of fear made his own breath feel short. Was Lauren allergic to beestings? She hadn't been as a child. He remembered both of them getting stung, more than once, since they spent the whole summer outside. Nanna Vera had some concoction in a little glass jar in her fridge that always took away the heat and pain. Lauren hadn't been allergic then, but people could change. And the number of stings and exact type of insect could trigger anaphylactic shock.

Lauren. He'd rejected her apology a few nights ago. The thought left him cold as he sped toward the emergency. He'd had plenty of time to mull over his feelings for the Benedict family over the last decade, had felt unsettled and without closure. And now that closure was a possibility, he'd turned away from it. What if he didn't get a second chance?

Seth drove through the park gates as fast as he could without causing a hazard to pedestrians and other cars. It was so early there was almost no one around. Questions—How long ago was the hornet attack? Who called it in? Were they already too late?—raced through his mind.

"Over there," Bear said, pointing to a UTV parked haphazardly. And a park ranger vehicle was rapidly approaching, lights flashing, from the opposite direction.

Seth could see two people on the ground. One of them was waving. As he drove closer, he recognized the white shirt of a parks uniform on the person waving. He saw long auburn hair as he closed the distance.

Lauren. If she could wave down the emergency responders, she wasn't the victim.

He parked and left the squad running. Chief Bear grabbed a bag out of the back while Seth dropped to his knees beside Lauren and a pale blond woman on the ground. He took a quick assessing glance. Judging from the red welts, both women had been attacked by hornets.

"She's allergic. I used her EpiPen at 7:02 because she couldn't breathe," Lauren said, her words calm but quick. "She has at least three hornet stings I can find. Ground hornets."

His partner was already uncoiling oxygen tubing as Seth put his fingers on the woman's wrist and checked her pulse. Her breathing and pulse were fast, but she didn't seem to be struggling to breathe.

"Good work," Seth said, meeting Lauren's eyes. "Are you okay?"

"Stung a bunch but okay." Now that he listened, her calm seemed almost eerie considering the red welts on her face, neck and arms. She sat back on the ground and pulled her knees up, hugging them as Seth and Bear took over. Two more firefighters arrived with a second ambulance and the chief directed them to grab the gurney and ready the patient for transport to the hospital. They worked fast, and the jogger was on the gurney when she reached out and grabbed Lauren's arm again.

"Thank you," she rasped out.

Lauren squeezed the woman's hand. "You're welcome. They'll take good care of you."

Another park employee, a woman with a name tag that identified her as Barb, arrived in a park vehicle and ran over to where Lauren still sat on the ground, knees against her chest. "Oh, my god. Are you okay? You must have been stung a dozen times."

"I'm okay," Lauren said.

Seth and the chief exchanged a glance and the chief guided Barb a few steps away. Seth vaguely recognized her as the grounds supervisor. Bear would get the information to write a report, and Seth needed to make sure Lauren was really all right.

"Do you feel able to get up?" he asked.

She nodded.

He offered her a hand and pulled her to her feet. She wobbled, her knees shaky, probably from sitting on the ground and the aftereffects of adrenaline. Seth had experienced the rush and fall of adrenaline many times, and he knew the quivering empty space it left in your body when it departed. He wrapped an arm around her shoulders and steered her to a nearby bench.

The ambulance with the jogger drove off and Seth heard them turn on the siren when they reached the park exit. They'd be at the hospital in minutes where doctors could assess the victim and decide on further treatment.

"Don't move," he told Lauren. He jogged over to the remaining ambulance and opened the side compartment to retrieve two ice packs. He squeezed and activated them, then laid one on Lauren's arm where a string of red welts had swollen. He sat next to her on the bench and held the other one to her temple.

"We'll need information for an official report, but right now let's just talk about what happened."

Lauren drew a deep breath. "I was cutting back an overgrown bush near a trail and there must have been a hornet's nest under it. They came at me. That lady was jogging past, and I yelled for her to run. We both did, but they got us anyway. We jumped in my UTV, and I drove fast and I guess they gave up chasing us."

"Smart," Seth said.

"I saw she wasn't okay, and she pointed to her bracelet, which said she had a beesting allergy. I tried to get her out of the cart and get to this bench, but we didn't make it. The lady pointed to her fanny pack and I dug out her EpiPen and pressed it to her thigh. It was at 7:02."

"You told me," Seth said. "You did everything right."

Lauren nodded but didn't say anything. She was so calm it was scary.

Seth checked her pulse and assessed her breathing. He counted at least ten stings that he could see. "Are you sure you're feeling okay?"

"Yes."

"I'd like to take you to the hospital, just to be on the safe side."

"I told you I'm fine."

Seth sighed. "Lauren, do you remember that

time we were skateboarding down the hill by the old campground and crashed?"

The childhood memory had lain dormant, but Lauren's cool demeanor had revived it. She glanced at him and seemed to be seeing him for the first time. The shock of the last ten minutes had drawn a blanket over her emotions, but now she was starting to shake.

"Your arm was broken but you were so worried about the goose egg I had on my head that you ignored your injury until about an hour later," Seth said. "You never shed a tear until we limped back to your house and your mom saw your arm."

"I thought you'd cracked your skull," Lauren said. "And you had a bloody lip."

"I remember." He also remembered signing her cast and staying out of the lake the rest of that summer to keep Lauren company because she wasn't allowed in the water. "How are you feeling right now?" he asked. He took a blood pressure cuff from his bag and secured it on her arm.

"Fine."

Seth kept his mouth shut for a minute as he took her blood pressure, which was elevated but not dangerously so. He knew stress would do that…and pain. Those hornet stings had to hurt.

"It's okay to be rattled right now, Lauren," he said quietly.

She met his eyes and Seth believed he had her attention. Maybe she was about to tell him how she felt about being in a life-threatening situation, lean on him even. He would understand far better than most people. He was a rescuer. He wanted to help her right now.

"There's our hero," Chief Bear said, coming over with the park employee. The woman immediately sat on the bench on Lauren's other side and hugged her.

"Are you all right?" she asked again. Barb took Lauren by both shoulders, ignoring Seth, and looked Lauren over as if she were her own daughter.

Lauren nodded.

"You saved that woman's life," Barb said. "The fire chief just told me she could have died if you hadn't acted so fast. I'm so proud of you. I don't know how you did it, especially when you were stung so many times yourself."

"It was the training," Lauren said.

Barb put a hand on her heart. "I'm so glad we just did that a few weeks ago. Are you sure you're okay?"

"I think so," Lauren said.

Seth noticed that her voice quavered a little.

The adrenaline was definitely wearing off and she'd be feeling the pain of those stings hard now.

He stood. "I believe we should take her to the hospital," he said, seeing an opportunity for support from Barb, who he guessed was Lauren's supervisor, or at least a friendly coworker.

"No," Lauren said. "I'm okay. I'll just put something on these stings."

Again, Seth remembered that little jar in Nanna Vera's fridge. What was in that stuff anyway?

"I insist," Barb said. "You're going to the hospital as a precaution. This is a serious workplace incident and I won't take no for an answer." Barb looked at the chief. "I could drive her, couldn't I?"

"No," Seth said before his boss could answer. "Our reason for taking her is to make sure she's not going to have a delayed reaction. That's a lot of venom. She'll be safer going with us."

"But—" Lauren said.

"It's for the best," the fire chief reiterated. Seth got up and offered Lauren a hand. He waited while she stood and assessed her closely to make sure she wasn't going to wobble. He took her arm and led her to the ambulance. "You can meet us there if you like," he told Barb over his shoulder.

Lauren didn't object as Seth supported her and helped her into the ambulance. The chief got in front to drive. She sat on the cot where he pointed.

"This isn't necessary," she said.

Seth used his stethoscope to listen to her heart, which was racing. His own was racing, too, and he reminded himself that Lauren was just like any other patient he'd cared for. Except she wasn't. She was his childhood friend. Her family had shown him what family meant. He'd driven the thought clear into the back of his mind, but there had—at one time—been an unspoken belief in his heart.

That he'd always be with Lauren. She was his soulmate. And then he'd sacrificed the love he felt for her by trying to rescue her sister. He hadn't asked Lauren's permission. He'd never had the chance to ask her how she felt about it. The move had ultimately destroyed him… But had it destroyed her, too?

Seth took another blood pressure and pulse reading as the ambulance got underway and he carefully recorded his findings on the tablet they used for reporting. He called into the hospital emergency room with an en route report, just as he always did. It was a short trip. He could stay busy.

But then Lauren leaned back and closed her eyes. He touched her cheek. "Okay?" he asked gently.

She gave a tiny nod and a tear leaked out the side of her eye.

Rain splashed the windows on the ambulance, taking Seth back to rainy days when they were kids. He wanted to comfort her. She'd hardly changed in the last ten years. She still looked just like the friend of his youth. Back then, he would have wrapped an arm around her if she was sad and suggested they get ice cream or play a board game until the rain ended.

Things had been simpler then.

"I've been a firefighter for a long time," he said. "In the heat of the moment, I'm brave. It's only afterward that I start thinking about what could have happened."

Her eyes were still closed, but she nodded again. He watched her closely, counting her breaths, assessing her status.

"You did everything right and saved someone's life. You need time to process that." He should leave it at that. Lauren had a family and friends. Her boss was aware and clearly concerned. She had people to talk to. But would they really understand? He took a breath and added, "And if you want to talk, anytime, I'm available."

Lauren opened her eyes and blinked at him. He could guess what she was thinking. They hadn't talked in years, and when she'd tried a few days ago, he'd run inside his house and locked the door.

Seth heard the ambulance slow down, and he knew from long experience they were arriving at the hospital. He had no idea if Lauren would choose him to talk to, but he did hope she wouldn't keep this morning's trauma bottled up inside where it would gnaw away at her like an unhealed wound.

Talking could be healing.

He wrote down his cell phone number, gave it to her and watched her tuck it in her pocket just before the fire chief parked the ambulance and opened the back doors.

CHAPTER SEVEN

MARLIN AND THREE other park employees texted her before dinnertime later that day. Lauren didn't feel like talking to anyone. When the hospital released her, Barb drove her home and gave her a strict lecture about resting and calling if she needed anything. Barb called her two hours later, left a voice message when she didn't answer and then called her again.

She'd showered, napped and taken the antihistamines recommended at the hospital. And now she was restless. The morning had been all kinds of too much and her nerves were still on edge. Her personal collection of eleven hornet stings was a painful reminder, just in case she tried to forget any of it. Not that she would. The memory of the jogger's panicked face, the snap of the EpiPen when Lauren had injected the woman and then Seth arriving with his compassion and competence and offers to talk.

Where had that guy been a few days ago when she'd knocked on his door?

Lauren sighed and looked at Lord Henry, who stared at her from the top of a couch cushion. "Feel like talking?" she asked. "Got a favorite movie?"

The cat didn't react to any of those words, his usual favorite words being *dinner* and *salmon*.

She could call Seth. He'd encouraged her to contact him if she wanted to talk. And she did want to talk to someone other than her grandmother's cat. But Seth was complicated. He'd been nice, yes, but it was only the circumstances. There was still a hefty ten-year weight hanging between them, and she needed quick, uncomplicated comfort right now.

Lauren picked up her phone and texted Marlin. A tree specialist, Marlin had joined the Niagara Falls State Park staff only a year ago, but she and Lauren had connected through a shared love of the park, the outdoors and the incredible cupcakes at a bakery just outside the park's entrance.

Can I declare a cupcake emergency? Lauren texted.

She got an immediate response. I'll bring your favorites.

Are you still at work? Lauren asked. Her friend usually started and ended work later than Lauren, mostly by choice. It was almost five o'clock.

Yes. Leaving in a minute.

Then I'll meet you at Cupcake Heaven. I need to get out of the house.

Her friend didn't argue, and Lauren decided to walk to the bakery to burn off some of her nervous energy. She took a final glance at herself in the bathroom mirror before she left her apartment. It was only a few blocks to the cupcake place. Yes, there were red welts on her face, neck and arms, but she wasn't going to scare anyone too much. She let her hair down to help cover some of the red marks, and then she fed Lord Henry and started walking.

She thought about the jogger she'd helped. Was she okay? Lauren wished she could take her a cupcake or send flowers, but she didn't even know the woman's name. Seth would know. It had to be in his report. But Lauren was certain that would be a violation of patient privacy, and the fire department and the hospital would not release that information. She hoped the woman might contact the park office, or even that she might see the woman again on one of the trails. She didn't even know if the jogger was a local or a tourist. She saw lots of people jogging in the park. From now on, she was going to pay closer attention, just in case.

Cupcake Heaven had opened the previous summer, and it had quickly tapped into the sweet tooth of many a local and tourist. The bold pink awning shaded wide windows with cupcakes painted on them. Outside, a sign advertised the daily specialty flavors. Lauren paused to read it. Chocolate Waterfall. Bridal Veil Vanilla. Maid of the Mist Mocha. Swirling Water Strawberry.

"Yes to all four," she muttered to herself. She started to push open the door, but it swung open from the inside and revealed Marlin with a box of cupcakes and a drink carrier with two coffees.

"Beat you to it," she said. "I got all four daily specials. We'll cut them in half and share them so we won't even have to feel guilty about calories."

"You're the best," Lauren said.

"Okay to eat outside?"

"Sure," Lauren said. She glanced around, but it was a beautiful summer evening and all the outdoor tables were full. Lauren recognized a few locals who worked downtown or at tourist attractions. She didn't feel like talking to anyone else, though, and didn't want to answer questions about her red welts. "We could grab a bench over by the park entrance," she suggested.

"Okay," Marlin agreed.

Lauren reached for the cupcake box and carried it while her friend held their drinks.

"I got us both decaf. Figured you wouldn't want to add a sleepless night on top of the lousy day you're having," Marlin said.

"Thanks."

"Although you did get the day off," Marlin teased.

"And it was glamorous. I got a free ride to the hospital, answered a thousand questions and discovered that antihistamines don't make me sleepy like a normal person."

"I'm jealous," Marlin said.

They found a stone bench near the park entrance and opened the box of cupcakes between them. Marlin took a plastic knife and fork and sliced the vanilla cupcake in half. Lauren took the lid off her decaf to let it cool.

"Your stings don't look too bad," Marlin said.

Lauren gave a little laugh. "Good. I don't want to scare anyone away."

"The exterminators found and removed the hornet's nest. They kept that trail closed for a few hours, but it's safe now." Marlin took a bite of Bridal Veil Vanilla and Lauren helped herself to the other half. "Everyone is talking about you being a hero and saving someone's life," Marlin said. "I don't know if I would have thought fast enough to do it."

"I don't even know if I was thinking," Lauren said. "I was reacting. The lady who got stung did all the work. She pointed to her medical bracelet and then her fanny pack. I just connected the dots."

"Uh-huh," Marlin said. "You can downplay it, but I still think you're amazing and so does everyone else. Barb is probably going to give you your own parking space—not that you drive unless it's snowing—and she is certainly going to ask you to be the guest speaker at all future first aid trainings. No one will ever be able to complain about sitting through that training again."

Lauren laughed. She didn't want to relive the morning's events, but it did feel good to talk about it a little. The sugary cupcake plus Marlin's friendship was taking the tension out of her shoulders.

"Chocolate Waterfall is next," Marlin said. "I hope it has a gooey chocolate center."

"We deserve that," Lauren agreed.

Marlin cut the dark brown cupcake in half and chocolate oozed out. Both women got their hands sticky scooping up their halves and eating them.

"Coffee break," Marlin declared. "And then I'll be ready for more sweetness."

"Good plan." They wiped their fingers on napkins and sipped coffee. "I'm coming back to work tomorrow," Lauren said. "Not that I couldn't have come back this afternoon. We've all been stung in the line of tree and flower duty."

"Not eighty-five times."

"I only counted eleven stings when I checked."

"That's more than enough," Marlin said.

Lauren sipped her coffee and nodded. Her friend was right. The initial pain had faded, but she felt tender and raw. The jogger had to feel much worse. What were the aftereffects of getting hit with an EpiPen? "When I come in tomorrow, I'm hoping Barb will know something about the other woman. I just want to know how she is," Lauren said.

"I heard she was a tourist from somewhere down south, maybe Georgia. That's what someone at the office said, but I don't know how reliable that is. Maybe she'll get in touch with the office before she goes home."

"I hope so," Lauren said.

"I do, too. I'd feel awful if this ruined her vacation and she never wanted to come to Niagara Falls again," Marlin said. She cut the Maid of the Mist Mocha cupcake in half and picked up her share. "Oof. That is either the cutest or most pathetic little dog," Marlin said after she took a bite. "So ugly, it's adorable."

Lauren turned around to see what her friend was looking at.

Seth. He and his son were wearing matching Buffalo Bills T-shirts, and Teddy had Sparky on a leash. Teddy was pointing in the other direction where an ice cream vendor had a semipermanent structure. He didn't see her and Lauren on the bench because his five-year-old attention was mesmerized by ice cream and his role as dog walker. Seth, on the other hand, was a first responder who was apparently hyperaware of his surroundings. Lauren felt it the moment his vision swept the area and landed on her.

She expected him to look away, using the convenient excuse of his son's desire for ice cream. That would have happened a week ago. Even a day ago. But instead, he put a hand on his son's shoulder and redirected him. They were coming over.

"Do you know the adorably ugly dog's incredibly handsome owner?" Marlin asked. "Not that I'm looking for a man. They always seem to break my heart because they don't understand my sense of humor."

"Your dream man who gets your jokes is still out there somewhere," Lauren said. "And yeah, he's an old friend of the family."

Although they'd become fast friends in the past year, Marlin was not from Niagara Falls and didn't know all the locals. And Lauren had had no reason to fill her in on her childhood friendships and heartaches.

She sipped her coffee, hoping she didn't have any chocolate on her teeth. She shouldn't be nervous. Seth had seen her plenty of times at her worst and her best. This morning had been an odd combination of both.

Seth and Teddy were at their bench in seconds, and Teddy was the first to speak.

"Hi, flower lady. Do you need a Band-Aid?"

The boy pointed to the red welts on her face, neck and arms. His eyes were wide and his expression sympathetic.

"Hi, Teddy," Lauren said. "I don't think a Band-Aid would really help. I got a bunch of beestings when I surprised them at their house."

She didn't want to say *hornet attack* or make it sound dramatic because that could scare the boy away from the outdoors and flowers.

"Did it hurt?" he asked.

"Only a little. The hurt goes away fast. They just wanted to remind me that they live here, too."

Though Seth hadn't said anything yet, Lauren could feel him assessing her. Was he evaluating the appearance of her stings or counting her breaths? Could he tell her heart was beating faster than normal? Maybe she had chocolate on her upper lip. She resisted the urge to check.

"Hi," Marlin said, breaking the tension and reminding Lauren that she had not made introductions.

"Sorry," Lauren said. "Marlin, this is Seth Jones and his son, Teddy. That beautiful animal is Sparky."

Marlin held out her hand. "Marlin Fitzgerald."

"Nice to meet you," Seth said.

"Are you a firefighter?" Marlin asked.

Seth nodded. "For ten years now."

"Did you hear about my hero friend here and how she saved someone's life this morning?" Marlin asked.

Lauren felt her cheeks heat, which only made her beestings hotter.

"I was there," Seth said. "After Lauren had already administered the EpiPen and rescued the victim."

"You should recruit her," Marlin said.

Lauren gave a half laugh in objection. "No threat of that. This morning was way too much excitement for me."

Seth turned his intense focus back on her. "Are you okay?" he asked, his voice low.

She nodded. Teddy was too young to be aware of the tension, but Lauren was certain Marlin would notice it and ask questions when Seth walked away.

"I don't know how you do your job," Marlin said. "I was shaking all over just hearing about Lauren's morning. Sometimes I get a little taste of danger when a tree branch falls in a high wind, but generally, being an arborist is a peaceful job."

Seth gave Marlin a professional smile. "We

have a lot of training, and I have great partners on the fire department. It's not always dangerous, but it is always rewarding."

Lauren thought his answer sounded like a textbook firefighter answer, professional, confident and mature. She tried to reconcile it with the boy she had known who hid his feelings well with most people when they were young, but she had known how soft his heart was and how tender his feelings were because of his home life. Losing his mom and growing up with a neglectful father hadn't made him hard then, and he'd chosen an occupation in which he would help people. Save them. Maybe it was his way of gaining power over his own need to be rescued, especially after her family had abandoned him.

"The only hard parts," he added quietly, glancing at his son, whose attention was on the dog instead of the grown-ups' conversation, "are when you can't help someone or rescue them. Those days are tough."

"I can't imagine," Marlin said.

Lauren didn't want to imagine. She knew Seth had been on the call to her grandmother's house and had tried to resuscitate her. That had to be hard for him, knowing the victim. But she suspected his meaning was broader. There were a lot of times when you wanted to help someone and you just couldn't. Her mind leaped to how he'd tried to rescue her sister and the thanks he'd gotten for that.

Her heart wasn't racing anymore. Instead, it had settled into a quiet rhythm, and she was suddenly very tired. Today had been a lot. Even the sugar rush from the cupcakes had abandoned her. She straightened her spine and tried to look like she was okay. She didn't want anyone fussing over her. Seth would understand if she shared the way she felt, but there wasn't anything he could do about it. He was right about that—you can't always fix things.

"We still have a cupcake left, and I for one have had enough sugar tonight," Lauren said. "Would you like it? It's strawberry." She didn't have to add that she knew he loved that flavor. He looked surprised that she remembered.

Teddy's attention focused on the cupcake, but Seth put a hand on his shoulder. "We came here for ice cream."

Teddy nodded.

Seth turned back to Lauren. "Take some antihistamines tonight before bed. And keep an eye on your stings. If any of them continue to be red or hot, you need medical attention."

"Will do."

"Are you going back to work tomorrow?" he asked.

"Of course. My roses are waiting," she said.

"I love flowers," Teddy said.

Marlin smiled at Teddy. "I love trees especially, but flowers are nice, too."

"I come with my clubhouse friends sometimes and we smell them."

Seth's expression shifted and he looked troubled. He had to know about the camp the park was offering with the Rainbow Clubhouse. Last she'd heard, Teddy hadn't been on the attendance list. Although she knew he would love it and she liked seeing the sweet little boy, she was not his parent and she had no business getting in Seth's business.

"You are always welcome," Lauren said. "We have flowers blooming all summer and even in the fall."

"Time for ice cream?" Seth asked his son, who nodded wordlessly and gave Lauren and Marlin a little wave. They turned to walk away, but Seth stopped and turned back. "It was nice to meet you," he said to Marlin. He looked at Lauren. "Drink plenty of water to flush out the venom. You'll feel better tomorrow."

Marlin watched as father, son and dog crossed the wide-open area and lined up at the ice cream vendor.

"Is there a wife in the picture?" Marlin asked.

Lauren shook her head. "An ex."

"And am I imagining some tension between you two?"

"We were friends as kids, but that was a long time ago."

"Okay," Marlin said. Her tone suggested she had more to say, and Lauren braced for it. Luckily for her, Marlin shrugged. "He seems like a good guy, but I can't believe you offered him our last cupcake. You know this is my dinner, right?"

Lauren laughed. "Sorry."

"You're a hero, so I'm letting it slide. Want a ride home?"

It was only a few blocks, but the day had left her feeling like a deflated balloon, so she accepted a ride home.

Once inside, she drank a full glass of water, took two antihistamines and climbed into bed, where she tried to let all the emotions of the day wash out of her. Instead, she lay there thinking about how strange it was to be in contact with Seth again. She remembered the way he'd touched her cheek that morning, the way he'd cared for her. Yes, he was doing his job and she was sure he treated all patients with kindness and concern.

But she had to admit to herself that it had been nice.

CHAPTER EIGHT

"THE SECRET TO getting and keeping the attention of little kids is bugs," Lauren's boss, Barb, told her. "We've got ten kids enrolled, and Amber, our educational coordinator and interpreter, will be with you. Show them the bugs, and you'll be fine."

Lauren had no doubt she'd be fine. What could be more fun than hosting ten kids ranging from age four to eight? They were adorable and excited about her favorite subject—horticulture—and doing special duty just might get her out of picking beetles off the rosebushes. The special program with Rainbow Clubhouse was scheduled for three days a week for the rest of June and the first half of July. Maybe she would inspire a love of flowers and gardening in these kids, and someday it could be their career or at least a lifelong passion. She'd had her grandmother to inspire her, but not all kids are that lucky.

"Bugs. Got it," Lauren said, acknowledging

her boss's advice. She'd worked for Barb since she was a teenager and done her college internship under her guidance. She loved and trusted her boss, but she also hoped that the flowers would capture the kids' attention. Lauren could teach them about pollinators, annuals, perennials, how to weed properly, why pruning was healthy, which plants were medicinal and which were best to avoid. There was so much to share!

"Trust me," Barb said as she typed something on her computer. "I was a preschool classroom aide for three years when my daughters were that age."

Barb's office was in the corner of the park operations building. Some of the rangers stopped in for coffee or to use the restroom, and both the summer and year-round parks maintenance staff used the building as their home base. On the sunny June day, everyone else was out of the office and the building was quiet. Lauren watched dust dance in a ray of morning sunshine. She was anxious to get outside, but she was waiting for a roster of the day care kids who were signed up. Was Teddy Jones the tenth child on the list?

"That must have been fun," Lauren said. "Little kids are so excited about everything."

"And sticky and germy and they really tend to overshare. The other parents would have been aghast if they knew all the things their kids revealed at school about what went on in their households."

Lauren laughed. "I'll keep them busy with bugs and flowers so they don't reveal the family secrets." Her smile faded, though, when her thoughts turned to her own family secrets. She'd had a video call with her parents the evening before, just a check-in as they were all processing her grandmother's passing. Maggie was on the call, too, but she'd had to leave early to attend an evening school event for one of her children. Lauren had tried to keep the tone light by putting Lord Henry—usually just his tail—in front of the camera, but after Maggie left the call, her mom had directly asked if she had run into Seth lately and what she might do now that she knew the truth.

Barb looked up from her desk. "Thanks for taking this on. The hornet attack was only a few days ago, and I know you have a lot going on with your grandmother's passing. Are you sure you're okay with this extra work?"

"I like being busy," Lauren said. "It'll take my mind off deciding what to do with all the things Grandma left behind."

"Godspeed," Barb said, handing her a printed list. "I coordinated with the special programming office, and they'll have name tags for the kids. They'll also have reusable water bottles with each kid's name on them and handle taking attendance for our records. If this is successful, it's a nice feather in our cap when we lobby the park for more programming money and staff next year."

"I'll do my best."

"There could be some parent volunteers from the day care center. Not every day, but be prepared," Barb added. "I'd rather have kids than parents sometimes. Parents don't love the bugs."

Lauren resisted checking the names until she got outside and climbed into her UTV. She skimmed a finger halfway down the list and found the one she was looking for. She couldn't remember exactly when she'd met Seth and how old they'd been, but she did remember already knowing him on the first day of kindergarten when they were in the same class. They must have met by the time they were Teddy's age.

What a strange full circle.

The rose garden was in its second year at the parks and had been Lauren's special project the summer before. She'd held her breath all winter, hoping the new plants would tolerate the deep freeze that gripped Niagara Falls from Christmas until almost Valentine's Day. Of course, she'd chosen cold-tolerant varieties of roses, but it was still a huge relief when she'd examined each of the ten dozen rosebushes earlier in the spring and found signs of life on nearly all of them. She'd lost a few of the hybrid teas—yellow ones, which were notoriously weaker—but nearly every other rose had new growth.

In addition to neat rows of rosebushes in a variety of colors, pathways invited visitors to wind through the garden. Curved benches anchored the corners, and a large square of grass sat in the middle. Lauren had asked Jill from the day care center to meet her here with the kids for the first day.

Lauren parked her UTV near the rose garden on a parks maintenance trail hidden behind a large tree. She tugged on her hat and grabbed her bag and then claimed a bench near the grassy center of the garden. The sun warmed her shoulders, and she breathed in the scent of roses and earth. Not all the roses smelled the same, and she knew the plants well enough to discern the spicier ones from the muskier ones and also a hint of another scent she called velvet in her mind. Her thoughts drifted to a velvety red Mr. Lincoln, an old rose that had been in her grandmother's garden since she was a child. It grew near the back of the house where it got the heat from the dryer vent, and Grandma Vera had always claimed that was why it was so tall and happy.

The sound of children talking and laughing shook her out of her reverie, and Lauren opened her eyes to see Jill leading a group of kids. A parks employee, one of the summer programming workers, was with the group. Lauren knelt, feeling the grass to see if the morning sun had dried it enough for the kids to sit down for the initial introduction.

"Good morning," she said as the group approached. She waved to the kids and then smiled at Jill and Amber. "Are we ready?"

"The kids sure are," Jill said.

"Who's ready to learn about flowers?" Lauren asked.

One of the children was waving furiously at Lauren and she returned Teddy's wave.

"You have a fan," Amber observed.

"That's Teddy. He's really sweet but usually very quiet," Jill said.

Lauren considered Teddy for a moment, trying to decide if he looked like Seth at that age. She couldn't remember, but she knew she had pictures stored away somewhere. Her grandmother did, too. She'd found a big box of photos the previous evening while working at her grandmother's house. Inside, there were stacks of printed pictures—Grandma Vera always wanted physical copies of pictures instead of just looking at them on a screen—and at first glance, Lauren saw the photos went way back to her and Maggie as babies. They were the only grandkids, but if a stranger looked through the box, they would have assumed there was also a grandson.

Seth was in so many of the pictures. There he was at the picnic table on Lauren's sixth birthday and on the swing set with Lauren, his long legs trailing. When her dad had built a tree fort in a huge maple at the back of Grandma Vera's property, which adjoined the property where Lauren's house was, Seth was their first guest. In the picture, he wore jeans that were too short for him. His clothes always seemed to be too small, either because he grew too fast or his dad didn't notice he needed new ones.

The kids were gawking at her rose garden and wiggling, swinging their arms, chattering. They all looked happy and well cared for, as kids should be.

"Let's all sit down on the grass," Lauren said.

Amber instructed the ten children to sit criss-cross-applesauce and they looked expectantly up at Lauren and Jill. Jill gave Lauren a nod.

"Welcome to Niagara Falls State Park," Lauren said. "Raise your hand if you've been here before." Hands shot up from all the kids and Lauren feigned surprise. "Goodness. Maybe I should ask you to give me a tour." The kids giggled and smiled. *This was fun.* "I know you know all about the waterfalls, but I'm excited to tell you about my favorite subject today. Can anyone guess what that is?"

"Flowers?" one child volunteered.

"Waterfalls?"

"Sunshine?"

"Grass?"

Lauren smiled. "You're all so smart that you just reminded me I have more than one favorite thing, and all your suggestions are on my list. We're going to learn about flowers, but first we have to learn about something that is very important to flowers. Can anyone guess what that is?"

The kids forgot to raise their hands and, instead, shouted out suggestions including water, sunshine and butterflies.

"You're all right," Lauren said. She noticed that Teddy hadn't said a word. He waited, arms and legs crossed, smiling at her as if he expected her to impart ancient wisdom. "I need a volunteer," she said, and, finally, Teddy raised his hand. She jumped on the opportunity and called him up to stand next to her. "Teddy will be my announcer for today's topic," she said to the group. She leaned down and whispered into Teddy's ear, and he grinned broadly. "Tell them," she encouraged. "Nice and loud."

"Bugs!" Teddy said.

Lauren high-fived him and he sat down.

"I love bugs because they're good for flowers, and that's where we're going to start today." She tapped her phone's screen and cranked up the volume and, as the kids got up and danced to the bug song she'd queued earlier, Lauren felt like a child again, too, with all its wonder and joy.

AS A SINGLE DAD, Seth had to fit in grocery store runs whenever he could. Even though it felt like cheating, he liked to hurry home from work once a week, grab his car and hit the small local grocery while Teddy was still at day care. Not that he couldn't take his son along. Teddy was polite and obedient and rarely made any special requests for things he saw in the aisles. But, Seth had to admit, single parenting on top of a demanding job could be draining, and sometimes he needed a shortcut. If he was keeping an eye on Teddy in the grocery store, he tended to forget at least one ingredient for every dinner he planned to make that week.

He stood in front of the fresh vegetables, seriously considering which ones he could chop up and add to that evening's macaroni and cheese menu. Carrots went over pretty well, but they seemed like a weird choice for mac and cheese, maybe because they were in the same color family. Instead, he added fresh spinach to his cart, hoping it would blend in well. A shopping cart rolled up next to his, and Seth glanced over.

Lauren. Still wearing her work uniform, just like he was.

"Hi," she said. "I was just..." She gestured toward the produce as if she needed to offer a reason for being in the same space with him. It was not the first time he'd seen her at the grocery where the locals shopped, a few streets over from the tourist area. They'd crossed paths at restaurants and community events, too. She didn't need to offer an excuse for being there.

Seth didn't want to make small talk. Seeing her never got any easier, and each time it reminded him of that cavern his whole childhood had fallen into.

"Are you...feeling okay?" he asked. He pushed his cart backward and tried to extricate himself, but her cart was in the way. The wheels bumped and a glass jar of grape jelly clanged around in his cart.

She nodded. "All better." She pointed to her arm where only a faint trace of the red welts remained. "Like it never happened."

Seth clutched the handle of his cart. "It was a traumatic experience for you. You won't forget it happened."

"Neither will that poor lady who...you know. But there's good news. Her husband contacted the parks office to say thank you and he said she was released later that day from the hospital and she's fine."

Seth knew the woman had been treated and released—privacy laws were strict, but the department usually heard at least that much from the emergency room staff.

"Thanks to you, she'll be fine," he said.

Lauren gave him a half smile. He wanted to ask if she'd had any nightmares or moments when the hornet attack popped into her thoughts and stole her breath. Responses to emergencies, even ones that turned out okay, varied a lot and sometimes snuck up on people. That was why his fire department took a proactive and serious approach to the mental health of all the first responders.

"I saw your son yesterday when his group came to the park," Lauren said.

Seth nodded. "I know."

Not only did he know, he'd lain awake for an hour thinking about what his son had said about "flower camp" and, more specifically, the "flower lady." Teddy had even sung part of a song about ladybugs, but he couldn't remember the rest of it and they'd worked together to find it on the internet so Teddy could listen to it again. Seth had also heard about how bees and worms help flowers. His son had spoken more in one evening than he usually did in an entire month. It had been painfully wonderful—painful because Lauren had inspired all those words, not Seth. But still wonderful. He loved seeing his son inspired and excited.

"I hope he liked it," Lauren said.

"He did."

"I'm glad," Lauren said. "It's really fun to see kids enjoying the outdoors."

A volume of unspoken words hung between them. They'd had a lot of fun outdoors when they were kids and then teenagers together. Right up until the great separation happened. There had never been a proclamation, a scroll unfurled banishing Seth from the Benedict family forever. But he'd felt it anyway, and it was real. They'd taken Maggie's side and he'd backed away and withdrawn into himself to protect his heart as best he could. That isolation and reflexive protecting had been part of why he'd married someone who—in retrospect he could see it now—wasn't a grand passion. He hadn't given his whole heart to the marriage, and neither had she.

He was giving his whole heart to Teddy now and never letting him down.

"We only had ninety minutes, so we never made it out of the rose garden," Lauren said. "There were plenty of bugs to talk about there, and I got to show the kids a lot of different kinds of roses in bloom. There's a great variety."

"Oh?" He felt like he had to say something.

"Yeah. I planned and planted that rose garden last year, and I was really happy the hard winter didn't kill off any of the plants."

She stopped talking and seemed a little breathless, as if she'd rushed out the words but now found herself at a dead end.

"So many roses," she added, her voice low.

"I heard."

And he had heard. Teddy had told him about how the roses were only two years old, younger than the kids in his group. And he'd told Seth the colors and had even smuggled a yellow rose petal home in his pocket. Teddy had a lot to say, but Seth's tongue was tied at the moment.

It wasn't lost on Seth that he was being just as untalkative as his son usually was—and how that could make someone feel. Not that he'd asked her to describe flower camp, but he knew how it felt to be on the receiving end of a cold shoulder. He didn't want her to feel awkward or rejected. It was the same impulse that had driven him to become a firefighter, serving and protecting his fellow humans, helping people who were hurt. One of the counselors who came to talk with his team on occasion, especially after a tragic accident or devastating fire, had told him and his colleagues that protecting others was noble, but sometimes they had to take care of themselves, too.

And while he might want to tell Lauren to keep her roses to herself and then seal up his heart and run away, he *was* grateful that his son at least had something to say last evening. Maybe it wouldn't hurt to be polite.

He sighed. "Thank you for inspiring Teddy. He talked a lot about you—about the flower camp—last night and sang the ladybug song."

Lauren's smile lit up her whole face. "I hoped the kids would like that. I don't have much experience with little kids, and it's been a while since…"

She trailed off as Seth's gaze locked on hers, and he felt the old tug of connection they'd always shared. This was getting dangerous.

His childhood bond had snapped when he'd tried to rescue Lauren's sister, and Lauren had clearly thought the worst of him all these years. In fact, she'd shoved her cart right past him in this very grocery store a few months ago without a word or a look.

He should walk away right now, but the scent of the earthy vegetables all around them took him back to summer days gardening or lying on the lawn. He'd missed those days so much, had let that bitter loss pile up with his other losses.

"Since we were kids," he said, finishing her sentence. *Why not*, he reasoned. The words were hanging in the air. Maybe voicing them would take away their power.

"Yes," she said. "But it's nice to…be talking to you again."

Seth swallowed. Lauren's visit to his house had made it clear she wanted to make some sort of apology, but he still wasn't sure what the point was now. Encouraging communication with Lauren now was just asking for trouble.

"I have to get going," Seth said. It had taken time, but he'd come to terms with his childhood trauma. He couldn't change the past, but he could build a solid, happy future with his son. Teddy was waiting for him at day care. Without another word, he untangled his cart from Lauren's and rattled toward the checkout, not slowing down to grab any other items. He had enough food for the next few days, and his only thought was escaping before Lauren dragged his feelings through the dirt again.

CHAPTER NINE

LAUREN AND HER mom were having a video call as Lauren ate take-out food at her grandmother's kitchen table. "Look," she said, shifting the phone so her mom could see Lord Henry sleeping on the kitchen chair next to her. "I brought him along for the evening sorting session, but I can't tell how he feels about being back here."

"It was his home for a long time," her mom said. "He's probably comfortable there."

Lord Henry opened one eye but performed no theatrics for the camera.

"He looks comfortable," Lauren agreed. "Oh, I was going to tell you—I saw our old house is for sale."

"It is?" her mom asked. "Real estate prices have gone up so much, I wonder how much the current owner is asking for it."

Lauren had seen the sign on her way to her grandmother's house. The house she and Maggie grew up in had a large backyard that adjoined Vera's. There had been no fence when they were kids, and it had all felt like one big piece of property. When her parents moved to Florida five years ago, Lauren hadn't wanted to buy the family home or even rent it from her parents. She'd been in her early twenties, seeking independence, wanting to make it on her own. Truthfully, she couldn't have afforded it anyway, and her parents needed the money from the sale so they could purchase their retirement home in Florida. The new owners had put up a backyard fence, and Lauren and her grandmother had planted flowers along it.

But now the house was for sale again.

"I looked it up on the Realtor's site before I called you," Lauren said. She told her mom the asking price, which seemed astronomical to her. She supposed it made sense though, since it was a four-bedroom home on a nice piece of property that included access to a small lake. But there was no way she could afford such a place on her horticulturist's salary.

"I'm glad this came up," her mom said. "We haven't talked about Mom's house."

"I'm cleaning it out as fast as I can," Lauren said. "On the evenings and weekends."

"Thank you, honey. We really appreciate that. But I'm wondering if we want to sell it or not."

"What…else would you do with it?" Lauren asked. Were they thinking of moving back home?

She felt her heart hiccup. Selling it, as far as she knew, had always been the plan. The house and her grandmother's remaining investments had gone to Lauren's parents because her mom was an only child. She knew her parents had a comfortable retirement, and the inheritance would make them even more comfortable. They deserved that.

"We want to be fair to you and Maggie, of course. We know Maggie is happy where she is, and you seem happy in Niagara Falls. I know you have a nice apartment, but if you wanted to consider taking over Mom's house, we could talk about it."

Her mother could usually read her thoughts just by looking at her face. They'd always been close, and Lauren tended to be an open book. But right now, her emotions were all over the place. She loved her grandmother's house. Desperately. It was a place of happiness and comfort, and every window and doorway and wall reminded her of Nanna Vera.

Lord Henry raised his head and perked up his ears.

"I don't know what to say," Lauren said.

"Just think about it. I wanted to bring it up at the funeral, but we all needed a minute to process. I thought we'd have a few more years with Mom, and it was quite a shock. It's only been two weeks now, but I wanted to start the conversation before you get too deep into cleaning it out."

"I'm sure this house would be really valuable on the market," Lauren said. "Out of my price range."

"Maybe," her mom said. "But it wouldn't be anywhere close to what our old place is listed at. It's cut off from lake access now because of the neighbor's fence, and it's small. We'd have to think of a good way to be fair to Maggie if we…transferred it to you, but it's a possibility."

Lauren's heart leaped at the thought of living here with all its comfort and familiarity. The garden in the backyard had been a joint labor of love between her and her grandmother, and she was already worried about moving a few of the beloved roses if the house sold later in the summer. Transplanting flowers at the peak of summer wasn't healthy for them. And who knew, the new owner might want the gardens kept intact as part of the deal. She didn't know much about real estate contracts or sales, but she knew there would be negotiations and the landscaping could be part of a potential deal.

"I don't know," Lauren said. "It sounds complicated."

Why was she hesitating? Taking it over meant she kept the gardens and the memories. Didn't she want to cling to those happy childhood days when she colored flower pictures at the table where she sat now, her take-out food getting cold in front of her?

"It could actually be really easy," her mother said. "But I'd want this to be what you wanted. I don't want you to feel obligated to keep the house in the family. Yes, we love it, but it's only a house. Your happiness is the most important thing to us."

Lauren and her mother chatted a few more minutes and then ended the call, leaving Lauren feeling a bit lonely as she continued her cleaning project. Her parents had always been kind, their support a rock there for her and her sister.

Which made it all the more upsetting that her sister hadn't trusted them when she found herself pregnant and afraid. Everything would have been so much simpler if Maggie had been truthful at the time. Lauren had never been in Maggie's shoes, so she hated judging her. But it did hurt that her sister had confided in Seth instead of her own family.

Seth had been a good listener. Lauren thought back on their tree house conversations and words exchanged as they passed each other on the swing set, each of them flying high but not always in unison. In her memories, she'd been doing the talking, and Seth had smiled and absorbed everything as if it were sunshine and he was cold. His son was an absorber, too. Which meant the other kids in the Rainbow Clubhouse group did most of the talking—sometimes a lot—and Teddy listened. He'd talk to her, one-on-one, about flowers and plants. And he had told her a funny story about his Chihuahua sitting in a chair at the kitchen table as if he was a person until his daddy made the dog get down.

And then Teddy had told her something that broke her heart. He said he tried to tell his daddy all the names of the flowers he saw that day and everything the flower lady had said, but his daddy had looked sad or mad, Teddy wasn't sure. So he'd stopped talking.

Lauren opened the closet door in the spare bedroom. Her grandmother had some ancient, dust-covered boxes in there she wanted to tackle. With Lord Henry watching from the nearby bed, Lauren opened two boxes and found odds and ends. A few half skeins of yarn in three colors, a cookbook that appeared unopened, a measuring tape, a puzzle, same paint sample cards and an old board game. Lauren remembered the board game well. She put the faded box on the bed and opened it. Just seeing the game board and playing pieces made her think of rainy days and the aroma of cookies in the oven.

The second box held a similar odd collection of items, as well as two baseball trophies. The trophies were for pitching, and the inscribed gold plate had Seth's name and the year—he would have been in seventh and eighth grade—on each one. Lauren was puzzled at first, but then she remembered that Seth had displayed them on her grandmother's mantel along with school pictures of Maggie and Lauren. She hadn't thought it was strange at the time, but now she wondered if Seth wanted to put them in a safe place or at least a place where someone would appreciate them.

He didn't have that at home. His father hadn't attended Seth's baseball games, but Lauren's family had. What should she do with the trophies now? Did Seth have other childhood mementos or had they been lost over the years? Maybe he'd want to show these to Teddy.

Lauren put the trophies and the board game in a box to take with her, and she sorted a few more items in the kitchen before scooping up Lord Henry and tucking him into his cat carrier for the trip home. She had to drive past Seth's house on the way, and she slowed down as she approached. If she happened to be outside, she might stop.

Even though that might be a mistake with her

feelings so close to the surface. The idea of moving into her grandmother's house had, of course, crossed her mind before. But she hadn't really considered it a possibility. She'd known it would be left to her parents, so it was their decision to make. And how would Maggie feel about it?

Lauren almost drove past Seth's place, but then she saw him in the garage. She was driving slow enough that he also saw her. She didn't want him to think she was spying on him or being weird, so there was no choice. She pulled into his driveway and popped the back hatch on her small SUV.

She realized Seth was putting away the lawn mower, and the smell of freshly cut grass filled her with happy summer memories. He had a few flowering plants around the home's foundation, too. She hadn't noticed that detail a week ago when she'd barged in with her awkward apology.

Lauren got out of her car. "Hey. I was cleaning out Grandma's house this evening. I'm doing a little bit at a time."

Seth wiped his hands on his cargo shorts and waited.

"I found something that was yours among her things," she said. "So I thought if I saw you some time I'd give it to you, and I was driving by and…saw you."

"Okay."

She wished he would say more, but when he didn't she walked to the back of her car and opened the box. Seth stood right next to her, also peering into the box.

"Your middle school baseball trophies," she explained. "I had forgotten she kept them on her mantel."

That was how much he'd been part of her family. The thought felt like an old scar for her, and she could only imagine what he must be feeling. Maybe this was a mistake. She could have thrown those trophies away.

"I remember playing that game," he said as he looked into the box. "Rainy days and cookies."

"Me, too."

"On rainy days, I play games with Teddy and I bake cookies out of premade dough," Seth said.

Lauren smiled. "It's a nice tradition."

His hint of a smile faded at the word *tradition*. Her family had had them; his had not. But she loved that he was trying to make traditions with his own son. He seemed like a wonderful father, a boy who'd grown up to be a good man. She'd known the boy, but she didn't know the man. She could only go on the scraps of information she'd discovered recently.

"I saw Teddy today at the park for flower camp."

He nodded. "He didn't say much about it this evening, not like he usually does."

"Did you ask?"

"I…tried."

She wasn't sure if she should tell Seth what Teddy had said. A friend would. But she was hardly a friend. Still, it seemed wrong to withhold the information. Secrets, large and small, could fester.

"He did say something to me today about… well, you."

"What?" Seth asked, his tone implying more of an interrogation than a simple question.

"Just that… He thought you weren't that interested in flowers."

Seth looked up at the sky as if searching for answers or meaning. "I'm interested in anything he'll tell me. Teddy doesn't talk much. He can, he just doesn't."

"That must be hard," Lauren said. The other kids at flower camp loved the songs and they also loved sharing information about what they had for breakfast or their favorite toys or their pets.

"For a few days, he talked a lot about—" Seth paused and blew out a breath. "Well, you. And flowers."

Poor Seth. Of all things he could get his reticent son to talk about, it was a member of a family that had mistreated him. He was probably tired of hearing about the flower lady.

"Oh," she said. "I see."

"I…miss that."

"So you want him to talk and you *are* interested in hearing about flowers?"

"If that's what it takes," Seth said.

"If you want to know what we did today, we looked at the stamens of some summer lilies. Their stamens are huge and dusty and will leave a rusty powder on your fingers. And they're so fragrant, almost overwhelming. You could see if he remembers any details about them. We have yellow and pink ones, and some have a wide stripe."

Seth nodded. "He's getting his thirty minutes of cartoon time after dinner right now, which is about as long as it takes me to mow the lawn, but I could ask him about it during bath time."

"Maybe I could…suggest things he could talk about at dinner. If you want." She knew Seth wouldn't accept her apology, but maybe he would accept a little help from her if it directly benefited his son. She couldn't repair the past, but she could be kind to Seth in the present.

"You could try that," he said.

His tone wasn't exactly encouraging, but it was permission.

"Okay. Anyway. Would you like these trophies?" Lauren asked.

Seth took them from the box and hefted one in each hand. "I'd forgotten all about them. I could show them to Teddy sometime. I don't have a lot of things from my childhood, and maybe someday he'll ask." Seth met her eyes. "Thank you for bringing them here."

"You're welcome," Lauren said. She waited a moment, but there didn't seem to be anything left to say. Reclaiming their old relationship was obviously beyond the statute of limitations.

She got in her car and drove away thinking about her own big box of school mementos and awards her mother had carefully preserved for her before they sold their house and moved away. Lauren had her childhood memories intact, except for the one big missing piece the size of Seth Jones.

SETH MADE THE desperate move of stopping for fast food after being the very last parent to pick up his child at Rainbow Clubhouse. He'd gotten off work late due to a house fire, and he'd nearly called in his childcare backup—the chief's wife—but he was able to grab Teddy just minutes before six.

They were both too hungry to wait for Seth to forage through the fridge and come up with something. At least the kids' meal came with apple slices, and he was too tired to cook. The house fire had started in one side of a duplex on the edge of town, and then it had spread through the attic to the other side. Hot spots in the walls had required them to pull apart the drywall and insulation, and both units were completely uninhabitable now. The fire department had helped the residents salvage some of their belongings, but everything was smelly and wet.

The kids stood on the lawn and cried. A single mom cried. The only redemptive thing about the whole day was that no one was hurt, and a local charity was finding temporary housing and clothing for both families. When Seth pulled into his garage, he spotted the trophies he'd stored on a high shelf two nights ago when Lauren came by. He hadn't wanted to show them to Teddy just yet or tell him the flower lady had brought them. That would require way too much explanation. He truly had forgotten them himself, but it was sort of nice seeing them again. He hoped the kids involved in today's house fire hadn't lost all their childhood memories.

"We could eat at the picnic table in the backyard where maybe the breeze will blow away my smell," Seth told Teddy as he helped him out of his child restraint and then grabbed the drink carrier and bags of food. "I know I smell like smoke and sweat."

Teddy giggled and pointed to Seth's face. "Dirt."

Seth laughed. "Come on. I'll share my fries with you if you'll give me an apple slice."

They set up their food on the picnic table and Seth took a big bite of his bacon cheeseburger. He'd missed lunch and was starving.

"The flower lady had dirt on her face today, too," Teddy said. "But that was only because there was a ladybug on her and she tried to brush it off with her dirty gloves."

Seth swallowed. "That makes sense."

"But it didn't get off and she thought it went inside her shirt but then she found it in her pocket and she put it on a leaf."

Someday, he would get past the genuine surprise and satisfaction of hearing his son's voice, but he relished it right now and hoped Teddy would continue. He wondered if this ladybug story was something Lauren had suggested Teddy tell his dad.

"Did you get to see a lot of flowers?" Seth prompted.

He knew it wasn't the right way to ask. He should be more specific with his questions.

To Seth's surprise, Teddy fished a paper out of his pocket. "The flower lady wrote down the hard words so I could remember to tell you." Teddy put the paper on the picnic table next to his hamburger and tried to smooth it out. "But you have to read the words and then I'll tell you about them."

Seth took a drink and then put his finger on the first printed word on the Niagara Parks notepad paper. "Hydrangea," he said. "That's a big word."

"They're bushes with big flowers and they even come in blue, which is my favorite color, but only sometimes and they have to have the right food to be blue."

Seth waited to see if Teddy wanted to reveal anything else about hydrangeas, but he was busy polishing off his burger. Whatever it was about the parks and flowers that inspired him, Seth would do almost anything to keep it going, even if that meant opening a closed door just enough to let little pieces of Lauren back inside. He just had to be careful to keep his hand on the doorknob, ready to close it if she got too close or the memories of losing his adopted family got too painful.

For now, the benefits for his son outweighed the risks to himself.

"Do you know the flower lady's real name?" Seth asked.

Teddy nodded and Seth reminded himself to

keep asking specific questions that needed more than a yes-or-no answer.

"What is it?"

"Miss Lauren," Teddy said.

"Good. Maybe we should call her that instead of flower lady."

"Why?"

"Because it's her name."

Seth waited for a question, but none came. Sometimes the simplest explanation with kids was the best. Teddy nodded again and took two fries from Seth's container.

"Ready for the next flower on the list?" Seth asked.

"Ready."

"Daisy," Seth said, and then he sat back and finished his dinner while listening to his son talk about daisies and then petunias and then coneflowers.

He wished there was an easy way to say thank you to Miss Lauren.

CHAPTER TEN

LAUREN HAD SPENT all afternoon the previous day getting a plot of ground near a children's play area ready. The Rainbow Clubhouse group would arrive any moment, and today's agenda was to plant hardy perennials in a bed that would get part sun and part shade. She had churned up the soil, making it loose and tillable, because she wanted the planting event to be fun for the kids instead of grueling work. If she fostered a love of gardening by helping them along with the tough parts, they might become lifelong planters. Her grandmother had done the same thing for her, selecting good locations and plants most likely to thrive so Lauren wouldn't be disappointed.

When she'd gotten older, of course, she learned and appreciated the hard prep work her grandmother had done, but by then the habit and the joy of working in the garden was already established.

Amber from the summer programming department parked in the small lot adjacent to the children's play and exploration area. The park planning commission had the selected playground equipment and overall design, and the area had been busy since its grand opening last fall. Lauren and Marlin had helped to select shade trees and ornamental grasses, but now it was time to add some color and beauty.

"Here they come," Amber said. "I made it just in time. We had a bird-watching group over on Three Sister Island this morning. Mostly older people with big cameras. I think they had a good time, and we did spot a few rare birds—at least I'm assuming they were rare because there was a lot of pointing and camera action."

"Not a birder yourself?" Lauren laughed.

Amber grinned. "Nope, even though I coordinate these events, I'm no bird expert."

"Still, that sounds nice," Lauren said. "We have a butterfly garden, but I haven't really been intentional about plantings that attract birds." She pondered it. "I might do some planning and research this winter and see what we can come up with."

"You're always thinking," Amber said.

Lauren laughed. "Today, I'm thinking about the kids' session and then cutting back the potted plants over by the snack bar this afternoon so we'll get another wave of blooms. The purple petunias are blooming like it's their key to heaven."

Amber shaded her eyes and then counted aloud from one to ten. "Looks like they're all here again. Thanks for doing the legwork to get the activity ready."

"No problem. Plus, it was your idea using the color-coded Popsicle sticks so the kids will know where to put the plants," Lauren said.

Lauren and Amber greeted the teachers from day care and then instructed all the kids to sit on the benches near the edge of the playground. Amber handed out kid-sized pairs of gardening gloves to each child and then stood behind the kids along with their teacher.

"We have a special job for you today," Lauren said. "I know you love looking at the flowers and smelling them, but there's more we can do." She paused for dramatic effect. "I have an important question."

One of the kids raised her hand even though Lauren hadn't asked the question yet, and Lauren wanted to laugh. They were so eager and excited about life. Her grandmother would be so proud if she could see what Lauren was doing right now. She thought about Vera all the time, especially now while she was spending her days teaching kids to love flowers and her evenings clearing out her grandmother's house and tend-ing her garden. It was a world of opposites—getting rid of things because Grandma Vera was never coming back, yet keeping her garden perfect as if she was. Again, her mother's suggestion that Lauren might want to move into the cute little house echoed in her mind, bringing a wave of bittersweet joy.

Lauren sucked in a deep breath and focused on her job and the children.

"Here goes," Lauren said, clapping her hands together. "Who's ready to help?"

All the hands went up and waved, and Lauren put her palm on her heart and feigned shock. "Do I really have that many helpers today? I'm so happy because I have a big job for us to do together."

The day care teacher reminded the children to put their listening ears on, and Lauren explained that they would be digging holes and planting flowers, and they would have to be careful to follow the directions. Each plant had a colored Popsicle stick in its container, and there was a corresponding colored Popsicle stick in the ground where Lauren had designated places according to a pattern—tall plants in the back and short ones in the front. The pattern also ensured that the shade and sun-loving plants were in the right places.

Marlin showed up just as they were getting

started, saying her boss had cleared an hour in her schedule for her to help out. Lauren suspected Marlin liked the kids despite her good-natured grumbling about their energy. Amber had rounded up extra trowels and small shovels, and the adults each took two or three kids and supervised their efforts. Lauren smiled at how clumsy the kids were, especially the younger ones, as they tried to dig little holes in the soil she'd already loosened. One boy put his foot on the shovel and pushed, but he fell over and rolled around on the ground, laughing.

Teddy was very serious. He got on his knees and used his small trowel, carefully scooping out dirt as if he was afraid to hurt something in the ground. He was in Lauren's group along with two girls, one of whom was singing the ladybug song to her waiting potted plant.

"It only takes three times as long with their help," Marlin said in a quiet aside to Lauren after half the plants were in the ground and the kids were having a snack and drink with Amber and their teacher. "But I do love their enthusiasm. I have some branches to cut up on the west side of the park. I wonder if I could teach them to use chain saws."

Lauren laughed and shook a finger at her friend. "Sorry, they're my helpers, and I'm not sharing."

She felt a hand slide into hers and looked down.

"I used the paper and explained all the flowers to my daddy like you said," Teddy said. "I think he liked it."

"I'm sure he did." Lauren could feel Marlin's eyes on her. Her friend knew who Teddy's daddy was, and she would probably have some questions later. But right now, Lauren had to focus on the boy. "Do you want my help writing anything down today?"

Teddy studied the garden where empty pots were stacked next to full ones. "I think I can remember."

"Okay," Lauren agreed. "What did he say when you told him about the flowers?"

"He mostly listened. But then he asked me if I knew your real name and I said I did and he said that I should call you Miss Lauren instead of the flower lady."

The other kids all called her Miss Lauren, but she didn't mind it when Teddy called her the flower lady. It was sort of cute and, technically, accurate.

"I like both names, but you should do what your dad says," Lauren said.

Teddy nodded and scrunched his brow so he looked very serious. "Should I save the paper and tell my mommy about the flowers later?

Daddy likes listening to me, but I don't think Mommy does. She's always busy."

Lauren sucked in a breath and exchanged a glance with Marlin. She didn't know what to say to that. She knew Teddy's mom was from out of town, and she had seen him with both parents at a distance a few times over the years. This summer, though, Teddy had only been with Seth. Did he have full custody? If so, why? She was debating about how to respond when Marlin jumped in.

"When I was a kid, I talked so much that my parents would sometimes offer me a quarter if I could be quiet for ten minutes," Marlin said. "I also had four sisters, so there was a lot of talking at my house."

Teddy smiled at Marlin. "I don't talk too much."

"Do you have brothers and sisters?" Marlin asked.

He shook his head.

"You get all the attention," Marlin said, giving him a thumbs-up.

Teddy gave her a serious look but didn't say anything.

"Why don't we work on a list, just in case," Lauren said. "I don't want your dad to miss out on the fun flower details."

She sat on the ground and got a notepad and

pen from her shirt pocket. She flipped past the first few pages where she had notes written for herself about fertilizer, water and some supplies she wanted to requisition.

"Let's start with describing our day. I'm going to write down that we were at the children's playground planting perennials. Can you remember what a perennial is?"

Teddy parroted back to her the same explanation she had given the group, proving that he was a good listener. "Good. Make sure you tell your dad that at dinner tonight. And now should we go ahead and list the names of the plants?"

Teddy remembered the names of some of the plants, and Lauren filled in the others. She wrote down butterfly bush, coneflower, shasta daisy, hosta, phlox, Russian sage and daylilies, reviewing the characteristics of each with Teddy as she wrote. She pictured dinner conversation at Seth's house. Would he and his son read the note together? She had no doubt that Seth would be patient and listen for as long as Teddy was willing to talk. Seth didn't want her apology or her friendship, but this was at least an avenue of communication with him.

She couldn't explain it, but ever since she'd learned the truth about Seth and Maggie, Lauren felt determined to fix things or at least right the wrong her family had caused. It was just hard to fix one half of something that was broken when the other half wasn't in the same place.

"We could add the part about the colored Popsicle sticks," Lauren said to Teddy. "I think Seth… I mean, your dad, would like to know about that. Maybe it's an idea he could use, and you could plant flowers in your backyard some time."

Teddy's expression illuminated as if the sun had just cleared the horizon. Lauren loved seeing the joyful look on his face, and she hoped she hadn't just created a problem for Seth. She had no idea what their backyard looked like or if they had room for plants. Did Seth even have time to care for flower beds with a full-time job and dad duties?

"Make sure you tell him Miss Lauren said it was okay if you don't have your own plants at home because you're always welcome to come here and see all the ones at the park."

The boy nodded, acknowledging her words, but Lauren still suspected she had planted a seed in Teddy's head that his dad was definitely going to hear about. She smiled. Maybe that wasn't a terrible thing. If Seth wanted his son to communicate, planting a garden with him might be the perfect activity.

AS AN EMERGENCY RESPONDER, Seth usually handled everything with calm grace, but the kitchen faucet coming off in his hand while he was trying to fill a pot to boil pasta for dinner... It was so unexpected that Seth could only stand there and stare for a minute while water gushed out of the broken pipe.

"Uh-oh," Teddy said. "Mess." His words jolted Seth into action, and he jerked open the cabinet under the sink and located the shutoff valve. Now he had two problems, dinner and plumbing. He foraged in the fridge and found leftovers to heat up instead. Three minutes in the microwave, and then he scooped enough chicken potpie onto a plate to satisfy his son. His own dinner could wait. He measured the pipe and rounded up tools from the garage while Teddy ate.

"Ready to hit the hardware store?" he asked when his son had mowed through his dinner.

Teddy nodded and got up. He put on his shoes without being asked and stood by the kitchen door. Seth was sorry he didn't get a chance to hear about flower camp over dinner, but the kitchen faucet wasn't something he could put off. He had to work the next three days, so he wanted to get it done tonight.

At the store, Teddy stood silently next to him in the plumbing aisle. Seth showed him several faucet possibilities and asked his opinion, but Teddy just smiled and shrugged. Seth gathered his supplies and headed for the register, where there was a line five people deep. Hands full, he watched the line creep forward while Teddy stared at all the impulse items—gum, candy and gadgets—in the racks at the checkout.

Seth finally got to the register and, with relief, laid all his supplies on the belt. His stomach growled, but he wasn't caving in to the candy bar aisle. No way was he setting that kind of example for his son.

The clerk began scanning his items, and Teddy chose that moment to pull a list from his pocket and hold it up. "Can we get these plants while we're here?" he asked.

"What?" Seth asked. "I mean… I…uh, didn't know you wanted to buy plants," he added, softening his tone. It wasn't his son's fault the sink was broken and he was hungry.

"We planted a garden today and I want to plant one just like it at home."

The clerk paused and eyed Seth curiously, clearly waiting to see if he would be diving back into the store to visit the garden center.

Seth sighed. The challenge and beauty of children, he thought, is their timing. Last-minute bathroom notifications, losing a tooth in the middle of a birthday party and having a growth spurt immediately after buying new clothes and shoes. These were all things no one tells you to expect as a parent.

He wanted to hear about Teddy's day. Wanted to show an interest in his son and encourage him to communicate. But, oh, the timing. He was getting a headache, and the clerk was still on pause. The line behind him stacked up and an old man cleared his throat impatiently.

"They have plants here," Teddy said, oblivious to the dilemma he was creating. "I saw them when we went by."

Seth grabbed a granola bar off the rack and a small candy bar, one of Teddy's favorites. He put them on the belt and nodded to the cashier to indicate he wanted to keep going. He put a hand on Teddy's shoulder. "I love your idea, but we should take time to plan together, and buying plants sounds like it could be its own special adventure another time."

"Tomorrow?" Teddy asked.

"We'll see what we can do, honey. But first, I'm going to need your help fixing our kitchen sink."

The clerk announced the total and Seth swiped his credit card. Teddy still held the crumpled paper in his hand. When they got to the car, he handed it to Seth, who folded it carefully and put it in his own pocket. "I'll keep the list safe so we can talk about it later." He smiled at his son. "I don't want you to get chocolate on it on the way home."

He buckled Teddy in and helped him unwrap his treat, and then Seth got behind the wheel and took a big bite of his granola bar to fuel up—as least partially—on the way home.

"Do we have any Popsicle sticks?" Teddy asked from the back seat.

Seth glanced in the rearview mirror. His son had chocolate on his face but also a big smile. "I don't think so," Seth said. "But we could get some."

"Okay," Teddy said.

Seth installed the new faucet seamlessly, thank goodness. He initially had a small leak, but he tightened the fitting, and everything seemed to be holding. Teddy watched him work and Seth included him by asking him to hold tools and the flashlight. Seth ran water in the sink, washed his hands and then high-fived his son.

"We did it."

"Can we look at Miss Lauren's list now?"

Seth put a hand on his son's shoulder. "Sure can." He got out the list and put it on the kitchen table. "Let me put some brain food on a plate for us so we can think better." He was still hungry, and he didn't want his hunger getting in the way of quality time with Teddy. Seth got precut cheese slices, grapes and olives from the fridge and arranged them on a plate, and then he opened a sleeve of whole grain crackers. He filled two glasses with apple juice, added a stack of napkins and then sat down next to Teddy. Sparky lay down under the table with his nose on Seth's foot.

"You're the flower expert," he said, ruffling Teddy's hair affectionately. "Tell me what I need to know."

Teddy smoothed the paper and studied it. He knew his letters and numbers and had a growing vocabulary of sight words, but Seth wasn't sure how much of Lauren's writing his son could actually read.

"I see the words *children's playground* at the top," Seth said. He pointed to the words and pronounced them slowly. "Hey, I thought you said you worked today. Were you actually playing?" he asked with a grin.

"We worked at the playground," Teddy said, emphasizing the word *at.*

"Ah, got it."

"And we planted a whole bunch of things. So many that they needed our help."

"How many?" Seth asked.

Teddy frowned. "Uh-oh. I don't know. I didn't count."

"That's okay. You can count next time or ask Miss Lauren. I'm sure she knows."

Teddy still looked troubled, as if he had missed

something important, and Seth tried to move on quickly so he didn't kill his son's joy.

"Wow. I hope you know about these plants because I sure don't," Seth said. "What on earth is a butterfly bush? Don't tell me it's a bush that can fly because that would be amazing."

Teddy giggled. "Silly. It's a bush for butterflies. They like to eat it and it makes them visit the garden."

"Interesting. What color is it?"

"It was just green right now, but Miss Lauren said it will be purple when it blooms."

"Nice," Seth said. "The next word is *coneflower.* Is it orange like a traffic cone?"

He was gratified to hear his son laugh again. Whatever it took to make a happy memory and connect with Teddy was fine with him.

"I don't know why it's called a coneflower, but I think it will be pink and it likes sunshine. Butterflies and bees like it."

"Bees are good," Seth said.

"Except when they sting. Miss Lauren got stung a bunch."

"I know. But those were hornets, a different kind of bee. I think your garden will have the nice kind of bees."

"I hope so. I'll ask Miss Lauren why coneflowers are called coneflowers," Teddy said.

"Should we make a list of things to ask her so we don't forget?" Seth asked.

Teddy nodded, and Seth got up and grabbed a notepad from the junk drawer. Sparky followed Seth to the drawer and back and then lay down again under the table. "How many plants did you plant at the playground?" he said aloud as he wrote it. "Why is a coneflower named coneflower?"

Teddy watched him write and then he pointed to the next word on the list. Seth continued reading the names and listening to Teddy's information about them. His son couldn't remember what the hosta or phlox looked like, so Seth added that to the list for Miss Lauren.

When they finished going through the list and making their own list of questions, Teddy pushed back from the table and stood. "Can we go buy them now?"

Seth glanced up at the wall clock. It was already past eight o'clock. He needed a shower, Teddy needed a bath and bedtime was looming.

"I'm excited about seeing these plants," he said, working up enthusiasm despite being tired at the end of a long day. "But I want to make sure we're doing it right if we're going to make our own garden. Planning is important."

Teddy looked disappointed for a moment, but then he brightened up. "Miss Lauren planned the garden we made today. She had colored sticks in the plants and we had to match them up with where they were supposed to go."

"Smart," Seth said. "I bet she put a lot of thought into it, and that's what we should do, too." He wasn't just buying time and stalling. He was no gardener, but he also didn't go at things haphazardly, either. Anything worth doing was worth doing right.

"She could help us," Teddy said, clearly latching onto the idea. "Maybe we can ask her to come see our yard. She has good ideas about plants."

Oh, boy. The father/son bonding experience was going to have another person involved. Seth was backed against a wall and two goals competed wildly in his heart. He could make his son happy or protect his own peace.

There really was no choice for him.

"I can call Miss Lauren and see if she has time to help us," he said.

Teddy clapped his hands excitedly, waking up the dog, who hopped around, enjoying the energy. Seth couldn't help smiling at their enthusiasm, even though his summer was getting a lot more complicated than he'd expected. Lauren's family was a painful part of his past, but he was an adult and he had plenty of practice compartmentalizing. Honestly, he didn't really know Lauren the adult, just as she didn't know him. It wasn't a terrible idea to get gardening help from a professional horticulturist, especially if he remembered Lauren was basically a benevolent stranger.

He was no longer stuck in the past. He was focused now on his future and his son.

CHAPTER ELEVEN

LAUREN MET HER friend Marlin at the bike trail that the parks system had opened the summer before. The trail had technically been available for years, but it had been rustic, with gravel, mud and holes, until one of the park rangers had taken on the project of making it accessible for all. Once a week, Lauren tried to do something that got her out of her horticulture bubble, and she was glad Marlin liked biking. She was also glad to have something to do outside rather than spending every evening sorting through her grandmother's things. Not that she had much left to do. Vera had never had many possessions, preferring the outdoors to a house full of things. She'd be glad to see Lauren biking tonight instead of sorting old Christmas decorations stored in plastic tubs in the basement.

"Are there any rules against dating someone who also works for the parks system?" Marlin asked as they rode under a tree canopy. "I think I have a link to the online employee handbook somewhere, but I confess I haven't read all the fine print."

Lauren laughed. "Marlin, has someone caught your eye?"

"Just answer the question. I figured if anyone knows, it would be you," Marlin said. "You've worked here for years and you always seem to do everything right."

"Hardly. I make my share of mistakes, but flowers are very forgiving and if I plant something truly unsuitable, I can blame the weather for the failure. Weather is an excellent scapegoat."

"And you've never dated anyone who works for the parks?" Marlin asked.

"No," Lauren said.

"Have you been tempted?"

The quick and honest answer was no, but she took a minute, thinking about why it was such an easy no. She was twenty-seven. What was she waiting for? She'd dated a few guys over the years, of course, but none of those relationships had lasted long.

"Not yet," she said.

"Maybe I should find out about the fraternization policy for sure," Marlin said.

They rode in silence for a moment, but Lauren's curiosity finally won out. "So, I'm assuming there's someone you have your eye on?"

"Maybe. But I don't want to get my hopes up if it's against the rules. I like my job."

"As long as this person is not a supervisor—especially not your direct supervisor—you should be okay. Or if it's someone who reported to you, of course."

Marlin laughed. "My direct supervisor reminds me of my grandpa Charlie, and there's no one else interesting and available in my whole department."

"So he's in another department," Lauren said, her interest piqued. "Don't tell me. It's more fun to guess and it takes my mind off my burning legs." When she rode her bike alone, Lauren liked a leisurely pace, but hitting the trail with Marlin elevated the experience to the category of actual exercise. She regretted planning this after a day spent squatting and kneeling among the beds of colorful annuals.

"Need a hint?" Marlin asked.

"Not yet." Lauren considered the question. What kind of man would interest her funny, free-spirited friend? "Is he full-time or seasonal?" The parks system employed dozens of people year-round, and the numbers tripled during the warmer tourist months.

Marlin flashed her a smile. "Full-time."

"That narrows the field. Plus, he's here to stay, which makes him more interesting." Lauren had dated a seasonal worker from a nearby hotel several summers earlier, but he'd moved on at the end of the season. She ran several possibilities through her mind. "Does he work primarily indoors or outdoors?"

"Indoors," Marlin said, surprising Lauren, who'd expected Marlin to choose someone outdoorsy like herself.

"Okay," Lauren said. "Does he wear a uniform?"

"No."

"Hmm," Lauren said. "So, he's a behind-the-scenes manager or supervisor of some kind. Not in the outdoor areas, so perhaps finance or accounting?"

Marlin shook her head and shifted as they cruised down a hill.

"Restaurant?"

"Nope."

"Special events?"

"Wrong," Marlin said.

"Publicity or public relations?"

"This is fun," Marlin said. "I may make you guess for the next three miles."

Lauren laughed. "My legs may give out before I solve the mystery."

"Well?" Marlin prompted.

"Retail," Lauren said, blurting out one of the departments she hadn't yet guessed.

"Finally," Marlin said. "Have you not seen the

buyer for the gift shops? The guy looks like he should be selling postcards with his face on them."

"I think people are here for the falls," Lauren said, grinning. "And the rainbows."

"They are here for the attractions," Marlin clarified. "And he's one of them."

"So how did you meet postcard man?"

"Last Monday. It was early and I was getting ready to go out with the maintenance team to address some tree growth too close to one of the gift shops. We had to trim it carefully to keep it from getting unbalanced, which wouldn't be very pretty at all and would ultimately weaken the tree. You know those ornamental cherry trees? I love them, but we have to be careful with them. If someone had asked me, I would have planted it five feet farther from the structure in the first place."

Lauren laughed. Her friend loved trees like Lauren loved flowers. "And the handsome postcard seller? How about him?"

"I don't know if he has an opinion about trees," Marlin said. "But I happened to be right by the gift shop, and I'd forgotten my water bottle at home, and it was already getting hot. I said I wished the store was open so I could get a water bottle—you know I hate using plastic throwaway ones—and he was there and said he could help me out."

"Darren was a year behind me in school," Lauren said.

Marlin hit her brakes and came to a squealing stop. "He's a local and you know him? Spill everything."

"I didn't know him well, but he seemed nice. A bit nerdy and academic, I think. His family moved in when we were freshmen, and I had my own circle of people I hung around with." She wasn't going to tell Marlin that her circle was really about the size of Seth and she'd been lonely when he was cut out of it for her last year in high school. She'd retreated to flowers and gardening. Now that Seth was back on the fringes of her life, she was glad. It was what she wanted, taking a shot at repairing her family's relationship with him.

But why was it so important to her? She didn't want to tell Marlin about it because her perceptive friend would ask questions. She couldn't talk to Maggie about it, although Maggie was exactly the person she should be talking to.

"What do you think I should do?" Marlin asked.

"I'm not a great person to ask for romantic advice," Lauren said. "But I do know his office window has an overgrown tree outside it. I noticed it when I was pulling weeds one day."

Marlin grinned. "An arborist might need to look at that tree, for its own good."

"You'd be providing a valuable service to the trees of Niagara Falls State Park."

They pedaled on in silence for a while, and Lauren just enjoyed her friend's company. She'd spent way too much time thinking about Seth lately. It was hard to put him out of her mind when she saw Teddy several days a week. And there were the notes going back and forth. Yesterday's note from Seth had included a question about whether these plants were resistant to rabbits eating them. Her mind had gone straight back to the little vegetable patch she and Seth had planted and which had gotten entirely decimated by local bunnies. Was he thinking about that when he asked the question? Did he even remember?

Lauren felt the breeze on her face, and she enjoyed the rest of the ride with her friend. It must be great to be Marlin and feel the rush of potential romance. Lauren hadn't felt that kind of rush in a long time.

Not since the last summer she'd spent with Seth, when she'd realized how much deeper her feelings ran for him. Before it all fell apart.

SETH WAS NOT going to ask Lauren for help. Apart from those years when he'd been closer to her family, he'd taken care of everything by himself. No reason that should change now.

Teddy had asked his dad if he'd called Miss

Lauren about the garden planning, and Seth felt a shiver of shame. He'd sort of lied to his son by telling him he hadn't had time. Then he'd doubled down on his lie by saying Miss Lauren was a very busy person and they should try to figure this out themselves. Guy project, he'd declared, hoping Teddy would latch onto that as a fun idea. It seemed to have worked, and Teddy was excited and kicking the back of the driver's seat on the way to the big home improvement store with the attached garden center.

Certainly there would be knowledgeable sales staff there to help him. Lauren Benedict wasn't the only person on earth who knew about plants. He heard paper crinkling in the back seat and hoped the list would still be readable by the time they parked the car.

At the store, Seth grabbed one of the low flat carts meant for loading things and carefully maneuvered it into the garden center. Row upon row of potted plants stretched before them. He glanced down at Teddy, who was wide-eyed, mouth-open at the sight. Teddy wordlessly handed Seth the list.

"We'll just get started at the top," he decided. "Looks like it's in alphabetical order. I wonder if this greenhouse is arranged in alphabetical order." The thought gave him a glimmer of hope and a potential map for navigating very unfamiliar territory. "Butterfly bush," he said, trying to convey confidence. He headed for the first aisle, but then noted that it was labeled sun/part-sun perennials. There was also a shade/part-shade aisle. And then an aisle labeled shrubs and another labeled vegetable and herb plants.

Oh, man. Was a butterfly bush a sun or shade plant and was it a perennial or a shrub? This was harder than he'd thought.

"Excuse me," he asked a worker wearing a red vest and a name tag that said Ava. The girl was probably just old enough to drive, but maybe she was a plant expert. "Can you tell us where to find butterfly bushes?"

"We don't sell butterflies," she said.

"No, I mean the plant." His hopes for Ava's help dimmed.

"I'll ask someone," the girl said, and she turned and disappeared into a row overshadowed by hanging plants.

"I don't think she knows," Teddy said. His brow was wrinkled and he looked troubled. The last thing Seth wanted was to kill his son's enthusiasm. He had to get it together.

"We'll just start going down rows," Seth said. "I bet we can find it if we read the tags."

"I'll help," Teddy said.

Just when Seth's hopes began to flag halfway down the sun/part-sun row, he ran across a tag with a familiar word on it. He showed it to

Teddy. "Coneflower! This is on our list," Seth said, his own excitement bringing Teddy back to life for a moment until Teddy looked closely at the plant's tag.

"This has a picture of an orange flower. The ones at the park are pink."

"Maybe there's more than one kind, and orange is nice, too."

Teddy shook his head. "Pink. Like the ones Miss Lauren planted."

"We'll keep looking," Seth said. He considered asking for help, but the teen girl was nowhere in sight and he might be better off figuring it out himself. If he could fight fires and save lives, he could certainly pick out some plants from a list and stick them in the ground wherever Teddy wanted. Their backyard was wide open. How hard could it be?

They continued down the row, and Seth found a group of phlox, a few of them already in bloom. "These are on the list," he announced to his son. "And they have a bunch of different colors." He picked up several pots and held them so Teddy could see the pictures on the tags. "See? White, pink and some with pink-and-white stripes. You have your choice."

Teddy considered all three but then frowned. "I can't remember what color we planted at the playground."

Seth's heart sank. Was this really going to be all about getting exactly what they'd planted at the park under Lauren's direction? He hated giving up, but it sure would be easier just to ask her for help.

"We could get more than one," he said, pointing to the sign that said the plants were $8 each or 3 for $24.

"Okay," Teddy agreed. "Two pink and one white. No stripes."

Seth didn't ask why his son objected to the striped ones. He was just happy that something was going onto the flatbed cart. He picked the plants that looked healthiest to him and were already blooming—that had to be a good sign, he thought, and it was clear they were getting the color they wanted. Planting this garden with his son was important, and he'd stay in the garden center for hours if necessary.

"I'm hungry," Teddy said.

"Me, too," Seth agreed. "But we still need to get more plants."

"We need Miss Lauren."

Seth's heart sank even deeper in his chest. His son was out of confidence now, and it was up to him—the adult—to restore it.

"Let's go to the shrubbery aisle," he said. "I bet the butterfly bushes will be there because *shrub* is just another name for *bush*."

"How do you know?"

It was true that he welcomed any communication from his son, but the almost accusatory tone hurt. "I know lots of words," Seth said. He sounded pathetic, assuring a five-year-old that he possessed a strong vocabulary.

Teddy stared at him for a moment and Seth turned away to face the shrubbery section. He took Teddy's hand and steered the cart with his other hand. The pink and white flowers bobbed cheerfully with the motion, but Seth felt anything but cheerful about this project.

In the shrubbery section, an older gentleman was watering and he paused, shutting off the water so Teddy and Seth could look at the plants. "Can I help you find anything?" he asked.

"We're looking for a butterfly bush," Seth said.

"Of course," the man said. "Right this way."

With great relief, Seth saw his son's clouded expression clear and they both followed the older gentleman.

"How big is your space?" he asked. "Some of these will get almost ten feet tall, but we also have dwarf ones if that suits your garden better."

Teddy turned and looked up at Seth, and Seth felt the full weight of having absolutely no idea where he was going to plant this bush—dwarf or giant version—and how the garden would look when it was finished. What if it was just a mess of plants in the ground and didn't even qualify as a proper garden?

"I'm not sure," he said.

The man's smile only faltered a little. "Well, how about color? Do you want a pink, white or purple one?"

"Purple," Teddy said.

"That helps. If you want purple, I only have the tall variety to offer you."

Teddy looked up at Seth again, and Seth felt pressured to decide. The pressure was worse than driving up to a fire and deciding how to attack it.

"Looks like we're getting a tall purple one," he said.

"Just one?" the man asked.

Seth thought about his large backyard. How much of it was he supposed to convert to garden instead of grass? Was there a ratio or guidance for something like that? Maybe he should have searched for backyard garden ideas on the internet. He took one of the plants the worker indicated and put it on his cart.

"Just one for now," he said. "We could be back."

The man nodded and smiled, and Seth felt as if he could see right through him. *Single dad, trying his best, floundering.* Could his son see right through him, too?

"Hosta is the next thing on our list," he said to the man. He held up the paper, trying to prove he did, indeed, have a plan. At least the framework of a plan. A list written by someone else—someone who would have been very helpful if he'd had the courage to ask her.

"They'll be in the shade/part-shade area over there," he said. "Do you have a certain variety in mind? I believe we have at least ten different ones."

The flash of confidence he'd tried to show faded at the thought of so many choices. This whole garden center was a minefield of difficult decisions out of his realm of knowledge.

"We'll figure it out," he assured the man. "Thank you."

Thirty minutes later, he and Teddy put exactly five plants in the bed of his truck and drove home in silence. He knew his son—quiet and observant—well enough to know that Teddy had no confidence in Seth's ability to pull off a garden like Miss Lauren could. And the boy was right. He could dig holes and put these plants in the ground…somewhere. But it wouldn't look like a real garden any more than a stack of lumber looked like a house.

He was down to a tough decision. Invite Lauren and her help into his home or disappoint his child.

CHAPTER TWELVE

IT HAD RAINED for two days, and Lauren was tired of spending her time in the park's greenhouse instead of outside in the gardens. The only bright spot was that it was a flower camp day, and the kids would be arriving at the greenhouse soon. If they had boots and umbrellas, she planned to take them for a brief walk outdoors so they could observe the ways flowers reacted to rain: Did their leaves shed water? Did they close up their blossoms? It would be a great lesson, if brief.

She was also looking forward to hearing from Teddy. Had he shared her note with Seth describing the children's playground garden? What had Seth said about it? She didn't know if he liked flowers or if he spent much time outdoors these days. As a firefighter, he was exposed to the elements, but did he like outdoor recreation? Was there a porch swing at his house or did he enjoy long bike rides on trails?

There was a lot she didn't know about him. Her information was a decade old, and people changed. Certainly getting married and having a son had changed Seth. Her family's treatment of him had changed him, too. For her part, getting the truth at last from Maggie had changed her. She was an adult but she didn't feel much different from the girl Seth had known. But they were strangers, no matter how odd that felt. She'd forced herself *not* to think about him for a long time, and she wasn't quite sure what to do with these feelings.

The small bus with Rainbow Clubhouse painted on the side pulled up in front of the greenhouse, and the kids clambered down the steps. Lauren and Amber held open the greenhouse doors and invited everyone in out of the rain.

She was eager to talk to Teddy, but there were nine other kids who deserved her attention. With Amber's help, they had put together an indoor activity that involved a scavenger hunt in the greenhouse. Each child would be given a chart showing pictures of various leaves, and they had to match the pictures up with the right picture cards she and Amber had placed on the corresponding plants.

"I don't know if this is going to take them five minutes or an hour," Amber confided after she and Lauren had given the kids detailed directions.

"Do we have a backup plan if it only takes five minutes?" Lauren asked. She and Amber had kid-proofed the greenhouse area as much as possible, putting away any chemicals and removing trip hazards. But still, they stood side by side, keeping a watchful eye on the kids. Rain continued to pound the greenhouse roof, and her hopes of taking the kids outside faltered.

Amber pointed to a big plastic tub on a table. "Coloring books and crayons. The coloring books are souvenir ones for the Niagara region, and we had a whole stack of them at the office. We could have them do the pages that are specifically horticultural, or just let them have fun."

"They could also draw flowers or make a garden plan," Lauren said.

"I like that idea. We could let them choose," Amber said. "Right now, I'm headed over to the corner where I hear a lot of giggling. If we're very lucky, there's a toad that's come in from the rain."

Lauren moved toward the middle of the greenhouse where Teddy and a little dark-haired girl, Ruth, were seriously pondering their leaves and picture cards.

"Can I help?" she asked.

"Would that be cheating?" Teddy asked.

"Not if I offer to help everybody with one thing," Lauren said. "Are you stuck on one thing?"

Both kids pointed to leaves on their chart. "I think it's this one," Ruth said while Teddy shook his head.

"You're right," Lauren said. She smiled at Teddy. "But I understand why you might have thought it was the other one. They're very similar. Just like people, some of them look a lot alike and some are really different."

Ruth took her paper and wandered off, but Teddy lingered.

"My daddy and I tried buying flowers," he said.

Lauren sucked in a breath but tried to keep a neutral expression. Was Seth going to plant a garden? "That's really nice. How did it go?"

"Terrible," he said. He put the chart on the concrete floor next to his feet and dug a paper out of his pocket. Lauren smiled at how adorable Teddy was with his skinny knees and legs showing above his red rain boots. He handed her the paper. "My daddy wrote our questions."

Lauren took the paper and read the questions about how many plants they would need for an average-size backyard garden and what percentage of shade is part shade. He also asked what color coneflowers there were in the children's playground garden. "Should I write my answers on the paper?" she asked.

Teddy nodded. "You can also tell my daddy when he calls you, but I like delivering the messages. Maybe I want to be a mailman when I grow up."

Seth was going to call her? She tried not to

show any reaction to that. After all, Teddy almost certainly didn't know that she and Seth had a history. She had to keep things professional for the boy's sake—and possibly her own. Wanting Seth's forgiveness was tricky.

"A mailman and not a gardener?" Lauren asked.

"A mailman and a gardener," he said. "And a fireman."

Lauren smiled. "You'll be very busy."

"My daddy is busy, but he's picking me up early today because he has the day off. He said I could come to flower camp, though."

"I'm glad you did. I'll write the answers and give you the paper before you leave today. That way you can be the messenger, just in case your daddy doesn't have time to call me."

"It's his day off," Teddy reiterated, clearly believing his daddy didn't have anything more pressing to do.

Lauren moved on to help a different group, keeping her promise to be fair. When most of the children had finished the activity, Amber switched them over to coloring and drawing. About fifteen minutes before dismissal, hints of sunshine streamed through the greenhouse roof. Lauren checked her weather app and then stuck her head outside to confirm. There was barely a sprinkle. If they went now, they could get some rain-free time outside.

She and Amber rounded up the children with Jill's help, made sure they had boots on and umbrellas in their hands, and then Lauren led them outside to a nearby perennial planting. She pointed out raindrops on broad leaves, a trail left by a worm and a flower that had closed its petals against the rain. They were only outside for five minutes when big raindrops began splashing around them.

"Umbrellas up!" Lauren said, cheerfully demonstrating by putting hers up and twirling it. "Rain is very good for plants." She looked toward the sky. "Thank you, clouds!"

The children also looked up and said thank you to the clouds, and then the adults led them back to the greenhouse. Lauren was glad they'd got a mini-lesson outdoors in addition to the indoor activities.

As she held the door for the kids, directing them to put down their umbrellas and stooping to help some of them with the tricky mechanisms, she saw a truck pull up. She knew that vehicle. She'd seen it parked in Seth's driveway. Teddy had told her that his dad was picking him up early, but she'd assumed he meant at the day care.

Seth got out of the truck and walked through the rain, seemingly unbothered by it. She knew he faced far worse conditions as a firefighter, and she did, too. It was something they had in common—working for the public good and being exposed to the elements. Did they have anything else in common these days?

Teddy had already gone inside and didn't see his dad approaching. Seth smiled as Lauren helped the last child attempting to bump inside with her umbrella up. He reached over Lauren and held the door so she could duck inside with the little girl. It shouldn't give her heart a little jolt as if lightning had touched down nearby. She had known Seth practically all her life.

Inside, Amber blocked the doorway. "Can I help you?" she asked Seth.

While Seth was no stranger to Lauren, Amber didn't know who he was, and the park's greenhouse was typically not open to the public, especially with a group of children inside.

"It's okay," Lauren said. "I know him. This is Teddy's dad."

"Oh," Amber said. She extended a hand. "Nice to meet you. Jill did tell me his dad was picking him up today."

Lauren wished she had gotten that information, but she was in charge of the plant and flower knowledge, and Amber was the overall activity contact with the day care.

"You're soaked, come in," Amber said.

"I don't mind the rain," Seth said, continuing to stand in the doorway as if he didn't want to intrude too far into a world that wasn't his. Would Lauren feel the same way at the fire station? Amber moved over to the area where the children were congregating and shaking off rainwater with the help of their day care teacher, leaving Lauren alone with Seth.

"Come on in. Teddy can show you the activity we did today."

"Okay," he said. He stepped inside and pulled the door shut behind him. "Can I ask you something?"

Lauren's heart had settled down, but it thumped a bit harder than usual inside her chest. "Sure. Of course, yes. Is it about the gardening questions you sent?"

"No. I mean, sort of yes."

He seemed nervous. No doubt he was a brave man. He risked his life daily to help and serve others. And she couldn't forget how he'd thrown himself at her sister's situation years ago. That wasn't the act of a coward. Only lately had she realized how brave it had been and how much he had risked. She'd been mad at him for so long, and it was strange viewing that summer from a different angle.

"Go ahead," she said. She glanced over at the kids. They were all on the other side of a row of tall plants and Teddy had not yet noticed his dad by the door. They probably only had another minute of alone time.

"You probably figured out that Teddy wants to plant a garden in our backyard. It's really not my wheelhouse," Seth said, speaking quickly as if he, too, knew his time was limited. "I was wondering if you could come and look at the space and help me figure out where and what to plant. If I'm going to do this, I want to do it right."

"I'd love to," she blurted. Not only would she love to help anyone with such a project, she adored Teddy and this was a way—a tiny way—to make amends with Seth. A garden couldn't erase the pain of the last ten years, but it could provide a soft place to move forward from.

"I have the rest of the day off," he said. "I know it's short notice, but—"

"I don't have any plans for after work," she said, her excitement growing. Sharing the act of planning a garden was probably the most healing thing she could do for herself and Seth. And it would help them bond. Gardens lasted a long time. He might need future help and advice with the seasons. Her grandmother had taught her many things, and the most important was nurturing growing things. Grandma Vera would be so excited to see her forging a bond with Seth. Was this what she had hoped for when she left Lauren that note? "I'm done at four, and the rain is supposed to stop after lunch," she said. "I could drop by this evening."

"I won't keep you long, and I'd be happy to pay you for your time," he said.

"No," she said. The thought of this being transactional would suck all the joy out of it. "I love sharing gardening advice. It would be my—"

Her words were interrupted by Teddy appearing silently by Seth's side and taking his hand. Other kids would probably have yelled "Daddy" from across the greenhouse, but not Teddy. This was why she wanted to be involved. For Teddy's sake. If he was willing to talk to her and she could help him find an avenue of communication with his dad, helping out an old friend would be doubly worthwhile.

"Wet," Teddy said.

Seth laughed and looked down at his son. "Did you know it's raining?"

"Rain is good for flowers," Teddy said. "We went outside and saw raindrops on leaves and some of the flowers curled up their petals and went to sleep because of the rain. And worms," he added. "Did you ask Miss Lauren about helping us?"

Lauren knew Teddy well enough to know that that was a lot of words for him. Seth's smile was so real and affectionate as he looked at his son—it warmed her own heart. The look of hope on the boy's face made her so glad she'd already said yes.

"I did. She can come over this evening for a few minutes."

"We're making pizzas," Teddy said. "They're really good."

Lauren exchanged a glance with Seth. Clearly, the child was inviting her for dinner. What should she do?

"I do love pizza," she said, opting for a truthful statement.

"I don't want to take up too much of your time," Seth said.

Lauren couldn't decide if he was hoping for a convenient way to un-invite her for dinner or if he was just being polite. It was his house, and the last thing she wanted to do was make him uncomfortable or add an obstacle to the slow de-thawing of their relationship. So, she waited for a count of five.

"But we will have plenty of food. If you won't let me pay you for your time, I could pay you in pizza."

She still didn't like the concept that Seth believed he would owe her for this. This kind of help was a natural thing between friends, and it only reminded her again that the ten years had made them strangers. Was it possible to begin again? Was that even a wise thing to do?

She looked at Teddy, reminding herself that this was about him, not his dad. "I'm usually super hungry after a big day of gardening, so I would love to have pizza with you and then help with your garden."

Teddy giggled. "I get extra cheese. You can, too."

The day care bus pulled up outside and Lauren heard the teacher instructing the kids to line up.

"So," Seth said. "We'll see you later?"

"I'll come straight from work if that's okay. That way I'm already dressed for gardening."

Seth nodded.

"Can you bring Popsicle sticks?" Teddy asked. "My dad said we don't have any."

Lauren smiled, delighted that Teddy wanted to try that method of garden planning. "I sure will. I know I have some extras around here somewhere."

Lauren held the door for the other kids, and Teddy glanced back and waved at her right before Seth closed the truck's door. Seth didn't look her way, but that was okay. Her summer plan to reach out to Seth on behalf of her family and somehow make an apology for a lot of lost years finally had an opening chapter.

IN THE TWO years Seth had owned the little house near the fire station, no woman had sat at this table. He and Hannah had rented a larger house just outside Niagara Falls where they could get more space for less money because it was farther from the tourist area. It was also farther from Seth's work, but he hadn't minded. He'd tried his best to make everything work, but he was the only one trying in that relationship. After the divorce, Hannah had continued renting the house—which Seth thought was good for Teddy because it removed one element of disruption—and Seth had bought the small house where he now lived.

The house had three small bedrooms and two bathrooms, all on one floor, and also a decent-sized eat-in kitchen and a nice living room. The back deck had taken some repair work, but it was nice now. The backyard, however, was as plain as a cardboard box. He mowed it and trimmed around the swing set, of course, but Seth hadn't spent any creative or physical energy on it.

Now, sitting on his back deck across the picnic table from Lauren Benedict, he felt as if he was about to ask Picasso's opinion on a paint-by-number project.

"I'm watching the light," Lauren said. "It's a bonus that the neighbor's trees shade part of the space but the rest is full sun. You can have a wide variety of plants that way."

She took a big bite of pizza and Seth felt as if

it was his turn to supply conversation. Teddy was eating, not talking. Either he was very hungry or he was listening. Teddy had a way of absorbing what was going on around him—hearing everything that was said and storing it away for later use. Knowing that made him very conscious of everything he said to or around his son.

"I wish I could say I planned it that way," Seth said to Lauren. "But I just got lucky when I bought this house two years ago."

"How do you feel about planting a tree of your own?" Lauren asked. "It doesn't have to be huge, but something with height would anchor that corner nicely." She pointed to a back corner where two sections of six-foot privacy fence met.

Honestly, the place looked like an abandoned playground with tall fences all around and one swing set plunked right in the middle. He did plan to add a kiddie pool when it got hot, but he hadn't even decided where to put it.

Teddy finished his pizza and then tossed a ball off the deck and it rolled halfway across the yard. Sparky jumped up and ran after it. His mouth was too small for him to pick it up and retrieve it, but the little dog pushed it around with his nose and then flopped down next to it as if his work was done. Teddy got up from the picnic table and went to play, too, rolling around on the ground with Sparky, and Seth groaned. "Grass stains."

Lauren laughed. "I'm sort of glad you don't have a puppy that digs or a massive dog that would flop down on tender new plants. Sparky will coexist well with a garden."

Seth had given up hoping that Sparky's real owner would come forth. He and Teddy had made space in their lives for the little guy. Teddy was enchanted, and Seth was somewhere between tolerating the Chihuahua and inviting him onto the couch.

"So, what do you have in mind?" Seth asked.

"I've been thinking about it since I got here," she said. "Even though this excellent food deserved my attention. I love your homemade pizza."

"I learned how to make pizza crust from my father-in-law," he said. "Former father-in-law." An awkward silence seemed to hang in the late afternoon air. "He owns a restaurant in Buffalo. That's where I met Hannah."

He wondered if Lauren even knew his ex-wife's name. Seth doubted Nanna Vera had passed along much about him to Lauren and her family. What would be the point?

Although Nanna Vera had left Lauren that letter. They wouldn't be sitting here finishing dinner on his deck watching his son and dog play in the yard if it hadn't been for that. Lauren would have kept on ignoring him for probably the rest of her life, and he would have been fine with it. He'd gotten used to covering up his childhood memories, and life was easier that way.

"I'm thinking about families," Lauren said.

Seth held his breath for a moment. Were they really going to have this conversation? He glanced at his son, who was too far away and too absorbed in Sparky's antics chasing a fly to notice.

"Planting several flowers from the same family is a nice way to organize a small space but still have variety," Lauren said, and he breathed out again. "For example, I think several varieties of ferns in the shady part would add color and interest in a subtle way. We can save the big color for the sunny section of yard, which I'm honestly glad is most of your yard. I love the shady plants, but my heart belongs to the big colorful flowers."

"Which ones?" Seth asked, hoping she'd just keep talking about flowers so he didn't have to think about what to say. He felt tongue-tied hearing her talk about where her heart belonged. He was keeping his life simple by letting Teddy be the sole owner of his heart and his time. He wished his own dad had been able to do the same.

"Roses, of course. Specifically the floribundas and climbers. I love their unbridled enthusiasm. The hybrid teas are dainty and beautiful, too, though."

Seth nodded.

"I also think that since this is a kid-friendly space, you should plant some sunflowers along the fence. They'll get way taller than the fence, but they look happy, like they'd like to be your best friend."

She paused and her expression clouded.

"Of course, daisies are cheerful, too, and there are plenty of varieties that are hardy in this climate zone. We definitely want to choose plants tough enough to make it through the winter. I don't want you to waste your money."

"Okay," Seth agreed. "I'm going with whatever you suggest because this is uncharted territory for me."

Lauren stopped talking and studied him for a minute. "There's a garden nearby that has a similar mix of sun and shade and has the kind of plants I've been describing. It might help to take a little trip and see it, especially because a lot of the plants are in full bloom or getting close."

"Okay," Seth said. He assumed she meant a nearby park or else a garden in the Niagara Falls State Park. Having her at his house felt very personal, and it would be good to go to more neutral ground.

"Are we going to see flowers?" Teddy asked.

Seth hadn't even noticed him reappearing on the deck, but now that Teddy had heard the plan he couldn't say no.

"If your dad wants to," Lauren said.

Seth tried to look enthusiastic for his son's sake. "It sounds like a good idea. Which park?"

Lauren bit her lip. "Not a park. The garden is actually…was actually my grandmother's. Grandma Vera and I worked together a lot in recent years to get it just right, although we weren't done when she…"

Her voice trailed off and in the awkward silence, Seth felt a slew of childhood memories involving that house assail him. He wished Lauren had told him that the garden was at Nanna Vera's before he'd agreed to it and before Teddy's enthusiasm got involved. He felt stuck.

"I have a grandma but she lives far away," Teddy said, his sweet innocence giving Seth a minute to calm his thoughts.

"That's nice," Lauren said.

"I don't know if she likes flowers or not."

Lauren smiled at Teddy. "You'll have to ask her next time you talk to her."

Seth really didn't want to have this conversation about his former in-laws who, in fact, did not live that far away. They never made an effort to see Teddy, or rather, Hannah didn't seem to want to make the effort to bring Teddy to see them. It had always seemed wrong to Seth, especially because they were his only grandparents. Would it be weird for him to reach out to them and make the connection? The summer, so far, had given him a lot of food for thought about relationships and who was responsible for keeping them up or letting them go.

"We should go before the light fades," Seth said abruptly, wanting to get this over with. He had dozens of memories of Nanna Vera's backyard. They'd mostly used it as a quick pass-through between Lauren and Maggie's big lake house and the warm little kitchen where Nanna Vera always had food available. Had there been a big garden there when he was a kid? It was not something he'd noticed on the way to the cookies and casseroles.

But now he was going down that memory lane. With Lauren. And with Teddy right there noticing everything that was said and done around him. Seth needed to keep it together, which meant keeping his head in the future instead of the past.

"That's a good idea," Lauren said. "Some gardens are beautiful at dusk or even later, but I'd like you to see this one with some sunshine on it." She gathered up the notes spread on the table.

"Can Sparky come, too?" Teddy asked. "Does your grandma like dogs?"

Lauren looked uncertain how to answer at first, but she managed, "My grandma isn't there anymore, but I'm sure Sparky would be welcome."

The dog in question had sprawled out at the bottom of the deck's steps and was fast asleep.

"Let's leave him here to enjoy the yard," Seth said. "We won't be gone long." There was no way he intended to linger in Nanna Vera's garden as the summer day faded. He certainly didn't want to be there when the first fireflies appeared, even though Teddy would love chasing them and catching them—for just a few minutes—in an old glass jar like the ones Nanna Vera used to save from pickles and peanut butter. His son deserved happy childhood memories like that, and it was Seth's job to ensure he got them. They just didn't have to happen in that backyard.

He'd do a quick tour of the garden, agree to whatever plants his son liked and Lauren thought would survive, and then he'd have his own backyard oasis for Teddy—no Benedicts needed for a happy childhood.

CHAPTER THIRTEEN

LAUREN HAD DRIVEN to work that morning because of the rain and then taken her car to Seth's place, so they drove separately to her grandmother's house. Seth hadn't offered her a ride in his truck, and she hadn't offered him and Teddy a ride, either. Planning a garden was personal. Visiting her grandmother's home and garden was very personal. If they rode together in the same vehicle, it was too personal.

And she might want to stay later anyway and continue her sorting project. At least that was what she told herself as she breathed deeply on the way there, thinking of Seth back in that house. Back in her life. She wondered what Maggie would say if she knew Lauren was opening the doors to Grandma's house, but she decided she didn't care.

Grandma Vera's house sat on a narrow lot and the houses were close on both sides, but there was still a pathway around the house to the back garden. They wouldn't even have to go inside.

Lauren waited for Seth to turn off his truck and get Teddy out of his seat.

Lauren grabbed the notebook she'd been writing in during dinner and got out of the car. "This way," she said, inclining her head.

Seth and Teddy followed her around to the back of the house, where early evening sun illuminated the warm colors of plants Lauren knew so well they were like mutual friends beloved to her and her grandmother. As if the plants had known how close they were and how much Lauren would miss Grandma Vera. She always felt a tug at her heart in this garden.

"Wow," Teddy said.

Lauren smiled. "You like it?"

"It's so pretty."

She nodded. "It is." Her eyes stung and she looked away so Teddy wouldn't see the shimmering tears there.

Seth saw them.

"Maybe this isn't a good idea," he said, his voice sounding thick. Was he also missing the woman he'd called Nanna Vera? Did being here in her yard bring back a swarm of memories for him?

He had a right to those memories, just as she did.

"It'll be fine," Lauren said. "We'll take a quick look at some examples here and I can suggest which ones will work for your space. Sort of a try-before-you-buy idea."

"That is an excellent life skill," Seth said. He grinned and it broke the tension.

"My mommy bought a car and she hated it," Teddy said.

"I told her—" Seth began, but then he stopped himself. Lauren was pretty sure what he'd been about to say, but he obviously didn't want to say it in front of his son. Or her? It was odd, knowing that the Seth Jones who'd spent over ten years as her best friend had gone off and married someone she'd never met and had an entirely different life for the last ten years.

They couldn't go back, and he didn't want to go forward. Did she? Could a friendship with him now work, and how long would it take before she knew the *man* Seth instead of relying on memories of the younger version?

"Daylilies," she said abruptly. "Boy, are they big bloomers, and hardy, too. You just have to be sure you love them because they are enthusiastic multipliers and you'll never get rid of them, even if you wanted to." She pointed and gestured for Teddy to follow her. "I'll show you."

Lauren led the way to an area by the back fence where green leaves filled in a broad area and long stems were topped with a variety of colored lilies.

"Orange is a common one, but there are also yellow ones and burgundy ones and striped ones. See?"

Teddy walked up and down the fence, inspecting the lilies. He nodded. "I like them."

"Excellent choice for the area by your own fence," Lauren said. "I'm writing it down."

Seth joined them and walked along a few paces behind Lauren and Teddy as if he wanted to let them decide and he was just along for the ride. They passed the hydrangea bushes in a partly shady part of the yard and then the butterfly bush in a sunny spot. A spotted butterfly landed right in front of Teddy and he spent the next few minutes engrossed in watching it as it opened and closed its wings.

"How do you feel about roses?" Lauren asked Seth.

"I don't know," he said. "How should I feel about them?"

"They're fragrant and beautiful, but some varieties are pretty thorny so I wouldn't put them in an area where Sparky and Teddy might get tangled up in them."

"Where would you put them?"

Lauren showed him the sketch she'd made of his backyard in her notebook. She pointed to an area near the deck but not along a walkway.

"You'll be able to smell them from the deck but they won't be in the way," she said.

"Okay," Seth said.

"Example," Lauren said. She walked him over to a yellow floribunda that both she and her grandmother had agreed was their favorite rose. It had dark green leaves and flowers with so many petals the blossoms practically burst with them, and it smelled sweet and summery. "A lot of people go for the red ones, but Grandma and I… This was our favorite."

Seth leaned over and smelled one of the roses, and Lauren felt as if Grandma Vera was right there with them, overseeing their very tentative reconciliation. Maybe it wasn't going anywhere. But perhaps they'd put some of the pain to rest, and that might be enough. She could help him with his garden, inspire his son to talk for the summer, and then she could go back to an existence where she saw Seth Jones from a distance but backed away from his life. Again.

But that seemed harder to do now than it had before. She knew him now. He was more than just a memory. He was a man with a heroic job who loved his son and made delicious homemade pizza. He was a man breathing in the scent of a rosebush on his day off because he wanted to plant a garden to make his boy happy.

The more time she spent with him, the more she regretted all the time they had lost.

"Can I get one like this?" Seth asked. "This one looks like it's been here a while, and I don't know if these are like cars, with new models coming out all the time."

Lauren smiled. "They do come out with new varieties all the time, but this one is only a few years old. Grandma and I planted it on her seventy-fifth birthday."

Seth swallowed, absorbing that information.

"I can always propagate a plant from a shoot off this one."

"You mean take a piece of this and transfer it to my garden?" he asked.

"Basically," she said. She found she liked that idea more than his buying a new plant of his own. Grandma Vera had left her that letter, after all, so surely that meant she would be glad to have a piece of her beloved garden growing at Seth's house. Then again, much as Lauren wanted to make amends with Seth, did she really want their past to become entangled with their futures?

"Let's continue the tour and finish the list," she said, resolving to keep this a matter of garden design business and not an open garden gate inviting her to wander down paths that had grown over.

THE NEXT MORNING at work, Seth mechanically inspected the trucks at the beginning of his shift. He'd been there long enough that he could do it without much thought, checking off the tools and supplies housed in each compartment. He liked the uniformity of it, knowing that the side compartment, passenger side, of the rescue truck would have road flares, heavy blankets and pry bars in three sizes. He'd used all of them in the line of duty where having the right equipment could mean the difference between life and death in an emergency situation.

So he did his work automatically but diligently, leaving him headspace to think about the previous evening—and what he'd promised to do the coming one.

"Morning, Jones," his boss said as he came around the front of the truck.

Seth nodded and returned the greeting.

Chief Bear leaned against the side of the truck. "Any chance you could pick up all or part of an extra shift today?" At Seth's obvious wariness, he added, "I hate asking because I know your situation this summer, but Grover's out of town and Murray had to take his daughter to a specialist in Buffalo. She broke her arm playing summer league baseball. He doesn't know what time he'll get back. You know how you have to wait at those places."

"I would, but Teddy—"

Bear cut him off. "I checked with Morgan already. She said she could take Teddy for the evening."

"That would be helpful," Seth mused. Teddy liked Bear and Morgan's son, who was about the same age. "And Teddy loves Morgan's cooking. Your wife can make vegetarian food taste like something even I'd want to eat."

"She's a gem."

"Plus, she puts up with you." Seth had known Bear and Morgan for a decade, and their wedding had been one of the first social events he'd attended as a member of the fire department.

"I sure won the lottery with her," Bear agreed with a laugh.

Seth didn't argue with that, but he sure wished his own marriage had been as simple as buying a winning lottery ticket.

The chief was awaiting his answer, though, and childcare wasn't the issue. It was the promise he'd made Teddy—that they'd take the very detailed list Lauren had written and visit the greenhouse she recommended. It wasn't a big-box store, but instead a smaller local nursery where someone knowledgeable would help him, especially if he mentioned Lauren's name. He wasn't the kind of guy who usually name-dropped, but he was sure he didn't want to let his son down.

Lauren had offered to go along when she got off work at four and had insisted it was no trouble at all, but Seth had already asked too much of her. He didn't want his son to think a list of plants was too daunting.

"I understand," Seth said. He calculated. The local greenhouse where he and Teddy were planning to shop was only open until six. If he stayed late to cover until Murray got back from Buffalo, he likely wouldn't be able to get to the greenhouse before it closed today.

"We could probably run the shift with one less guy, but I hate being bare bones like that," Chief Bear added, "with it being peak tourist season and everything."

"I know," Seth said.

This was the hard part about parenting, especially single-parenting. Carrying all the weight yourself, even if it was a precious burden he would never give up. He was lucky to have excellent childcare available, but it wasn't always just about having a safe home and a hot meal. He'd made a promise to do something special with Teddy. He could push off the flower shopping until tomorrow night—although they had planned to do the planting tonight and tomorrow night because five days of rain were in the forecast after that.

He pictured himself telling his boss the station would have to get by with a limited shift because he wanted to pick out daisies and lilies with his son. Bear would understand—he was a dad, too—but the point was that Seth felt like putty stretched so thin it was losing its elasticity.

The garden was supposed to be a special project just for him and Teddy, but he'd already had to ask for help. Would it be so bad to ask for a little more? He could take Lauren up on her offer to buy the plants today. He'd pay her back, of course. She was a professional. Was it wrong for him to call in a pro? And this way he could start planting them as soon as he got home. Maybe he'd even let Teddy stay up late to help. It was summer; they'd have daylight until almost nine.

"I think I can make this work," Seth said. "If Morgan can pick Teddy up from day care."

"She said she would," Bear said, looking relieved.

"Sounds like a plan," Seth said. "I'll stay until Murray gets here."

Bear clapped him on the shoulder and said thanks, and then Seth pulled out his phone. The day care had Morgan on file as an approved pickup person, but he wanted to let Teddy know Miss Morgan would be there for him. He didn't want his son to be surprised or upset, especially since they had plans that night.

He dialed Rainbow Connection day care and

asked to talk to Teddy. It would be a one-sided conversation, of course. Teddy was reluctant to talk in person; on the phone he was even worse.

"He's not here," the person at day care said.

Seth's heart shut down for a second before the woman continued. "He's with the group at the park, the flower camp thing."

"Oh, right," Seth said. "I can call back later."

He hung up, but then the radio traffic caught his attention. A neighboring department was being called out on a big fire. It was the kind of thing that sometimes ended up involving other departments. The nature of his job meant that it was unpredictable. It was possible he wouldn't be able to call the day care and speak to Teddy this afternoon.

But there was someone he could call that Teddy liked and trusted. She would deliver his message. She might even hand Teddy the phone. Seth couldn't believe he was dialing Lauren's number, but he was thinking of his son and making him happy while trying to balance his responsibility to the people of Niagara Falls. This was a solution.

Lauren answered on the second ring. "Hello?"

As soon as he heard Lauren's voice, Seth considered hanging up fast. But she had caller ID like everyone else on earth. He couldn't back down now, even if his brain had caught up with his emotions and was telling him this was a foolish entanglement. Hadn't he recently vowed to himself that he would ensure Teddy's happy childhood without needing the Benedicts?

As he had needed them. A long time ago.

"Hey, it's me," he managed. He could hear children singing in the background. Was that the ladybug song?

"Is everything okay?" Lauren asked.

"Yes," Seth said quickly. "Fine. I just…wanted to get a message to Teddy, and I thought he might be there with you and—"

"He is," she said.

Seth heard her calling Teddy's name and pictured her motioning him over to her, Teddy gleefully skipping toward his current hero, Miss Lauren, who liked his dog and pizza and flowers.

Before he could gather his thoughts, he heard Teddy's small voice saying "Hello, Daddy."

"Teddy, honey, I just wanted to call and tell you we have a little change of plans for tonight. I have to work late, so Miss Morgan will pick you up from day care and you'll have dinner at her house with Jimmy, and I'll get there as soon as I can after that."

"After dinner?" Teddy asked.

Seth could hear the disappointment in his son's voice.

"Yes. Hopefully right after."

"But we were going to the flower place."

"I know, honey, but I can't tonight. I'm sorry." This was breaking his heart. Flowers were the thing Teddy had shown the most enthusiasm about all summer. And Miss Lauren, Seth had to admit.

"That's okay, Daddy," Teddy said, sounding much brighter.

Seth breathed. Maybe this was going to be okay.

"Maybe Miss Lauren can take me."

Seth heard the sound of Teddy fumbling the phone, probably holding it mashed in his little hands, and then a conversation between Lauren and his son. He wanted to yell into the phone to get someone's attention. He didn't want Lauren taking his son on this errand.

Flashbacks of a thousand trips in the Benedict family car rushed over him. Take-out dinners, rides home from school, rides to the store to get his school supplies. Always belted safely into the back seat with Lauren and Maggie, and Mr. or Mrs. Benedict at the wheel. As a child, he hadn't realized how strange it was that his own dad wasn't driving him around and had basically allowed the Benedicts to be substitute parents.

He was not letting history repeat itself.

"Hey, Seth," Lauren said, her voice coming

through the phone clearly. "Teddy tells me you have to work late and there's a good chance the store will be closed when you get off."

"Yes, but—"

"I don't have any plans tonight," she said. "I don't mind helping out."

She hadn't had any plans the previous night, either, and that was how he and Teddy had ended up staying longer than planned at her grandmother's house, sitting around the familiar kitchen table while Lauren sketched out a garden design and wrote a list. Just being at that table had felt like being under a warm blanket—and that was dangerous.

"I'd love to take Teddy to the greenhouse and show him all my favorite—"

"No, thanks," Seth said. "I've got this. We can go tomorrow."

"But—"

"Lauren," Seth said, more harshly than he intended. "You don't need to drive my son around and do things for him. I'm his dad. That's my job."

He noticed Chief Bear across the station, watching him with concern. With the high metal roof and concrete floors, everything echoed in there. Bear could probably hear this whole conversation.

"Of course," she said, and Seth could feel the hurt over the phone. He knew what hurt felt like, too.

"I'm…" The word *sorry* was on his lips, but what was he apologizing for? Lauren could not sweep in like her parents had done for him and rescue another generation of sad little Jones boys. Teddy was not abandoned. Seth was not like his own father. Nothing was the same as it had been.

"I'm handing the phone back to Teddy now," Lauren said.

Seth wanted to tell her to wait, partly because he didn't want to be a jerk to her and partly because he didn't know what he was going to say to his son. Miss Lauren was someone he knew and trusted—someone who'd been at their house and eaten with them the night before. Teddy wouldn't understand why Seth was saying no to this outing.

There was silence on the other end of the line, but he knew Teddy was there.

"Teddy, honey, I'm sorry we can't go to the greenhouse tonight, but I want to be the one to take you, so I said no thank you to Miss Lauren. I promise I'll take you tomorrow, and I know you'll have a great dinner with Miss Morgan."

More silence.

"Okay?" Seth asked.

"Okay," he heard the tiny voice of his child

answer, and Seth wanted to race to his son and hug him, but he couldn't.

He didn't let himself think about Miss Lauren comforting a disappointed little boy, even though he knew in his heart she probably was.

CHAPTER FOURTEEN

THE RAIN HAD a good sense of timing, Lauren thought as she opened the door to the small, attached garage at her grandmother's house. She had two days off from work, which meant she didn't have to weed the flower beds along the falls in the rain. And she wouldn't have to water the dozens of hanging baskets filled with colorful annuals spread throughout the park. Mother Nature was doing her job for her. Which was fine with her because she had her own place to clean, a cat that needed cuddling and her grandmother's house and garden to take care of.

She didn't mind, since the rest of the family lived out of state. But she did wonder if she was just the convenient choice, not the best choice to care for her grandmother's legacy. Not that it mattered. Her parents and sister seemed to be in a waiting mode, and she was also in limbo. Was that a natural part of grief? Did the survivors wait for the calendar pages to turn, holidays to pass, seasons to change, as they continued their journey toward acceptance that their loved one was never coming back?

She turned her mind to more practical matters, peering at the breaker panel in the garage. Which was the right breaker? She had no idea why her grandmother had never had an actual light switch installed and instead just flipped a breaker in the garage's electrical panel when she needed the lights. As a child, Lauren had been afraid of the electrical panel, certain that she would touch the wrong thing and be electrocuted. Grandma Vera had no such issues with it and had managed everything around her house for years by herself. Lauren's grandfather had passed years earlier, before Lauren was born.

The older woman had been a combination of fiercely independent and nurturing at the same time. During the early spring, Grandma Vera had always parked her car outside so she could start seedlings in the garage under a heat lamp, but she had also been brave enough to set the fledgling plants outside to make it on their own when the time came. "Gardening teaches you a lot about life," Grandma Vera used to tell Lauren. "Plants need nutrients and water, but not too much, and plenty of sunshine but also not too much. They have their own cycles, just like people, and some of those cycles are prettier than others."

Lauren smiled, remembering her grandma's lectures about plants and people having a lot in common. As a nurse, Grandma Vera also knew all about nurturing but empowering the patient to stand on their own two feet. Being in this small garage with the empty potting table made Lauren's heart ache for one more conversation with her grandma.

Instead, she flipped several breakers in the box, and a lamp came on—its dim light barely enough to chase away some of the rainy gloom. She moved an old bicycle away from a stack of plastic bins and took the lid off the top one. Porch decorations. Of course. Grandma Vera was serious about seasonal decor inside and outside. The box was marked February-May, and at the top was a big red heart with a glittery cupid on it. Lauren remembered being able to see that decoration from all the way down the street on snowy winter days. Under the heart, she found a familiar St. Patrick's Day wreath with a green shamrock and a rainbow—also very glittery and visible from a distance. For April, there was a tulip wreath in the box and two inflatable bunnies, carefully deflated and packed away for next Easter.

There was nothing in the box for May, and Lauren realized the May wreath with spring flowers was still on the front door of the house, even though her grandmother had passed away during the first week of June. She should have realized her grandma wasn't feeling well—Vera was never one to let the calendar change without updating her porch decorations.

Lauren sighed. What was she going to do with all these things? The bigger question—Did she want to move into the house and take over where her grandmother left off?—weighed on her. She could be the one putting up the July decorations and maintaining the garden, which could be right outside her own back door. Lord Henry could move back in and take up his spot by the bay window in the living room. She could just…go on, following her grandmother's paths through the garden.

But a lot had changed with the Vera's passing, starting with the letter. Those words, that knowledge, couldn't be packed away like seasonal decorations. Rain pounded harder on the garage roof and the chill made her think of fall nights. She used to love the firepit by the lake in her parents' backyard. Seth considered it his duty as the guest to gather armloads of firewood from a nearby stand of trees that always seemed to be shedding branches. Lauren could vividly recall his face with warm firelight reflecting on it as he laughed at something she'd said. He used to laugh a lot with her family, but he seemed much more serious now. Was it parenthood that had made him so serious?

She skipped the tub marked June-September and went straight for the October-November one. December would have its own dedicated bin of decorations because Christmas was huge for her grandma. Lauren took the lid off the October-November bin and found fall wreaths in colorful oranges and reds. She also found the plastic pumpkins she and Maggie had drawn silly faces on with markers. Lauren flipped one over and found her name on the bottom in her childish handwriting. She got out her phone and texted Maggie a picture of the one that had her sister's name on the bottom.

Do you want this? she asked.

While she waited for a reply, Lauren found another plastic pumpkin in the bin with a face drawn in black marker—a careful face, as if its artist had put some thought into proportional eyes, nose and mouth. It had Seth's name on the bottom. Would he want it for Teddy?

She considered texting him, but before she could type it out, her sister called her.

"I can't believe Grandma kept all that old stuff," Maggie said instead of a greeting. "I must have been about five when I drew that face on."

"Hi, Maggie," Lauren said as she opened a folding chair and sat down. "I think we were a little older because…" She paused. She knew Maggie must have been at least six because Seth started hanging around with her family when he was five. Even though Maggie apparently considered the whole Seth saga water under the bridge, Lauren still felt weird bringing it up—almost guilty, as if she was the one who'd done something wrong, but also still protective of her sister's feelings, especially now that she knew about the miscarriage.

It still stung that Maggie had told Seth about it but not her. She'd taken Lauren's best friend into her confidence, and simultaneously taken him away from Lauren. It was a lot to think about, and Lauren knew she was letting things get even more complicated by rekindling a relationship with Seth—however tenuous it was. He was clearly keeping her at arm's length, though, and had been quick to turn her down when she suggested she could take Teddy plant shopping. Was she a fool to think she could reclaim what they'd lost—or at least make amends?

Luckily, Maggie marched on with her end of the conversation. "You don't have to keep any of that old stuff and you shouldn't feel guilty just donating it or pitching it," Maggie said. "I honestly don't want anything."

"Okay," Lauren said.

"How's everything else going?" Maggie asked.

"Fine. It's raining today, and I'm glad I'm not at work."

"Instead you're in the damp garage with the shady electrical sorting through junk," Maggie said. "I owe you."

Lauren stayed silent, but her eyes roved over her grandma's prized potting table, garden tools and other things she had loved—not junk, at least not in Lauren's eyes.

"Mom told me you might be interested in having the house," Maggie said. "And I think you should take it—if you want it."

"I don't know," Lauren said.

"I'm not coming back to Niagara Falls to live," Maggie said. "And anytime Mom and Dad visit or I bring the kids, we can always stay with you, right? So you might as well keep the lights on there. It can be like a family house."

"It's always been a family house," Lauren said. Didn't her sister remember how many meals they ate in the kitchen, evenings sprawled on the carpet in front of the television or helping put up the Christmas tree in the front window?

"You know what I mean," Maggie said. "Like a next-generation family house. My kids will love being able to see it when we come visit, so that's a big advantage of keeping it in the family."

Lauren knew what her sister meant, but she

also felt a stab of frustration. It felt like you had to have privileged access to get to the Benedict family now, like there was a wall around them all and a guard at the door. Did they need to keep some things in the family and keep some things—some people—out? She wanted to ask her sister what she would think if Lauren invited Seth to family events at the house in the future, but she stopped herself.

It would never work. She couldn't bring Seth back into the family without also bringing up a tough time in her sister's life. And he didn't seem to want to climb back over the family wall anyway.

"I'm glad I have you on the phone," Maggie said. "I'm planning to come for your birthday in July, so that will be a good opportunity to catch up with you. We were so busy when I was there for the funeral."

She wasn't wrong, but the family secret had changed Lauren's summer almost as dramatically as her grandmother's death. Suddenly, Lauren felt that she needed to say something for her own peace of mind, even if she risked hurting her sister.

"Maggie," she began, "if Grandma hadn't left me that letter, would you ever have told me the truth about your engagement to Seth?"

She heard her sister suck in a breath. Lauren hated conflict and was sensitive to everyone else's feelings… But just this once didn't her feelings matter, too?

"I… I don't know," Maggie said. "The past is the past. I thought it was best to leave everything there."

It was on the tip of Lauren's tongue to say that was easy for Maggie since she lived far away. For Lauren, Seth had been right there all along, and lately she'd been finding it very hard not to see him in the present tense.

RAIN DRIPPED DOWN Seth's face and ran off the brim of his baseball cap. His T-shirt under his rain slicker was already soaked and sticking to him. Teddy had a wide-brimmed waterproof hat, but his cheeks were wet with rain. And pink. And his eyes were bright with enthusiasm.

"Take a picture, Daddy! I'm a gardener," Teddy said, holding his arms wide as he stood in front of the flower bed along the back fence. Seven entire unsolicited words from his son completely removed the irritation from water running down the back of Seth's neck. Teddy's boots were so caked with mud Seth doubted the boy could take a step. But, wow, did he look happy.

Seth shielded his phone with one hand and took a picture. Gray sky and gloom framed his son in a bright yellow raincoat with a radiant smile. The contrast almost made it seem as if Seth had used some trick of photography or special filter. It was a picture he wanted to save…or share with someone. But who? He had no family. His ex-wife and her parents would be interested, but would they see the magic in the photo?

"Can I see it?" Teddy asked. He tried to move quickly, but his boots made a loud sucking sound in the mud.

"I'll come to you," Seth said.

He bent down and held the phone for Teddy to see. The boy nodded and asked, "Can you send it to Miss Lauren so she knows we made the garden?"

Seth hesitated. She would love the picture, but he couldn't send it to her. They had a very shaky connection of late, a flimsy shadow of what they'd once shared, but they were hardly "text a cute picture" friends. And they never would be.

Still, he appreciated the purity of his son's question and the logical assumption behind it. And she'd shared a lot lately, but there was still a ten-year gulf separating them.

"How about I send the picture to your mom?" Seth said.

Teddy shrugged. "Okay."

"I could send it to Grandma and Grandpa, too," Seth suggested.

Another shrug. "Okay."

"And then you can tell Miss Lauren about the garden next time you see her. It's nice to tell people things in person if you can instead of sending a text or picture."

Seth thought he was teaching his son a valid life lesson about communication. And it was true. In person was always preferable.

Teddy tilted his head and rainwater ran off the side of his hat. "But you like writing notes to Miss Lauren, and that's not in person."

He was being called out on his logic by a five-year-old child. The fact that his son was engaging with him—even making a valid oral argument—made Seth focus on who was really important in this conversation, and it wasn't him.

"That's a good point," Seth said. "I'll send Miss Lauren the picture, but I'll also include a message telling her that you'll give her all the details next time you see her. That way we cover all our bases."

Teddy nodded vigorously, throwing raindrops everywhere.

"Can we get back to work?" Seth asked.

More nodding.

They'd already planted a butterfly bush in the location Lauren suggested where it could spread out its branches and butterflies would feel safe visiting. As a surprise for his son, Seth had brought home a birdbath he picked up at the home improvement store. They settled it into place near the butterfly bush, though Seth knew he was going to have to give it more solid footing with some brick pavers once the rain stopped.

He would much prefer saving the whole garden project for a nice day, but days off didn't correspond with good weather in the near future, and the plants needed to get in the ground and Teddy was so eager to start their project. Seth had checked online about the wisdom of planting in the rain, and the general opinion was that the plants would enjoy the extra drink, and it was better than planting in the blazing sun.

"Coneflowers," Seth said. He picked up a black plastic pot in each hand and placed them near their corresponding Popsicle stick. Luckily, he and Teddy had done the measuring and placed the markers the previous evening during a break in the rain. So he had the hand-drawn garden plan, courtesy of an expert, and the list of plants, which had all been available at the garden center Lauren recommended. All he had to do was put the plants in the ground and remember to water them all summer. Easy.

"I'll dig the hole this time," Teddy said.

Seth smiled encouragingly, despite knowing

it would take five times longer if he let Teddy dig. It was priceless seeing his son's excitement, and it wasn't really possible for him to get any wetter. He reminded himself to enjoy the journey of parenthood instead of worrying so much about what was for dinner or finding the right words for everything.

"Can you do a movie of me digging?" Teddy asked.

"Sure can," Seth said. He again shielded his phone and took video of Teddy using his small shovel to take tiny little bites at the soil. It was a memory he wanted to treasure, a special snapshot of time that was just for him and his son. The garden would—should—last a long time, and he hoped Teddy would remember this day. If not, the picture and video would remind him that he and his dad could manage pretty well together.

Seth had believed he needed Lauren's help for the whole project, fearing a failure would disappoint his son, which was the last thing Seth ever wanted to do. Sure, Lauren had been very helpful, but he was managing just fine. Better yet, Teddy was talking—not just talking, initiating conversation, speaking up, asking questions. Seth felt as if he'd unlocked a parent achievement, inspiring and motivating his son.

And he didn't need Lauren to be there helping.

But as he looked at the muddy mess in his backyard and the determination on his son's face as he shoveled, Seth found himself wishing Lauren was there to see it. She'd loved playing in the rain when they were kids, stomping through puddles. He wondered if she still loved the rain, or if she ever thought about him when it rained.

He thought about her sometimes. He always had. Even though he'd been quick to shove those thoughts away. Today, he was okay with thinking about his childhood and his friend. Maybe he didn't have to crush those memories to be able to live with them.

He didn't need Lauren's help to plant a garden with his son, but looking around his rain-soaked yard with a happy, wet kid in it made him realize it would be nice to share this moment with the woman who had inspired it.

CHAPTER FIFTEEN

LAUREN TOOK THE long way around to Terrapin Point, looping past Three Sisters Islands on the south side of the Niagara Falls State Park. When she was a child, she and her family would often walk the pedestrian paths throughout the park, and she'd loved exploring. In the springtime, geese would work together to shepherd dozens of baby geese near a grove of trees by Three Sisters Islands. It always felt like a quieter, almost private area of the park that was near rushing water but at the end farthest from the actual falls. Lauren stopped her UTV near a picnic table where she got out and picked up some fast-food bags left by visitors. Her job was flowers and shrubs, with the occasional flowering tree, but she cared about everything that happened at the park.

She remembered having a tenth birthday party near this picnic table. Her parents had packed a picnic basket and her grandmother had brought a cake. One of her presents was a hula hoop, which her parents didn't even try to wrap. She also received a lawn game that she played with Maggie and Seth after they ate.

Lauren got back in her UTV but took one last look at the picnic table. Her twenty-eighth birthday was coming up in a few weeks, and her parents and sister were planning to visit. Maybe she'd ask them to re-create that birthday picnic with her.

Although Grandma would be missing. And Seth.

She drove toward Terrapin Point, a falls overlook that was very popular with tourists. It was technically right on the edge of the Horseshoe Falls and offered a spectacular view across the gorge of the Canadian side. With its long slope down, there was plenty of viewing available along its accessible walkways. It was also the location of a spectacular bed of annual flowers—red begonias, multicolored snapdragons, dwarf sunflowers and zinnias. The van from Rainbow Clubhouse would drop off the flower campers nearby, and Lauren was ready to teach the kids an important lesson about gardening—knowing when and how to prune.

Marlin met her near the visitor's snack bar and restrooms where ornamental cherry trees grew. She paused, tree trimmers in her hand, as Lauren approached.

"I have news," Marlin said. "Big news."

"You're going to lumberjack school. Finally," Lauren said.

Marlin laughed and shook her head.

"Building tree houses and renting them out," Lauren guessed.

"You're killing me with your goofball guesses when I have something very serious to impart," Marlin said.

Lauren smiled at her friend. "You don't look serious."

Marlin put down the tree trimmers and did a little twirl. "I went out with Merchandise Man," she said.

That had actually been Lauren's first guess, but she wanted her friend to have a little fun with the big reveal.

"I hope you didn't call him Merchandise Man."

"*Darren* and I," she said, emphasizing his name, "had a lovely dinner in Canada last night at a winery near Niagara-on-the-Lake."

"Bummer," Lauren said. "That doesn't sound romantic at all."

Marlin crossed her arms, not taking the bait. "You know you want to hear all about it."

"I do. Desperately. I bet those ten kids would love to hear it, too," Lauren said, pointing behind Marlin at the string of kids approaching.

"I will find you later," Marlin said, "and gush

about it. In the meantime, prepare yourself for a save-the-date notice. Darren is the one."

"What is the name of this winery where you had dinner?" Lauren asked. "It must be magical, and I could use some of that magic."

Marlin raised one shoulder and shrugged. "The winery doesn't matter. I would have fallen for him if we got hot dogs at the visitor center."

"Wow," Lauren said. Could Marlin be serious? A person couldn't fall for someone in a matter of hours. Relationships should take weeks, months, even years.

"I think he's the one. I hear birds singing when I'm with him."

"Well, yeah. You both work at the park, so of course you hear birds singing."

"Mark my words." Marlin picked up her trimmers and lopped off a low branch, a huge smile lighting her face. Lauren wanted to advise her to guard her heart, go slow, be careful… But then she remembered that she wasn't exactly qualified to write an advice column on finding true love. When was her last date? An even better question would be when was the last time she'd been so excited to see someone that it made her cheeks flush and heart race?

The memory of Seth getting out of his truck in the rain and meeting her at the greenhouse door washed over her. She'd felt flushed. Her heart had raced. But that didn't count. Seth wasn't a new acquaintance, someone she barely knew but wondered if there might be a connection with.

Their first meeting had been more than twenty years ago. There would be no chance for a lightning strike, a love-at-first-sight moment.

"Daddy wrote you a note."

Teddy's voice interrupted her thoughts as Lauren watched her friend saw away at the low branches. She turned and found Teddy at the front of the line of kids, his face pure sweetness and joy. He looked so much like Seth had at his age, and Lauren wished she could go back and relive those childhood days, changing the bitter ending this time.

"Oh," she said, unable to resist a smile despite her thoughts about the past. "I can't wait to see it. He sent me a picture of you and your garden, but his message said you would be the one to tell me all about it."

Teddy nodded vigorously, but the rest of the class crowded around. She would have to make sure she found time to hear from Teddy before the morning's camp ended, Lauren thought. She listened to her colleague remind the kids that there were two weeks left of flower camp after today. Considering how well it was going, Lauren and Amber had discussed running another camp right afterward or even later in the fall.

Happy kids were good for the present and future of the parks system, and Lauren's boss was a big supporter of programming.

Teddy shoved a note into Lauren's hand, and she slipped it into her pocket without reading it. The whole group deserved her attention at the moment, but butterflies flitted in her stomach with the anticipation of what Seth had written to her.

"Let's start with these pretty marigolds," she said as she bent down and touched the velvety yellow flower. "Did you know these help keep mosquitoes away because the insects don't like the smell?"

One of the girls in the class got down and smelled the flower, and then all the other kids did it, too.

"What do you think?"

"I think it's pretty," the girls said.

"Me, too," Lauren said. "But I'm not a mosquito."

"Mosquitoes drink blood," one of the boys said. "One time, my cousin had this huge bite and—"

"Jason," their teacher said, interrupting what was probably going to be a gross story. Jason had already told some whoppers in the previous two weeks. "Let's keep our thoughts and words on the lesson."

"Today's lesson," Lauren said, "is about annual flowers. *Annual* means once a year, and these flowers are very pretty, but they usually only live for one year."

"Perennials live a lot of years," Teddy said.

"Yes," Lauren said, giving him a high five. "These annuals only bloom for one year, but they will often bloom more than once if I do my job watering them, fertilizing them and deadheading them."

"Dead-head," Jason whispered enthusiastically.

"In plant terms, that means I cut off the old flowers so the plant spends its energy making new ones," Lauren said. "Other words you might hear are *pruning*, *trimming* or *pinching back*. These all mean basically cutting off the dead flower heads, one at a time."

"Doesn't it hurt the flowers?" a girl asked.

"Not at all. It's good for them to get a chance to start over and bloom again. Their old blooms would hold them back, so it's my job to give them a second chance."

If only that were true for people, she thought. Just snip off the old and rebloom, even better than the first time.

Lauren demonstrated cutting spent flowers off dozens of annuals in the big flower bed at Terrapin Point. She usually enjoyed the tedious labor, sometimes listening to music with her earbuds, sometimes just listening to the thunder of the nearby falls. Today, that note from Seth was burning a hole in her pocket. Was there a chance their friendship could rebloom?

"We're going to have you work with an adult partner and help us find all the flowers that have already bloomed so we can cut off the old blossoms. Ready with your eagle eyes?" Lauren asked.

The kids formed groups of two or three with an adult and went to work. Teddy and Jason ended up in Lauren's group. Teddy took the work seriously and knelt down to spot the flowers with spent blossoms. Jason made sword motions as if he was chopping the head off a whole company of flowers. Now there was a kid who could probably benefit from nurturing a garden at home.

"It rained the whole time we were planting our flowers," Teddy said. "My boots got stuck and Daddy had to pick me up but one of my boots stayed in the mud. Sparky got in the mud, too, and he had to stay outside until I was done with my bath. We only have one bathtub."

"Do you think Sparky had fun planting in the rain?"

"Uh-huh," Teddy said.

"And did your daddy have fun planting, even though he had to do a mud rescue?"

Teddy giggled. "I think Daddy was happy. He took pictures and made a video so he could always remember it."

"I'm glad," Lauren said. "Make sure you tell your daddy that the new plants will need to be watered almost every day unless it rains a lot. Just until they get used to their new home."

"Are you going to write my daddy a note for us to read together tonight?"

Lauren made a quick grab for her pruning shears that Jason was about to pick up. She clicked the safety catch to make them kid-proof. Jason redirected his focus and picked up a worm and—to his credit—held it gently cupped in his hands while he watched it wriggle around.

"Of course," she said to Teddy, taking off her garden gloves and pulling the note from her pocket. She glanced at it and smiled at Teddy. "Can you read these words?"

"Not really. But Daddy told me what it says. He just wrote it in case I forgot."

Lauren pointed out the words and pronounced the first sentence carefully. "Thank you for your plant suggestions and plan. We planted in the rain, which I'm sure Teddy will tell you all about." She glanced up, and Teddy smiled at her. "Check," she said. "The next two words have question marks after them. *Fertilizer* and

Mulch. I'm guessing he'd like to know what to do about those two things?"

Teddy nodded.

Lauren paused to help Jason find a nice pile of dirt to rehome the worm in rather than putting the creature in his pocket. "Okay," she said to Teddy. She took a pen from her shirt pocket. "I'm writing down the kind of fertilizer and how often to use it, and I'm putting a *yes* next to mulch. It helps prevent weeds and keep moisture in the ground. You can pick the color you like, red, brown or red. I like dark brown, but that's just me."

"Daddy might like red, like fire," Teddy said.

"Maybe," Lauren agreed with a smile. "You two will have to decide that."

Lauren tried to imagine the scene at Seth's house. She hoped she was helping bring happiness to both father and son. After all, wasn't that what nature did? Seth was probably only going along with the interaction because it was bringing Teddy out of his shell. It had nothing to do with her or the way they'd felt about each other a long time ago.

It was worth it anyway.

She added an extra note after his questions. It was taking a chance, but she was going to act on a feeling that had been growing since her grandmother's death. Putting things right wasn't easy, and it may not even be possible. But trying made her feel that she could breathe into the childhood memories again, reviving them instead of just keeping them stored away like boxes in a garage.

Your son reminds me so much of you when we were kids. He's bubbling with joy, even though he's quiet. When you first started hanging out with me, giving me a playmate who also loved the outdoors, I remember you didn't talk much but you seemed to see everything. Teddy seems like that to me.

Also, if you're going to fertilize, don't get the mulch with the fertilizer built in. It will be overkill.

SETH SMILED AT the practical ending to the note, but he couldn't help going back and rereading the first part. Had he really been like that as a child? Do children know how they appear to others? For that matter, do adults? He remembered lots of laughter and fun with Lauren, but had he started out quiet, like Teddy?

There was no one to ask. His parents were gone, and the only people who'd really known him as a child were the Benedicts. He could have asked Nanna Vera, but she was gone, too. His connection to his childhood was Lauren.

He hadn't even realized he *wanted* a connection to his childhood until recently. *Maybe having a son and watching him grow and develop takes your mind back and makes you wonder what you were like and how the people around you shaped who you became.*

But this was a new generation, and it was the present that mattered. His son waited expectantly while Seth read the letter.

"She wrote a lot of words," Teddy said.

Seth nodded. How much of this did he dare to share with his boy? If Teddy knew all the things he and Lauren had done together as kids, he'd want to do those things, too. He'd wonder why they couldn't all be friends and go paddling on the lake and have campfires and play tag until it was too dark to see.

"She gave me very specific instructions about fertilizer and mulch," Seth said. "She wants us to get it right so our garden will be nice."

"Can she come see it?" Teddy asked.

"I don't know," Seth said. Those pathetic words popped out like a reflex. Along with "we'll see," they seemed to be parental filler that allowed time to think—or waffle. Seth did know it was possible for Lauren to come see their garden, obviously. What he didn't know was whether or not it was a good idea. His son was getting attached to her. What would happen when flower camp came to an end in a few weeks? It was safer to limit the interactions. After all, this summer was his time to bond with Teddy and increase his self-confidence before kindergarten began, along with the back-and-forth of shared custody with Hannah. He didn't want to confuse Teddy with an extra relationship with Lauren.

"It would be fair," Teddy said, bringing him back to the present. "She helped."

The boy was right. Also, Seth had to admire him sticking up for someone. And he didn't want his son thinking Seth was unfair or unappreciative of others.

"I'll write her a note and ask," he said.

"Now?" Teddy asked.

Seth needed to consider what he'd write first. "Right now, we should go to the garden center for fertilizer and mulch, and then we have to eat dinner, and then we'll both need baths because I bet we're going to get our hands and knees dirty in the garden this evening."

Teddy giggled and smiled, and Seth resolved to sit down and write the note after his son was tucked into bed that night.

AT THE NEXT flower camp day, Teddy was waving a folded note before Amber even had time to welcome the kids and take attendance. It was a special day because they had T-shirts for all the kids with the logo of the Niagara Falls State Park on the front and Garden Helper on the back. The shirts were green, the same color as the pants and hats Lauren and her coworkers wore as part of their uniform.

"Thank you," she said, taking the note from Teddy.

"There are a lot of words, but I know what some of them are. Daddy told me."

"Okay," Lauren said. Amber was working with the day care teacher to hand out the shirts and help the kids pull them on over their clothes, so she had a minute to read the note as Teddy got in line with the other kids to get his shirt.

Thank you for the recommendation on fertilizer and mulch. We bought some last night and put it all down before bedtime. You're right about Teddy. He's quiet but he sees everything. I'm glad he's like that, most of the time. It's nice that he sees beauty and details. I remember making lots of noise when we were young, but I also noticed everything like how the world looked blue for about ten minutes every evening before the light was gone. It was my favorite time of the day.

Teddy would like you to come see the garden now that we've planted it. You don't have to if you're busy. We'll be home this evening.

Lauren felt her face heat and then cool and then heat again as she read the note. Seth talking about when they were young brought back all the feelings she'd had for him—playmate, friend and then the brief hope of something more until it was crushed. She knew now that it wasn't his fault, that he'd made a somewhat rash decision to help Maggie, and that her family had turned away from him afterward. She still expected something better from her sister, though. Was it wrong to forgive him and want to wrap her arms around her memories of him while still being irked by her Maggie's deception?

She remembered how he'd loved that ten minutes of blue every evening. She still tried to notice it as an adult. Often, though, she was busy, and suddenly the world outside was dark, and she'd missed the steady passing of daylight into starlight. She was going to make a better effort this summer not to let those hazy blue minutes escape unnoticed.

Teddy broke off from the group and stood in front of her, standing up straight in his new green shirt. "Can you come?" he asked.

She had plans for the evening. She'd put her grandmother's car up for sale on a few online sites, and a potential buyer was going to meet her at Vera's house at six. But summer evenings were long, and depending how the meeting went, she'd have time to stop by to see the garden. She couldn't say no to the invitation, for Teddy's sake.

"I'll try this evening," she said. "I have an appointment but I think I can come by later, okay? I'll write a note to let your dad know."

"You don't have to write that," Teddy said. "I can remember and tell him."

She was almost disappointed not to have a reason to write back to Seth. The notes were quaint, a bit old-school. Personal. But she couldn't argue with encouraging Teddy to use verbal skills and talk to his dad. That had been where all this back-and-forth had started.

"Even better," she said. "Please tell him I'm trying to sell my grandmother's car tonight, but I'll come over if there's still daylight after."

SETH TILTED HIS head and considered the vehicle that had just parked in his driveway. It was Lauren's car.

"Hello," she said as she got out, but then she paused. "You look confused. Didn't Teddy mention the plan?"

He laughed. "Teddy said you'd be driving your

grandmother's car because you had to drive it in the daylight."

Lauren chuckled. "He was close. I told him I had an appointment to sell my grandmother's car and that I would come over if there was still daylight after."

"Ah," Seth said. "Maybe we should stick to the notes for clear communication."

"Maybe. Although it's sort of fun this way."

She wasn't wrong. For weeks Seth had been taking full-time fatherhood very seriously, worrying about getting everything exactly right instead of just letting himself go along for the ride sometimes. Letting go—to an extent—was freeing.

"So did you sell the car?"

Lauren's expression turned cloudy and she sighed. "No. The guy showed up late and then hassled me over the tires and the price. He wanted to look under the hood, but I honestly don't think he even knew what he was looking at. He just wanted to find a reason to make an insultingly low offer. After a while, I told him he could shop elsewhere. I just wanted to get rid of him."

Seth felt his chest tighten. "Was he rude to you?"

"Yes, but I think he was just trying to get a bargain. I sent him on his way."

"I could...help you with that, if you needed

someone to be with you when a stranger is coming to your house." He didn't like the thought of Lauren being pushed around by some random man looking for a cheap car. As a general safety concern, of course. He was a public servant. A protector. He would offer to do the same for anyone.

"My grandmother's house," Lauren corrected. "And I was fine. I've been on my own a long time."

Seth's jaw was still tense, but he forced a smile. He didn't have any claim over Lauren. He understood she could take care of herself, but it was good to have support, too. She didn't have any family living in town anymore. Who would she call if she really needed help? He and Lauren had always had each other's backs when they were kids—even the time Seth accidentally knocked over Mrs. Benedict's favorite lamp and shattered it. Lauren had taken the blame and hadn't even told her sister. They'd stopped having foam dart wars in the house after that, no matter how cold it got in the winter and how desperate they were to burn off energy.

"Is this a bad time?" Lauren asked, prompting Seth to remember she was there because he'd invited her to see the garden.

"No," he said. "Definitely not. We finished dinner and did the dishes, and Teddy is getting his allotment of TV time while we waited for you."

Lauren smiled. "Only thirty minutes, right?"

"Absolutely."

"You're a tough dad. On rainy days, remember how we watched movies for hours in the basement?"

He could still smell that basement. It was clean and dry, but there was always a hit of must and laundry aroma in the air. There were also comfortable chairs arranged on a rug in front of a television. On rainy days, he still thought of how cozy it was, he and Maggie and Lauren watching movies or old TV shows, whatever they could agree on. Maggie liked teen drama movies, Lauren liked the nature channel and Seth was just glad to be included, seldom making a request because it wasn't his basement or his television.

Seth shrugged. "I'd rather do things together than watch TV."

"Agree," Lauren said. "Unless it's *really* raining hard and I have the day off. The travel channel had a whole series on private gardens at European mansions and castles. A girl can dream."

Her smile lit him up inside. She had a wide smile and a way of scrunching her nose just a little. Her hair had usually been loose and wild when they were kids, but she wore it tamed in a ponytail these days. It had darkened a little, too. Still brown with a reddish tint, but mellower.

Did he look the same as he had as a teen? It was hard to say about yourself. Sometimes, looking at Teddy felt like watching a movie of himself at that age—or at least how he thought he might have been. Lauren had seen the resemblance, too. It was strange having someone who had known him so well as a kid but hardly knew him now.

"Come in," he said. "We'll let Teddy know you could make it. He'll be excited to see you."

Seth held open his door for Lauren and they went through the living room, where Teddy hopped up, completely abandoning the cartoon race car show.

"Did your gramma's car run on daylight?" he asked.

Lauren put a hand on Teddy's shoulder. Affectionately, Seth thought. Like a mom would. And his son looked up at her as if she was the sun.

"Plants run on daylight," Lauren said. "And I can't wait to see the work you and your dad did. Am I even going to recognize your backyard?"

Teddy laughed and tugged on her hand, pulling her toward the French doors leading to the back patio.

When Lauren got outside, she shook her head. "Nope. I don't think this is the same yard you showed me before. Do I have the wrong address?"

"It is," Teddy said. "There's the fence and the swing set and our dog."

"But it looks magical now," Lauren said.

Seth scanned the yard, taking in the small plants in their curved beds with mulch. Instead of grass imprisoned by a fence, the yard looked like it belonged to a home now. Lauren was next to him, close enough to touch, and the blue dusk was lit by fireflies. He remembered other summer nights just like this one at a different home just across town.

"Magical," his son said, and Seth felt his heart tip over a ledge and start to fall right toward the beautiful woman standing next to him. It was like a fire that had suddenly rekindled, and Lauren's warmth felt so good beside him. It was almost too easy to forget how cold he had been when her whole family turned their backs on him.

CHAPTER SIXTEEN

ON JULY 3, Lauren had a special job for the flower camp kids. Armed with a crate full of small flags on wooden sticks, she waited for Marlin to pick her up for the short drive to the Bridal Veil Falls, where they would be meeting the group. One of the other horticulturists had Lauren's UTV because he'd turned his ankle playing backyard volleyball with his kids and needed easy transportation for a few days.

"We're getting married," Marlin announced when Lauren got in her UTV.

"Who's getting married?" Lauren asked, balancing the big box on her lap.

"Me and Darren."

"What? When?" Lauren asked.

Marlin shrugged. "I don't have a date, but I'm just letting you know it's going to happen, that way you won't be too surprised. I might even have you do the floral arrangements in addition to being in my bridal party."

Lauren opened her mouth but closed it again.

Her friend was making a lot of assumptions. For one thing, Lauren didn't do flower arranging. That was an entirely different skill from being a horticulturist and nurturing living flowers. But that wasn't really the part of Marlin's proclamation catching the most of her attention.

"I can see from your fish imitation that you don't believe me, and that's fine," Marlin said. "But remember I told you I was going to get a grant to plant all those willows, and I did. And I also predicted Stacey and Kelly would call off their wedding last summer, and they did. And who told you months ago that the park would do its own July Fourth street fair this year to compete with the cool Canada Day one across the border?"

Lauren wasn't going to argue with those points. Marlin had indeed seen the writing on the wall with Stacey and Kelly, and she was also a good grant writer, so there wasn't a lot of voodoo involved in those predictions. And, yes, the July Fourth street fair thing was going to be amazing, but it was just logical that both sides of the international border would celebrate the first weekend of July, since July 1 was Canada Day.

It was the suddenness of this marriage declaration that made her pause.

"What makes Darren the one?" she asked carefully.

"We like a lot of the same things. He appreciates my sense of humor. He makes me laugh."

"And?"

"There is no *and*," Marlin said. "Isn't that enough?"

"I think you have to be in love with someone to marry them," Lauren said.

"Of course." Marlin's expression turned serious. "You know about that guy I dated last summer even though I knew from the start there were no sparks."

"I remember."

"And I told you about the other ones who were about as important to me as…well, as having nice floor mats in a car. Who cares about those, right?"

"Not sure where you're going with this," Lauren said.

"I've never been with anyone who made me feel this way. Darren treats me as if he's been waiting for me his entire life."

"Oh," Lauren said, her throat suddenly thick.

"And he gets my jokes and I… Well, this is what love is supposed to feel like."

"How…do you know?" Lauren asked.

Marlin propped her elbows on the steering wheel as she drove and held up one hand. She put a finger in the air as if she was about to launch into a detailed explanation and said, "First of all—"

Lauren laughed and steadied the wheel until her friend put her hands back at ten and two o'clock. "Wait, you don't have to explain yourself. I'm happy for you."

"Thanks."

"I was just surprised because you've only known him for a few weeks."

"How long is it supposed to take?" Marlin asked. "Is there an average?"

Lauren thought back to two nights ago at Seth's house, standing with him in his garden during the blue period right before nightfall. She'd known him almost her entire life. She'd loved him as a friend until that last summer when everything went wrong. She'd realized she loved him as more than a friend just in time to see him get engaged to her sister. A wave of heat rushed over her at the humiliating thought.

"I honestly don't know," Lauren said.

"No one knows," Marlin said. "That's the fun part."

They passed under a stone arch at the park's entrance and drove along the trolley path to the busy area where tourists accessed the Bridal Veil Falls. The kids from Rainbow Clubhouse were already sitting on benches, swinging their legs, while Amber and their teacher stood over them.

"Thanks for the ride," Lauren told her friend.

She grinned. "And let me be the first to congratulate you on your upcoming wedding."

"Too late," Marlin said. "I called my mom last night and she's so excited. She can't wait to meet him."

"In that case, I agree with you on the fall wedding. I've seen plenty of those, pretty much every weekend in the fall and even some during the week," Lauren said. "Just text me the date when you know."

Marlin laughed and drove off, leaving Lauren with her box of flags and a group of kids anxious to have something to do.

"We're decorating for the Fourth of July holiday," she announced. "Everybody gets five flags, and it's your job to stick them in the flower beds so they'll look pretty. I'll demonstrate with this flower bed so you'll get an idea of how far apart the flags should go."

Teddy bounced on his feet as if he wanted to say something, but he kept his mouth closed and watched as Lauren carefully stuck the little flags between the annuals planted along the path, one flag every five flowers. Lauren counted out the flowers, placed a flag and did it again, hoping the kids would do well with the task. If not, she'd just rearrange the flags after the kids left, though she would never tell them that. She wanted them to be confident in their abilities. A great trait to have—unless a person is rushing headlong into marriage two weeks after their first date.

Was Marlin really serious? And what about Darren? For both their sakes, Lauren hoped they were on the same page. Was it really possible to fall in love that fast? She pondered it with every flag she sank into the soil.

The kids paired up and placed their flags, and then Amber rounded them up for a Popsicle treat—red, white and blue—on the benches by the quick-serve restaurant. Families in disposable plastic raincoats emerged from the elevator down to the wild, slippery decks along the falls and walked past them. There were tourists from all over the world enjoying the natural wonder of the falls, and Lauren was accustomed to hearing many different languages every day.

"Guess what?"

She turned toward Teddy, who had red and blue around his mouth and Popsicle juice running down his hand. She grabbed a napkin and caught the drip before it got on his shorts.

"What?" she asked.

"I get to ride in the fire truck."

It took Lauren a second to realize what he was talking about. "In the parade?"

Teddy nodded. "My daddy is driving the fire truck and I get to ride and throw candy."

Lauren smiled. "You're going to have the best

Fourth of July. Especially if you get to blow the horn on the truck."

"I do," Teddy said. "I asked and Daddy said I could, but not too much."

"I'll make sure I watch for you if you promise to throw some candy my way," Lauren said.

"And then we're going to the road party."

Lauren nodded. "The street fair. I'm going, too."

"With us?"

"I…with everyone. Everyone gets to go, if they want to."

Lauren had already seen the blocked-off streets in downtown Niagara Falls and the food trucks—at least ten of them in addition to the ones that were usually parked there—lined up and ready. The weather was going to be hot and sunny, perfect for an outdoor celebration, and it was all happening close to the entrance of the park. She was looking forward to it—and she had backup plants in the greenhouse just in case any of the flowers near the entrance got trampled.

Teddy handed Lauren his Popsicle.

"No thanks," she said as gently as she could. "Can you hold it?"

She took the stick, conscious of the stickiness but forcing herself not to flinch. She'd touched a lot worse things as a gardener. Teddy produced an envelope from his pocket and gave it to her.

"Daddy said you don't have to write back. You can just tell me yes or no and I'll tell him."

Lauren assumed the note contained a question about his garden that only required a simple answer, but then why the sealed envelope? She assumed Teddy could only read a few words, but maybe his dad knew something different. She unsealed the envelope and read the note.

Teddy and I are going to the street fair at five o'clock on the Fourth of July. Would you like to meet us there? I would like to buy you dinner to say thank you for all your help.

She felt a thrill, just for a moment feeling like he was asking her out. Of course, he'd made it clear the invitation was to pay her back for the garden help, and the street fair was a safe place to buy her dinner. It would be crowded and noisy and impersonal.

Lauren considered the question. She would have the day off and was planning to go to the parade and the fair anyway. It wouldn't be out of her way. Marlin already had plans with the man she insisted was her future husband. In past years, Lauren had spent the holiday with her grandma, having a barbecue and pie—Grandma's famous cherry pie—and then watching the fireworks later from Grandma Vera's back deck. This year was going to be sad and strange without her.

Teddy took back his Popsicle and stared at her, waiting for an answer. Lauren tucked the note into the envelope and slid it into her pocket. "Please tell your daddy the answer is yes."

Teddy nodded and went back to licking his red, white and blue treat. Clearly, he didn't know what the note said. Seth had probably decided not to tell the boy in case she said no.

For the past almost month, the ice had slowly been melting away from her relationship with Seth. The gradual softening had been gentle, leaving room for either of them to retreat and refreeze the memories.

Having a sort-of date on a holiday known for heat and fireworks might accelerate the melting… or cause a reverse reaction. She'd begun the summer hoping Seth would accept her apology on behalf of her family, but spending time with him, and with his sweet child, made her want her old friendship back with him. And more. She understood he was being cautious, having been burned before and also because of his son.

But he was the one who'd sent her a sealed invitation. The flutter around her heart told her to be careful, but she'd already given Teddy her answer.

"READY, PARTNER?" SETH ASKED his son, who was belted into the passenger seat of the huge red pumper truck draped with flags.

"Ready."

"Remember, you have to stay in that seat. The window will be down so you can throw candy, but no hanging out the window. Butt in seat. Okay?"

Teddy nodded, looking solemn as he clutched the bowl of candy in his lap.

Seth reached over and ruffled his hair. "Safety first, but have fun," he added. He had avoided driving the fire truck in the parade for the past five years, but it was his turn. As a new firefighter, he'd loved representing the department, waving at parade-goers, maybe even inspiring some young people to choose the fire and rescue service as an occupation. It had made him feel valuable and valued. The fire department had become his family when he was barely nineteen and just out of the fire academy. In those early years, his coworkers, partners and their spouses and kids had filled the hole left by the Benedict family.

Then he'd gotten married and, he thought, made a forever family with Hannah, then Teddy. He believed he'd been all in on the marriage and thought it would fill his craving for someone to love, someone who would love him in return. The marriage had gone okay at first, but when Teddy came along, Seth noticed the cracks. His ex-wife didn't deserve all the blame for the divorce, but having a child showed him that she was a bit of a child herself. Her parents had given her everything and she liked being the center of their world and then Seth's. Sharing that circle of attention with a toddler had further strained their relationship.

He'd tried to fix it, putting both Hannah's and Teddy's needs before his own. He wanted to protect his new family, but eventually he realized he needed to protect his son and that was best done separately from Hannah.

And now he was driving the parade truck again because it would delight Teddy. He glanced over at the boy's shining face. "You could pull the air horn if you want," Seth said. "Just one short blast, okay?"

Teddy reached out and pulled the string Seth had tied to the air horn cord so it would be within his son's reach. Teddy gave it a tentative tug and jumped at the loud noise. Then he laughed, and so did Seth. Seth kept an eye on his son but most of his attention was on the street ahead. He was moving slowly in a long parade snaking through Niagara Falls. The parade route would end near the street fair, but he would continue past and return to the station at the end of the parade.

"Are you too hot?" Seth asked. The fire truck technically had air-conditioning, but at the slow speed and with the windows down, it wouldn't work very well. It was the middle of the afternoon and the temperature was in the mid-eighties with humidity.

"No," Teddy said.

Seth pointed to a bottle he'd filled with ice cubes and cold water before leaving the station. "Drink."

Teddy balanced the candy bowl and took a quick drink and then went back to waving enthusiastically with his entire arm and throwing candy with the other hand. The boy was never going to make it to the fireworks at dusk, Seth knew from experience.

A high school band a few places ahead of them in the parade stopped periodically to play a song and do a show and then started moving again. They were keeping the overall parade pace slow. Seth felt sweat running down the back of his neck, and he wished he'd remembered cold water for himself.

Teddy unwrapped a piece of candy and ate it, smearing melted chocolate on his face. Candy and heat...not a great combination for a lot of reasons. A group of baton twirlers following the high school band paused and did a show right in front of the fire truck. Seth closed his eyes for just a moment while he was stopped to block out the blazing sun.

A crashing sound got his attention. A baton

bounced off the windshield of the fire truck and skidded across the pavement.

"I don't feel good," Teddy said. He put his hand to his mouth.

Seth reached over and removed the bowl of candy, setting it in the back seat of the truck's cab. "Take a sip of water and then some nice deep breaths," he said. He sounded calm, but his thoughts raced. The heat was too much for Teddy. What could he do here? He was going to have to abandon the candy-throwing responsibility, roll up the windows and crank up the air-conditioning.

He couldn't escape the parade with the huge fire truck, and there was a long way to go. They were still in the old part of town where locally owned restaurants occupied storefronts, many of them with apartments overhead. A few residences and apartment buildings were interspersed.

The parade started moving again, and Seth hoped a slight breeze would revive Teddy, but he was still searching for a solution and considering turning down the next side street that came up. He'd be letting down anyone in the second half of the parade route who expected to see and hear a fire truck, but he didn't want Teddy's memory of this day to include vomiting in the truck.

Suddenly, he saw Lauren in a folding chair

under a small shade tree, watching the parade from the sidewalk in front of an apartment building. He knew she lived in this part of town, and seeing her looking cool and comfortable was like that balm Nanna Vera had kept in a little glass jar in the fridge for scrapes and stings. He wished he'd asked her what that concoction was.

Seth stopped the truck. Whatever fears he had about letting Lauren back into his life and his heart, his son came first. "Lauren," he called.

He didn't need to get her attention. He was driving a very visible truck and she was already waving at him. He gestured for her to come into the street. She glanced both ways first, clearly aware that he was holding up the parade, but then stood outside his window and looked up.

"Teddy is overheated, and I don't think he's going to make it to the end of the route," he said.

Lauren stepped up onto the running board and looked into the cab. Her cheek was so close he accidentally brushed it with his lips. Heat rolled over him and he wasn't sure he was going to make it, either.

"Hi, Teddy, want to watch the parade with me? I have a chair and my own shade tree."

Teddy looked at Seth and there were tears in his eyes.

"It's okay, honey," Seth said. "You were my copilot for half the parade, but you only get to see what's right in front of us when you ride in the truck. I heard there were horses and big balloons in the back of the parade, and you'll get to see them if you watch with Miss Lauren."

A tear mixed with the chocolate on the boy's face, but he nodded. Seth knew the parade was backing up behind him. He couldn't wait much longer.

"I'm sorry in advance," he whispered to Lauren. "I think he's sick to his stomach."

She smiled. "No problem," she whispered in his ear. "Remember the time you threw up on me in the back seat of my parents' car?"

"No," Seth said.

She laughed. "Yes, you do." She jumped down and went around to the other side of the truck, where she opened the door and held out her arms to Teddy. "Did you save me that piece of candy I asked for?" she said cheerfully.

Teddy opened his fist and produced a piece of candy that was almost certainly a melty mess in its wrapper. Lauren took it. "Awesome. Thanks. I'll help you hop down and then we'll watch the parade and then meet up with your dad in a little while."

Seth leaned over. "I'm worried about some mild heat exhaustion, so—"

Lauren smiled. "I've had first aid training.

Small sips of water, ice pack, shade and moving inside as needed, right?"

Relief rushed through him. "Right."

Seth waited until Lauren and Teddy crossed in front of the truck and he saw Teddy settled in Lauren's chair. She got an ice pack from a cooler and put it on the boy's neck, and he looked up at her in adoration.

It took every ounce of professionalism Seth had to put the fire truck in gear and drive away at a snail's pace behind the band and the batons. It wasn't just the difficulty of trusting his sick son to someone else. It was the feeling that he'd like to be there in a chair next to Lauren, watching the parade with her and Teddy. The girl who had been his beloved childhood friend was now a woman who was just as sweet and kind and loyal as that girl had been.

He needed time to think about what he should do, but he had to meet up with her after the parade. Even if he wanted to chicken out on his invitation, there was no backing out now that Lauren was in charge of his son. Seth smiled and waved to people lining the parade route and blew the siren occasionally as he sweated in the truck, but all he could think about was the strange feeling of being young again and cool summer nights with Lauren.

CHAPTER SEVENTEEN

LAUREN WAS PURPOSELY trying not to read too much into it, but having Seth trust her with his son—literally handing the heat-sick child off to her in the middle of a parade—had to mean something. When she'd first learned the truth, she'd made it a summer goal to apologize to him and make amends for the way her family had treated him. She'd meant to apologize on behalf of all of them.

But, with each day that passed, she knew it was more personal than that. Her parents and sister were happily going on with their lives. She knew they weren't heartless, but Seth didn't figure in their memories the way he did in hers. Her kind parents surely felt a tug when they thought of that poor boy, Seth Jones, whom they'd misunderstood. Her sister, Maggie, though, was a puzzle. Maggie had made a desperate choice and, as far as Lauren could guess, hadn't regretted it enough to right the wrong.

So, Lauren had felt it was up to her. But she

wasn't fooling herself anymore. She was extending an olive branch for herself, not her family. Or not just her family. Losing her grandmother had shifted the earth underneath her and left her feeling alone. Left her missing someone who knew her—really knew her. Or at least had known her. Could she and Seth connect now as adults and have a relationship that was not based on being childhood friends?

She reached over and stroked Teddy's hair. Heat no longer rolled off his head, and he didn't look as if he was going to lose his lunch anymore. He looked happy, waving at the parade royalty in convertibles, the big-wheel bike team doing tricks and the floats representing various community organizations. He was delighted with the large balloons and horses at the end of the parade, and she loved seeing it all through a child's eyes.

As the parade ended, she got a text from Seth. He asked first about Teddy, then let her know that he'd made his way back to the fire station and needed to refuel the vehicle and make sure it was ready to go back into service. Lauren assured him the boy was much better and looking forward to the street fair.

Seth liked her reply but used the heart emoji instead of a thumbs-up. He loved the good news, of course. There was nothing more to it than that.

Are you okay with him for an hour while I run home and let Sparky out? Seth texted.

Absolutely. We'll suck up some air-conditioning in my apartment, then walk downtown.

Another heart acknowledged the message, and Lauren's own heart gave a little flip.

"Would you like to meet my cat?" Lauren asked Teddy as the crowd around them began to fold up their chairs and pack up their coolers.

"You have a cat?" he asked, instantly at attention.

"Yes. He believes he's a very important cat because my grandmother named him Lord Henry. But he's still lovable."

"Where is he?" Teddy asked.

Lauren pointed at the six-story building behind them. "My apartment. I live in this building on the sixth floor."

Teddy turned around and looked up. "Wow. It's big."

Lauren laughed. "My apartment is only a small part of it, but it's nice and cool. I texted your dad and said we'd hang out here for a bit and then meet him at the street fair."

"Cool," Teddy said, and Lauren wasn't sure if he meant the temperature or his opinion of the plan. She didn't have many little people in her life, just her nephews, whom she saw a few times a year. It was fun having Teddy around. It made her feel like a kid again.

Teddy carried her cooler and she carried the chair, and they went into the building and used the elevator. Lauren often took the steps unless she was carrying groceries, but she didn't want to wear Teddy out after his heat exhaustion. Plus, if Seth was planning to let him stay up for the evening fireworks, the child needed to conserve his energy.

When she opened her apartment door, the cat was waiting on the doormat as usual. Lord Henry had excellent hearing, and it was quite heartwarming that he greeted her every day. Teddy dropped to the floor and held out a hand to the kitty.

"Hi, Lord Henry."

The cat pushed his nose against Teddy's hand, and the boy giggled. "He's bigger than Sparky."

Lauren laughed. "Lord Henry is a big cat." She wasn't sure he was larger than Seth and Teddy's Chihuahua, but it would be close. "I wonder if Sparky and Lord Henry would like each other."

Her cat was accustomed to being the only pet in the home, ruler of his kingdom, but he might tolerate a visitor.

"We could bring Sparky next time," Teddy said. "To say hi."

Next time. Lauren wasn't sure there would be a next time. She was just helping Seth out—he'd clearly been desperate to get his son out of that hot truck.

"I'll ask Daddy," Teddy said. The cat walked in a circle around Teddy, sniffed him all over and then returned to pushing his nose against Teddy's hand.

"Why don't you use the bathroom and wash your hands," Lauren suggested, "and I'll get some cheese and crackers and water ready for us in the kitchen."

"I'm not hungry."

"You're still cooling off. I think a tiny little snack would be a good idea before we meet your daddy downtown. Sometimes the lines at the food trucks are long, and we don't want to get hangry," she said, putting her hands over her stomach and making a funny face.

Teddy laughed and let her steer him into the bathroom. Lauren heard the toilet flush and then the sink running. Was that the ladybug song she heard him singing as he washed? She smiled. It was nice having him there.

"Right?" she asked Lord Henry, who had curled up on a kitchen chair while she sliced some cheese and got out a sleeve of crackers. She filled two glasses with cold water and had the table ready when Teddy came in. His hands were clean, but his face was still a bit chocolaty.

Lauren wet a paper towel and wiped his chin. "That's better," she said.

"Now I'm hungry," Teddy said.

Lauren smiled and they sat down for a nice late afternoon snack. Afterward, they toured the apartment so she could tell him all about her houseplants. Lord Henry trailed after them, clearly interested but trying to look nonchalant. Lauren got a text from Seth.

Want me to pick you up?

Lauren thought about it for a minute. She'd been in his home. He'd been with her at her grandmother's house. But the apartment she'd made her own for the past eight years? Having him there felt like inviting him deeply into her life—although she was caring for his son there… How much deeper can you get? Plus, Seth might be worried about his son getting overheated or tired.

Sure. Park in back and I'll buzz you in. Come up to the sixth floor. Apartment 602.

His first concern was, of course, his son. But as soon as Lauren opened the door and he saw

Teddy, Seth knew the boy was just fine. His face was clean, eyes bright, smile huge.

"We had snacks and petted the cat and Miss Lauren showed me her plants," Teddy said.

Seth wrapped an arm around Teddy and smiled at Lauren. "Thanks a million."

"It was my pleasure," she said.

Seth took in the clean simplicity of her apartment—mostly whites but with plenty of green plants—and sucked in the fresh, cool air. Was this the kind of place he imagined Lauren living? He knew the Lauren of old times, but did he know the current one? More and more, he was finding that he wanted to, and that thought was like a roller coaster. Exciting but dangerous… But was the danger actually real? The worst thing that could happen had already occurred, with Lauren abandoning him along with the rest of her family. She couldn't do it again. Not in the same way. He was a grown-up now, a professional, a dad, a homeowner. Only his heart was in any danger.

He looked at his happy son. Well, maybe Teddy's heart, too.

The cat stepped forward and sniffed at his shoe.

"This is Lord Henry," Lauren said.

Seth knelt. "I wondered what had happened to you."

"What—" Lauren began, and then it must have dawned on her that Seth had seen the cat at her grandmother's place.

"Do you want to get going?" Seth asked. He hadn't made it past the entryway.

"Sure, but do you need a snack or a drink first?" Lauren asked. "We have cheese and crackers and ice cold water."

Seth was starving, and he'd made the mistake of eating some of the candy in the fire truck. The sugar rushed him and then left him worse off. He felt weirdly light and giddy, but he didn't want to hold up Lauren and Teddy.

"Thanks, but I'll be fine when we get to the food trucks," he said.

"Corn dog," Teddy said.

Seth wanted to model rephrasing that statement into a complete sentence, but it was a holiday and the day was already strange enough.

Lauren grabbed a small purse and looped the strap over one shoulder and across her chest. "Ready," she said.

They got in the elevator and Seth had the oddest feeling as if they were a family. Teddy took his hand, but he also reached for Lauren's as they descended. Maybe they were getting in too deep. On the car ride to the visitor parking lot by the park entrance, Teddy sat in the back and kicked Seth's seat as usual, but there was a whole different energy because Lauren was in the passenger seat.

Lauren reached over and gave Seth her employee ID at the gated lot entrance. “We get free parking in the visitor lot after four o’clock,” she said. “It’s a nice perk, and I often come back in the evening and walk the trails.”

“We can walk Sparky with you,” Teddy volunteered from the back seat. Seth had become so accustomed to his child actually speaking when it involved something he was excited about that it hardly even registered with him. The past month had brought a lot of improvement to Teddy, and he had Miss Lauren to thank for some of it.

“Sure,” Lauren said. “I would love that.”

Seth parked and they crossed the lot toward the noise and excitement of the street fair just outside the entrance. Lights flashed, music played and hundreds of people filled the sidewalks and streets. He held Teddy’s hand tight because of the crowd, and the boy again grabbed Lauren’s hand, connecting the three of them.

It wasn’t a bad idea. It would be easy to get separated in the crowd.

They lined up at a food wagon first, picking one that offered corn dogs, burgers and fries. Seth insisted on paying for Lauren’s food and then sought out a table. The place was busy, so the only table they could find had two chairs.

Seth put his son on his lap and sat across from Lauren as they ate. It was date-like, except for the child on his lap.

Afterward, they wandered through the fair. Teddy wanted to try some of the carnival rides, but Seth looked them over carefully first. They were probably all safe and assembled correctly, but Seth had seen a lot of things in his decade of being a first responder and he didn't take chances with his son. There was only one ride he was willing to strap Teddy into, a mini-train that followed a track that was safely on the ground.

As he was standing with Lauren outside the ride and watching, Lauren leaned close to speak over the noise. "Remember that time we went to the amusement park and you barfed on the scrambler?"

Seth laughed. "Why do all of your childhood memories of me involve vomit?"

Lauren shook her head. "Not all of them." Her smile faded and she looked thoughtful. "I have so many memories of us doing things together, I usually just pull up the one that's appropriate at the time."

"So, say we were riding bikes," Seth began.

"I'd ask you if you remembered that time we rode way out into the country but then I got a flat tire and we had to walk our bikes back. It got dark, and I wanted you to go ahead and ride home, but you wouldn't leave me."

"I remember," Seth said.

"My mother was frantic and my dad was out with the car looking for us."

Seth remembered that, too. He also remembered that he'd gotten home well after dark and his father was watching television, drink in hand. He hadn't even known Seth was out. Anything could have happened to him. At the time, he'd thought it showed how much his dad trusted him and also the Benedict family. Now, as a dad himself, Seth knew he would never be able to relax unless he knew exactly where Teddy was and if he was okay.

Yet, he hadn't been worried about Teddy after Lauren took charge of him this afternoon.

"Are we watching the fireworks tonight?" Lauren asked. "I have specific childhood memories of that, too, you know."

So did Seth. There were fireworks over the falls every night during the summer, visible from all over town—including the Benedict home. It had been a hot summer night with fireworks in the distance when he'd come across Maggie crying in a secluded area by the lake. He'd been on his way to pick up Lauren to get ice cream. He never made it for the ice cream because that was the night Maggie told him her secret and he hatched a plan to try to help her. Save her, he thought. Looking back on it, would he have done the same thing again?

"It might be too late for Teddy," Seth said. And that was true, but watching fireworks with Lauren might be a bridge too far for Seth himself. Maybe he should take his son and go home. Watch the fireworks from his back deck, although they would light up the garden Lauren had helped create. She was already entwined in his life, it seemed.

"Oh," Lauren said. "I understand, of course. I might just wander down and watch with two thousand tourists later." She smiled. "I know where to stand near the mosquito-repellent flowers I planted."

He didn't want Lauren to watch by herself or feel lonely. Or abandoned. He remembered that first summer when the Benedict family had dumped him, he'd seen Lauren watching the fireworks out at the park. He'd assumed she was with her family—that they were all together without him. But what if she'd been alone? What if he'd abandoned her that summer, too? The shock of that simple realization thundered through him. He'd spent the past decade feeling that the Benedict family had dumped him, but suddenly he saw it from Lauren's perspective. Had she felt abandoned by *him* as he had felt abandoned by her family?

"Maybe we could stand there with you," Seth said. "Teddy isn't going to sleep early tonight anyway."

"I'd like that," she said, her voice soft.

Teddy was still riding the train and suddenly Seth saw only Lauren, despite the swirling lights and sounds all around them. "I would, too," he said.

Was she holding her breath just as he was? If this was any other woman and a different situation—if this was a date—would this be the moment he would kiss her? The thought was exhilarating but dangerous, like teetering on the edge of a waterfall.

Lauren cleared her throat and adjusted the strap of her purse. "We probably have at least an hour until the fireworks," she said. "Any suggestions?"

Seth was relieved the moment had passed, but also disappointed. Was it such a terrible idea to take a chance on falling for Lauren?

Yes. He had to remember his top priority: Teddy. "I believe my son could be talked into ice cream."

"No persuasion necessary here," Lauren said. "I have never outgrown my love of it."

"I'm glad," Seth said, remembering very well how getting ice cream was an event with her and her family. They'd drive an hour sometimes to find the best flavors, and "going out for ice cream" was the cure for everything from boredom to bad weather to a tough day at school.

Teddy came off the ride, flushed and happy, and then their trio indulged in ice cream and strolled the busier-than-normal pathways through the state park to find the viewing location Lauren suggested near Terrapin Point. From there, they could see the Canadian falls and the fireworks, and benefit from the mosquito-repelling flowers. The air was heavy with humidity, even though it had cooled enough that Seth kept a close arm around Teddy to make sure he was warm. He felt Lauren's own warmth next to him.

"Any minute now," Lauren said when she turned her wrist and her smartwatch lit up with the time.

Even though they were prepared for it, the first crack of the fireworks startled Teddy, and Seth and Lauren moved at the same time to reassure him as he stood between them. Seth's cheek touched Lauren's and she turned into it. His heart raced. It was dark, his son was mesmerized by the show and Seth had a hand on his shoulder so there was no danger of him getting separated. He was free to think about the woman who was practically in his arms, her cheek next to his. He turned at the same time she did, and maybe it was timing or fate or intention, but their lips met and Seth lost himself in her kiss. Lauren responded and moved a hand up his shoulder, resting it on the back of his neck as if she didn't want him to move away an inch.

He could hardly hear the fireworks or the falls because all his senses were filled with Lauren and everything they'd meant to each other, all the time they had lost and the incredible sweetness of possibility in the here and now.

CHAPTER EIGHTEEN

THE KISS STAYED on Lauren's lips for days, lingering like a summer evening and reminding her that Seth was a man—not just the boy she'd loved growing up. He'd been the first to make a move, but she had definitely made her assent clear by putting her cheek against his and standing close enough to breathe in his scent mixed with flowers and fresh mist off the falls.

They'd broken the kiss and Seth glanced down at his son, who was engrossed in the fireworks. Seth's eyes had met hers, and she'd given the slightest nod, inviting him back for another kiss. The grand finale of the fireworks show reminded them where they were, and they moved apart before Teddy turned around. Although Seth had offered her a ride home, she'd walked, enjoying the summer night with the stars overhead.

That was three days ago and there was no word from him—aside from a brief text an hour after the kiss to ask if she'd gotten home safely.

"Happy birthday!"

Lauren recognized Marlin's voice and turned. There was a whiteboard in the parks office that her boss updated at the beginning of each month with all the staff birthdays, so Lauren wasn't surprised to see Marlin holding up a box from Cupcake Heaven. Her friend had the window rolled down on her green pickup truck. The bed of the truck was loaded with a chain saw and ropes.

"There are two different cupcakes in there, both mostly chocolate." Marlin handed Lauren the pink-and-white box.

"Thanks," Lauren said. "You know me so well." She pointed to the truck bed. "It looks like you have a busy day."

"Just giving some silver maples a trim."

"How's the love affair?" Lauren asked. Even with the lid down on the cupcake box, she could smell them, and she considered taking a bite before the flower camp kids arrived. It was her birthday, right?

Marlin shook her head. "*Affair* is the wrong word. It makes it sound temporary or forbidden. Darren and I are the real thing, mark my words."

Lauren smiled. "Consider them marked."

"Are you celebrating your birthday with anyone special?" Marlin asked.

"My parents and sister are coming into town for a few days."

"So they'll be here for the hero award tomorrow night? I'm coming to that, too."

"I'm not really a hero."

"Tell that to the town council and to the woman whose life you saved," Marlin said.

The hornet incident seemed so long ago, even though it was only weeks. A lot had gone on since then, but Lauren was pretty sure she'd always remember every detail of that morning.

"I have to go," Marlin said. "If I stick around, I'm going to steal a cupcake, and that would be a lousy thing to do to you on your birthday."

Lauren smiled. "You know I'd share."

"I do, which is why I have to leave before I'm tempted. Enjoy!" Marlin said and she waved and drove off toward a wooded area of the state park.

Lauren drove her UTV to the perennial garden where she and Amber had planned to meet the day care group. It was a beautiful July morning, and the kids were walking in a line, each of them carrying the water bottle they'd been given the first week of camp. They also wore their matching T-shirts, but Lauren could still pick Teddy out of the lineup right away.

"Welcome," she said cheerily to the kids. It was her first time seeing Teddy since the fireworks. Would he have a note from Seth? He stayed in line with the other kids and listened for directions—today they were measuring moisture levels and watering plants with a variety of watering cans she'd gathered. It had been hot and dry for days, and even some of the established perennials were looking wilty. Teddy wiggled his knees and bounced on his toes as if he had something to tell her, and Lauren was almost as anxious.

"A plant died," Teddy said as soon as the group broke up to get busy.

"Oh, no. Which one?"

He screwed up his face, thinking. "I can't remember the name."

"Did your daddy write me a note maybe?"

He shook his head. "I asked him to write you a note, but he said he didn't want to bother you. He said we've bothered you enough this summer."

Lauren sank to her knees in front of Teddy. Even though the words stung, her main concern was reassuring the boy. "You have absolutely *not* been bothering me. I love talking about flowers and helping plan gardens, and I love seeing you…and your daddy."

"He's busy at work. I had to go to the babysitter for dinner yesterday."

"Oh," Lauren said. "Maybe there are a lot of fires this time of year. It's been very dry and hot." She smiled and tried to sound cheerful and steer the conversation to something safe, for her own sake and for Teddy's. "Which is why I'm glad you're here today because my plants are also hot and dry, and they need us to come to the rescue."

Teddy didn't move toward the row of watering cans. "My birthday is tomorrow," he said.

"Really? Are you going to be six?"

Teddy nodded.

"Can you believe my birthday is today? Happy early birthday!" Lauren high-fived Teddy and he smiled. How strange that their birthdays were only one day apart. She hoped that Seth's work would slow down and leave him time and space to celebrate his son's birthday.

"How old are you?" Teddy asked.

"Twenty-seven."

"My daddy is twenty-eight."

It was on the tip of her tongue to say, "I know," but she didn't.

Lauren kept her mind on her work and creating a fun and educational experience for the flower campers, but her thoughts were on Seth. She believed that he must be very busy at work. It sounded like going to the babysitter was outside the norm for Teddy. Maybe that was all his message had meant.

She couldn't let herself get preoccupied. Today was a happy day. She had flower camp this morning and plans with her family later. She was excited about her birthday because she loved any excuse to eat cake and her mother was a very good gift-giver, always choosing something both practical and indulgent. And she was looking forward to the "local hero" award she would receive at the city council meeting for helping the jogger who had been attacked by hornets.

But she was also nervous about seeing her family. They would want to know her decision about the house, and her feelings on that and everything else were tangled up with Seth and the past and summer nights then and now. *And that kiss that felt as if it had been decades in the making.* Had he and Maggie ever kissed or was their engagement purely for show? What if Maggie's pregnancy hadn't ended as it did… Would they have really married and stayed together, raising a child—her niece or nephew?

It was too strange to think about. She wasn't even sure she was going to tell her family that she'd reconnected with Seth. Maybe there was nothing to tell anyway. They hadn't spoken since the kiss.

Later that afternoon, Lauren drove to her grandmother's house. Maggie was driving from Indiana and stopping to pick up their parents at the Buffalo airport on her way into Niagara Falls. All Lauren had to do was wait.

She prowled the house. She'd done a good job cleaning it out, she thought. It still had enough furnishings to act as a guesthouse for visiting family but felt lighter without her grandmother's personal possessions. Lauren went out to the garden to take some calming breaths. She was looking forward to seeing her parents, but why did she dread seeing Maggie?

"We're here!" her dad's voice called through the open windows of the house, and she straightened up from the rose she'd been sniffing and headed inside.

"Happy birthday!" her mother said, pulling her into a hug. "I can't believe you're twenty-seven."

Lauren laughed. "Last year, you said you couldn't believe I was twenty-six."

"And I was right," her mother said. "Time goes too fast."

"We picked up a cake on the way here," her dad said. He set a bakery box on the kitchen table, and Lauren recognized the pink-and-brown box from the bakery where her parents had been buying birthday cakes for years. They'd always gotten her chocolate ones, Maggie vanilla ones, and Seth strawberry ones.

Her dad hugged her and then Maggie did, too, but she felt a little distance in the hug from her sister. Lauren wasn't sure if that distance was coming from Maggie or from herself, holding back a little and preserving a space inside to process all the changes over the past month.

"You've worked hard," her dad said. "This place looks like my mother's house, but not totally. It has her warmth and character but your appreciation for minimalism."

"Wow," Lauren said. "That's a big observation, and you've only seen one room."

"Am I wrong?" her dad asked with a smile.

"No," Lauren admitted. "I've been busy. And I've got a lot to talk to you about."

"Let's put our stuff in the bedrooms and then go out to dinner," Maggie cut in. "My stomach's growling after that long drive."

Lauren didn't want to think negatively, but Maggie had just neatly pulled the attention from Lauren to herself. Maybe she should be grateful because she wasn't ready to spill the tea on the whole Seth connection or the kiss. Not yet. Maybe not at all.

"Can we order in?" her mom asked. "Your dad's ear is bothering him from the flight, and I'm afraid he won't hear well if we go to a restaurant. You know how busy they are during the summer."

"Sure," Lauren agreed. Maggie had already gone off to claim one of the bedrooms.

"Are you doing okay?" Lauren's mom asked her. "You seem…well, not at ease somehow. Like something's on your mind. Is it this house? You can take all the time you need."

"It's not that," Lauren said. "It's everything I had to process since Grandma died. It's only been five weeks."

"Have you been able to do anything about the letter?" her mother asked.

"You mean reaching out to Seth and righting Maggie's old wrong?" Lauren asked.

Lauren's parents exchanged a glance, and her dad picked up their travel bag and went down the hallway.

"This is a long story," Lauren said. "We should order food. Maggie said she was hungry."

Her mother nodded and said, "Just tell me one thing. I'm guessing from your expression that something, either good or bad, has been going on with Seth."

"We sort of reconnected. I went to his house right after the funeral to apologize on behalf of our family, but he didn't want to hear it. But then his son is in a special program I'm running for kids who like horticulture, and that has brought us back into contact."

"And have you gotten him to accept an apology?"

Lauren shrugged. "Not in so many words. I haven't pressed him, and maybe I shouldn't since it really was a long time ago. I think he wants to move on, and I'm sure that's what I should be doing."

"Okay," her mother said, drawing out the word slowly.

"There's no way to go back to the friendship I had with Seth before…you know."

"Before I ruined everything," Maggie said from the doorway.

Lauren and her mother whipped around. "You didn't—" Lauren began.

"Yes, I did," Maggie said. "I got pregnant and the guy I thought I had a future with left town rather than dealing with it. So I took the easiest way out I could live with."

"Getting married isn't an easy way out," their mother protested.

"I thought it was," Maggie said. "And I'm sorry, okay? I know you're all disappointed with me and upset or just plain mad. I get it. If I could go back and do things differently, I would, all right?"

Lauren was accustomed to her sister being assertive and speaking her mind, but this speech had an edge to it, a layer of anger. Whom was she mad at?

"I think we all would," Lauren's mom said.

Maggie snorted. "How could you? You didn't know what was going on, so there wasn't much of a choice for you except to be happy I was engaged to someone you all loved like he was a member of the family."

Lauren didn't miss the "you all loved" part of her sister's sentence, said almost as if Maggie hadn't loved him like the rest of them.

"We were surprised, of course," her mom said.

"Why?" Maggie asked.

Their mom sent a questioning glance at Lauren. Lauren had kept her mouth shut and her feelings hidden deep a decade ago, but the events of the summer had loosened her grip on them. That was the summer Lauren had realized she loved Seth right when it was too late. She'd squeezed those feelings into a tight, hidden space for years. Why shouldn't she say what she felt now when everything was said and done, deep in the past?

"Because Seth was mine," Lauren said, the sentence so brutally simple that tears sprang to her eyes and she sat down hard in a kitchen chair. Silence hung over the kitchen for a long moment.

"Finally," Maggie said. "Finally, someone said it. I know you were all thinking it back then, but you didn't know…" She crossed her arms over her chest and her eyes glistened with tears. Neither Lauren nor her mother moved, perhaps because they all knew this conversation had to happen. The words had lain dormant too long.

"You didn't know how confused and foolish I felt and then how guilty I felt about using Seth and letting him take all the blame." She stared down at the floor. "The cost of self-preservation is high, but I thought I'd paid it all or it had been written off at some point. But Grandma made sure I wasn't getting away scot-free."

"That's not fair," Lauren said, finding her voice. "Grandma wanted the truth to be known."

"Why?" Maggie asked. "So I could be humiliated all over again?"

Lauren stood up. She noticed her mother hadn't said a word, even though she was standing between the sisters, clearly absorbing the shocks from both sides.

"Maybe it's not about you this time," Lauren said. "Maybe Grandma wanted *me* to have a chance to know the truth."

"Why?" her sister challenged. "So you get to be happy knowing that Seth really did love you and not me back then and he was only engaged to me out of pity."

"No," Lauren said, her voice high and shaky. "I just want him to know we don't hate him for what happened. That we know the truth, that he was doing something nice and it all got misunderstood and screwed up."

"I suppose you're running around with him again, then, hanging out like old times, thinking you can just pick up where you left off before your stupid sister ruined everything."

"Wait…no. We haven't even talked about you. It's not like that," Lauren protested.

"So you've been talking," her sister said.

"We live in the same town. His son is in my program at the park. We—"

Lauren felt as if she were defending herself, and she hated the feeling of being on the defensive. It was a terrible place to argue from, and she was afraid she was going to say something hurtful. She glanced at her mother, hoping she would intervene.

"Grandma kept in touch with him, too. Just a little," their mom said.

"That's fine," Maggie said. "It's pretty obvious that I've moved on from all that, so you can all just go get stuck right back in the past if it makes you happy."

"We're adults now," Lauren said.

She stopped, almost shocked at the truth in those words. Her mother and sister also looked surprised, and Maggie's posture relaxed a little but she still seemed ready to either attack or defend.

"And who is Seth Jones now?" Maggie asked.

"He's a good man who rescues people and loves his son more than anything. He dug up his backyard and planted a garden because his son wanted him to." Her voice shook. "That's who he is. The boy who grew up with no mother and an awful father is now an excellent parent himself, which takes a lot of love and courage on his part."

"I see," Maggie said after a long pause. "Sounds like you know a lot about him. Just be careful and think about your reasons, and his. Maybe he just wants to feel like part of our family again, and he sees you as a way to get back inside."

Her sister's words hit Lauren like a blast of heat and made her question everything. Was she seeking a relationship with Seth just to make herself feel better? Worse, was he just being nice and pitying her because her grandmother was gone and her parents and sister moved away?

"It's Lauren's birthday," her mother said, her voice quiet as if she was comforting someone who was wounded. "This isn't the time to dredge up things from the past."

Maggie relaxed her frown a bit. "Sorry," she said, but she didn't elaborate and she didn't sound sorry, in Lauren's opinion. She sounded like she wanted to escape from the conversation, just as she'd looked for an escape years ago.

Lauren's dad whistled as he came down the hallway and popped into the kitchen, where he announced he'd ordered pizza from his favorite hometown restaurant and he'd gotten everyone's favorites, which he listed off to prove he remembered. His tone implied that he hadn't heard anything that was said between the three women in the kitchen, and no one enlightened him. He suggested they all go out on the deck to enjoy the summer evening while they waited for food.

As Lauren watched the fireflies from the back deck, she wondered if her older sister might be right—that she was reaching out to Seth to assuage her own guilt about siding against him a decade ago.

It was some birthday.

CHAPTER NINETEEN

HANNAH PARKED AT the curb in front of Seth's house, not even committing to the driveway.

"Your mom's here," he called to Teddy, turning from the door where he'd been watching for his ex-wife. Teddy had been playing with Sparky, throwing one of his indoor toys while he waited for his mom to pick him up for dinner for his sixth birthday.

"Can you come, too?" Teddy asked.

The sad look on his son's face sliced Seth's heart. He was glad Teddy wanted him to come along, but the reason was sad. Either he wanted his parents together or he was more comfortable with Seth than with his own mother. Which would make going back to the shared arrangement in the fall tough. They'd been existing on a two-week rotation for the past two years, and it was honestly exhausting. Having Teddy for the whole summer—with the exception of this prearranged birthday visit—was easier, at least emotionally.

"This is your special time with Mom," Seth said, kneeling and hugging his son. "You'll have a great birthday dinner together, and I have to go to a work event this evening. We'll both be back here in time for bath and bedtime. I promise."

Teddy nodded, and Seth was disappointed that he wasn't getting a full sentence out of his son. He'd gotten almost accustomed to his son talking over the past two weeks, but not today, apparently. Even though it was his birthday. Seth considered telling Hannah that if she wanted Teddy to talk, she should ask him about the flowers and gardens, but he hoped she'd figured that out already in her weekly calls with Teddy.

Seth tried to smile as he took his son's hand and walked him out to the curb, where he made sure Teddy was secured in an appropriate child restraint in the back seat before waving goodbye to him. He and Hannah barely spoke.

After they drove away, Seth tried to remember a typical day during their marriage. What had they talked about? A cold feeling gripped his chest. They had hardly talked for the past few years of their marriage, and that was Teddy's environment. No wonder. Seth felt his eyes sting and his face heat. He'd been blaming Hannah for poor communication, but what if he was just as much to blame?

Everything was different this summer, and

he'd thought it was because he had Teddy full-time. But in his heart he knew there was another reason he felt more talkative and alive than he had in a long time. Lauren.

She would be at the city council meeting tonight, of course, because she was being honored with a citizen lifesaver award along with a local fisherman who'd rescued someone from drowning. Maybe he could ask her out for coffee afterward. He'd been avoiding her since that electrifying kiss because he didn't know what to say. Suddenly, he felt like talking to her and telling her everything he'd been feeling.

Seth went back inside, put on his dress uniform and checked the mirror. He could use another shave. He took off his shirt and laid it on his bed, shaved, got dressed again and readjusted the pin on his badge until he got it straight.

He felt as if he was going on a first date.

When he walked in the door of the city council building and turned down the hallway toward the meeting chambers, he recognized a local reporter hovering outside the meeting doors. Seth took a deep breath and reminded himself this meeting was not about him or his feelings. It was about honoring quick-thinking locals who'd saved someone's life. His chief would read the proclamation, and Seth would hand out the actual awards—behaving professionally toward Lauren and her co-honoree.

But he was still going to ask Lauren for coffee afterward. With Teddy away for the evening, this might be his only guilt-free chance. He was picturing a quiet corner table in a downtown bakery open late—imagining them laughing over an old memory, perhaps even sharing a kiss when they parted—when he stopped dead in the aisle.

Lauren was there in the front row, and so were her parents and Maggie. He could only see them from behind, but he knew who they were.

Seth's legs were lead, and he had to force them to move toward the second row, where Chief Bear sat. He wanted to run. He'd gotten so accustomed to being with Lauren that the pain and awkwardness of his lost relationship with the Benedict family seemed like a distant memory.

That memory was back, gushing over him as if someone had opened a fire hose. For years he'd tried to forget his childhood, escaping those memories, dulling the pain by force of habit. But he was sorely out of practice now.

He slid in next to Bear, who boomed "Seth! There you are."

The chief's words brought all four Benedict heads around to face him. He'd battled flames, floods, snow, darkness and death in his role as firefighter, but he didn't feel like a brave rescuer now. He felt like little Seth Jones in clothes he'd outgrown having a ham sandwich at the Benedict family table.

A lifetime ago.

He avoided their glances, even Lauren's. Bear gave Seth a questioning look. "Stage fright or something? I'm the one who has to do the talking. All you have to do is look pretty and hand over the plaque."

"I'm ready," Seth said.

"Well, get comfortable. We're the tenth item on the list and it'll probably be an hour before they get to the awards. I think they save the good stuff for the end so the reporter will stay."

Seth stared at his hands all through the first part of the meeting with its call to order, Pledge of Allegiance and reading of the previous meeting's minutes. He endured listening to a long presentation about a proposed zoning change to the city's east side that would allow for more transient rental properties. There were several votes on minor language in the city's charter, and all throughout, Seth kept his eyes down, not daring any glances toward Lauren, who sat on the aisle just feet from him.

Chief Bear, who was following along with the meeting on a handout, elbowed him. "We're next." He pulled a box from under his seat and handed it to Seth.

When the president of the council announced the Citizen Lifesaver awards, Chief Bear stood and Seth followed him to the front. The fire chief read a general proclamation about the award itself and then gave specific details about the hero fisherman. The man came forward, and Seth presented him with a plaque and shook hands with him. Then they posed for a picture along with the chief.

There was no avoiding what came next. The chief read the details about how Lauren had driven the jogger away from the hornet nest and then used the woman's EpiPen to save her life. Even though Seth was determined to be stoic and detached as a means of self-preservation with the whole Benedict family looking on, he couldn't be cold about it. What Lauren had done had been noble and brave. She deserved the accolade and more.

Seth's eyes met hers as she rose from her seat when Chief Bear invited her to come forward. He felt her family watching him, but he kept his attention where it was deserved. He reached for her hand and held it a moment longer than he had the fisherman's. He stood next to her for the photograph and tried to give a genuine smile despite the shock of her family being there. People in row three applauded loudly, and Seth recognized several of them as Lauren's coworkers, including her boss and the other facilitator he'd seen at Teddy's flower camp.

But it was her family he was trying to avoid facing. Had they come just for this ceremony? It was a big deal, of course, but Florida was a long way away... And then a memory hit him. The date. Yesterday was Lauren's birthday. He remembered it being just a few days after the July Fourth holiday, like his son's. He remembered the tent her dad set up one year in the backyard so she could have a campout on her birthday. Maggie had gotten tired of it and gone inside during the night, but Seth and Lauren were still there in the morning when the sun came up.

She was turning away from him to return to her seat when he said "Happy birthday" so quietly he wasn't sure she could even hear it. But she stopped moving and glanced up quickly at him, a gentle smile curving her lips.

She'd heard.

They returned to their seats, and he let go of his earlier intention to ask Lauren out for coffee. She would have plans with her family, and there was no way those plans could include him.

THERE WAS NOTHING like the relief Lauren felt when she heard the words *meeting adjourned.* She'd known there was a strong possibility Seth would be at this event, but she'd underestimated the impact of having her whole family in the room with him. But she'd wanted reconciliation between them all. Or at least redress for a past wrong. Even if she was the only member of her family who was willing to make the effort.

They were all along for the ride now. As soon as everyone got up, Seth and the fire chief scooted out the end of their row as if they were escaping something. She could let them go. Could go out for dessert and coffee with her family, who'd come to celebrate her birthday and this special award.

But Seth was her family, too.

"Wait," she called. "Seth."

He stopped midstride and Lauren felt her sister tense next to her. "What are you doing?" Maggie whispered.

Good question.

SETH FACED THE whole Benedict family and waited.

"Hello, Seth," Lauren's dad said, approaching Seth and extending his hand as if they were old friends casually meeting outside church. "How have you been?"

Seth shook her dad's hand and nodded. "Fine. How about you?"

"Retired and living in Florida, so I can't complain."

After barely a moment's pause, Lauren's mom

approached Seth and held out her hand, too. This felt so strange. Mrs. Benedict had hugged Seth so many times when he was little. Was she holding back for herself or was she respecting Seth's boundaries?

"I'd love to see a picture of your son," she said.

Seth tried to keep his confusion at bay, glancing toward Chief Bear. But the chief waved and left along with most of the crowd. Seth's eyes landed back on the Benedicts. Maggie stared down at the evening's printed program and didn't look at him. In the past ten years, he would never have imagined this exact scene or any kind of reconciliation with the Benedict family. He'd wished for it desperately at first and then hardened himself against their memory.

But he was a grown man now. Would he want his son to see him shying away from a tough situation like this? He got out his phone and scrolled to the picture of Teddy on the night they'd planted the garden in the rain.

Mrs. Benedict smiled. "He looks like you did at that age."

And those words almost broke him. He was, once again, the motherless kid going school shopping with Mrs. Benedict. He couldn't breathe. He wanted out of that public space, somewhere out of the public eye where he could pull himself inward and protect his heart.

"Teddy also laughs like Seth," Lauren said, filling in the silence while Seth tried to find his footing. "He's a cutie."

The hallway outside the meeting room was almost empty now, leaving Seth with the found family of his youth.

"Listen, Seth," Mr. Benedict said. "I know this isn't the time or place for this conversation, but ten years is a long time and maybe we should talk, you know, sometime, if you want to—"

"Stop it," Maggie said. "Everyone just stop dancing around the fact that I'm standing right here and now you all know the truth."

A door slammed at the other end of the hallway, echoing the length of it.

"Don't," Lauren said with a pleading expression as she put a hand on her sister's arm. Lauren clutched her hero award in her other arm, and Seth's heart ached for her. This should have been a happy night. She deserved that.

"It's time to rip off the Band-Aid," Maggie said. She glanced around at all of them. "Isn't that what you want? Don't you want to hear me just say it, once and for all?"

"No," her parents said at the same time, and her dad added, "No one is blaming—"

"I lied, okay?" Maggie said. "I was young and stupid and desperate, and I lied about the engagement and then the breakup." She jabbed a finger in Seth's direction. "You didn't have to play the victim all these years. You could have ratted me out."

Seth shook his head, too numb to speak.

"And you moved on, too, just like I did. Got married, had a family of your own. You can see why I kept quiet. You kept quiet, too," Maggie snapped.

Seth's feet were glued to the floor and his mouth was dry. The long-held secret was already out, so what was the point of Maggie's outburst?

"But keeping quiet didn't change the one big thing," Maggie went on.

Lauren's face had gone white, and her mother's hand shook as she reached out for Maggie.

"Sweetheart, stop," Mrs. Benedict said. "There's no point in this."

"Yes, there is," she said. Maggie squared her shoulders and faced Seth. "I knew you and Lauren were in love. I *knew* it. Everyone knew it. But I took your ring anyway."

Lauren gasped and then silence hung over them all like a cloud. Seth was sure they could all hear his heart beating. He felt as if the air had been knocked out of him, leaving him hollow.

"I thought you'd both gotten past it, but I'm not blind," Maggie said. Her voice softened. "You're still in love." She glanced from Lauren to Seth and back again. "I'm sorry, okay? I'm sorry for messing everything up for you two." She turned and walked down the long hallway, her footsteps echoing.

Seth felt as if all his anger and angst from the past decade was walking down that hallway, getting softer with every echoing step. He'd seen a lot of brave things in his life, but what Maggie had just done was one of the bravest.

It was freeing.

She'd set him free.

The tension in his chest uncoiled, and he almost wanted to laugh aloud, even though this was not the time and place. There was too much hurt hanging in the air, but his own pain was gone. Just having Maggie acknowledge what she'd taken from him had given him the ability to reclaim it. Lauren had loved him, but he hadn't believed he deserved her. And then everything went wrong, but none of it was his fault.

Did he deserve Lauren now?

Lauren and her parents stared at Seth. They were shocked into silence, but Seth felt clarity. "You should go after her," he said, willing to let them go right now because he felt peace for the first time in a long time. He would be okay if they walked away. It wasn't about him right now.

No one moved for a moment, but then Lauren turned to her parents. Seth waited for her to decide what to do.

"You go," Lauren said. "I'll talk to you later."

Seth barely had time to process Lauren's words as her parents walked quickly away and Lauren faced him. She was staying this time? When her whole family walked away a decade ago, she had, too.

But things were different now. Suddenly, Seth viewed the past from a different lens, as if he'd been wearing sunglasses indoors and finally remembered to take them off. He and Lauren had been in love—something he'd refused to acknowledge for ten long years. He'd sacrificed any chance he had at having her and it hurt too much to think about. But now her own sister had said the words aloud. The same person who had robbed him had given him that gift back. Finally.

Lauren held her plaque in one hand, but Seth reached out and touched her empty hand. She didn't move away, and so he wrapped his fingers around hers.

LAUREN WATCHED HER family walk away, but she didn't feel alone. Instead, it felt right to stay there with Seth.

"Do you want to go for a walk along the falls?" Seth asked.

It was such a casual question. Such normal words for a situation that was so wildly emotional. At least for her. Why did Seth seem so calm? Was it his long experience with high-stress situations as a firefighter or did he not feel the tight coil of tension she did?

"Okay," Lauren said. She needed to move. That long, echoing hallway was no place for these feelings or this conversation. Her parents and sister were gone, probably on their way back to Vera's house. She was very thankful she had her own place. Her quiet apartment with only Lord Henry, who couldn't ask questions or dredge up the past.

She pulled her hand from Seth's so she could slip the small plaque into her purse. She felt its weight tugging the strap on her shoulder, but it was nothing like the weight of what her sister had said.

That he'd loved Lauren. And Maggie had known it all along. Knowing that, Lauren felt a pang of guilt—not just for Seth and Maggie, but for herself. She hadn't understood what Maggie had been dealing with back then, hadn't seen the pressure or fear Maggie faced. And yet Maggie had seen what was in Lauren's heart and still made her choice. Lauren closed her eyes and tried to remember that summer. Had she really been so wrapped up in her own world that she missed everything else? And what about now? Was she looking at this reconciliation with Seth only from her own perspective, ignoring Maggie again?

She didn't know what he was feeling, but she could guess why he'd stayed behind. Seth was a rescuer. He'd sent her parents after her sister, and now he was hanging around to make sure she was okay. It was what he did. He had tried to deescalate the situation just as he'd tried to rescue Maggie years earlier.

They left the city council building. There were only a few vehicles in the parking lot. Lauren had ridden with her family, but she wasn't worried about getting home. It wasn't that long a walk, and there was always Seth to the rescue. His truck was in the parking lot.

"Where is Teddy tonight?" Lauren asked, mostly just to have conversation that wasn't laced with past drama. Teddy had been the initial connection this summer, after all.

Seth paused at a cross street, looked both ways and was safely on the other side before he answered. "With his mother."

"Oh," Lauren said. "I thought—"

"He's mine for the summer, but she came to take him to dinner for his birthday and they're going to a park afterward."

"That's nice," Lauren said.

"It should be," Seth said quietly. "I told her I wouldn't be home until nine."

Lauren glanced over. "Did you think the city council meeting would last that long?"

He shook his head and stopped walking. They were nearing the entrance to the state park and could already hear the music of the water rushing over the falls. "I knew you'd be there, and I planned to ask you out for coffee afterward."

Lauren was glad Seth had stopped because his words put her off-balance.

"Why?"

He turned and continued walking. He kept his eyes straight ahead, but he began talking. "In my job I'm very good at compartmentalizing, putting feelings away until it's the right time to deal with them, which is sometimes never. I've done the same thing in my personal life." He paused and glanced at her for a brief second. "And that's something I never realized until this summer. You made me figure that out."

Lauren walked alongside him, unsure if she should interrupt. As much as she was confused, she wanted Seth to have a chance to clear the air and get all the past trauma off his chest. He deserved that. He deserved better than the way he'd been treated.

"I thought my marriage failed because Hannah didn't put herself into it, and maybe she didn't entirely, but I don't think I did, either. I was afraid of giving all my love, knowing it could be taken away. The only exception for me was Teddy, but I suspect he knew there was something missing anyway." Seth looked at her again. "He's blossomed this summer."

"I…love your use of a flower metaphor," Lauren said. It was the only thing she could think of to say. Where was Seth going with all this?

"It's fitting," Seth said. "You had a lot to do with that. You made him happy and helped him find something he was excited about, but you also opened up my heart, which helped me and Teddy a lot."

These were the words she'd wanted to hear. The apology she felt compelled to offer Seth weeks ago had actually taken root. She'd helped him. He didn't have to formally accept her apology or say he forgave her and her family. This admission from him was enough. She should be happy and walk away. She should leave Seth alone to figure out his life now that she'd helped free him of the past.

That was all she'd wanted after she'd learned the truth, and she didn't deserve any more from him. He'd given her family enough. Too much.

"I'm glad," she said. They were passing a rosebush she'd planted three years earlier and which had grown a bit large for its location. A pink rose dangled from a branch, clearly broken by a passerby. She stopped and snapped it off the rest of the way. A thorn got stuck in her finger, and Seth took her hand.

"Let me help," he said. He extracted the thorn but continued to hold her hand. "Lauren, we need to talk about us."

She shook her head slightly. She was still reeling from the whole evening.

"What your sister said tonight about us being in love when we were kids," he began. "Was it true?"

Lauren felt as if she were a rose with its delicate petals fluttering in the wind. "Was it true for you?" she asked.

Seth stood up straighter, still holding her hand. "Yes," he said. "But I didn't know if you saw me as anything but a good friend. Plus, I didn't offer much. I had nothing, and I had no idea where I was going in life. I thought you deserved someone better."

"But you proposed to my sister," Lauren said.

"She was desperate."

"That wasn't fair to you. None of it was."

"I made my own choice back then. I could have done things differently."

"You made a promise to Maggie, and you didn't go back on it," Lauren said. "You're a good guy."

"I was a coward," he said. "I was afraid to betray Maggie's secret because I thought that would make you hate me even more than you did."

"I never hated you," Lauren said.

Seth raised an eyebrow.

"I didn't. *Hate* is a terrible word. I just felt that you were lost to me. Like one of those branches that goes over the falls. Just gone. It was only my grandmother's passing that jolted me into trying to reverse everything that happened."

It was just dark enough for the lights to come on over the falls, a soft pink glow tonight, and Lauren heard the crowd's reaction from a distance. The lights came on at the same time every night, but tonight felt as if everything was being lit up and changed.

"Do you want to try to go back to that summer?" Seth asked.

Lauren shook her head. "You can't go back." She swallowed and tried to compose herself even though she wanted to cry. "My family thinks I ought to take over Grandma Vera's house and keep on living there with her cat and her garden as if nothing happened."

"And what do you want?" Seth asked.

She wanted him to say he loved her. Now. Just as she was. Not as some memory or ideal or treasured heirloom from the past. But she'd already asked enough of him. He had a son and life and now that he was set free from the past, he deserved a chance to give himself fully to his own life.

She deserved that, too. She realized this was why she was resisting what her family thought was the easiest thing in the world—just move into a beloved family home and carry on. But now that knowing the truth about the past had set her free, too, she wanted the chance to see herself in this new light. Not as the little sister who thought she was protecting her big sister, the loyal granddaughter or the grown woman who was the apologist for the family. But as Lauren Benedict, a woman.

She had loved the boy Seth had been, and she was falling in love with the man standing before her, but she wasn't ready. As Seth had said himself, his marriage had failed because he hadn't been able or willing to give his love entirely. She needed to be ready or she'd end up hurting him and herself.

"I want us both to be happy. We'll never be as carefree as we were as kids, but I want you to give yourself to Teddy and make sure he is a happy and carefree kid. You both deserve that."

"What about you?" he said, squeezing her hand.

Lauren thought about it for a minute. What if she put her arms around him and kissed him and told him she'd been in love with him then and that those feelings were all back but stronger and different now? She had a feeling he'd return the kiss…maybe even the words. But so much had happened this evening. She didn't want to act out of impulse and leave Seth regretting anything. He'd suffered enough and so had she.

"Remember how I liked to take long walks after dark and smell the earth and hear the insects?"

He nodded.

"That's what I'm going to do now. We both need some time to process this. You need to get home, and please tell Teddy happy birthday from me."

Seth still held her hand and he was so close she was tempted to take that kiss, but she didn't.

"Are you sure that's what you want to do?" he asked.

"For now, yes."

She didn't know if Seth believed her or not, but he nodded, squeezed her hand one last time and walked back toward the direction they'd come. Alone.

CHAPTER TWENTY

LAUREN'S PARENTS AND sister stayed another day, and Lauren took a vacation day from work to spend with them. Now that everything was out in the open, the level of tension between Lauren and Maggie had dissipated.

The two sisters were browsing the shops in Niagara-on-the-Lake, and Maggie held up a hat in one of the boutiques.

"Try this on," she said. "I have the wrong-shaped head for hats, but you always looked good in them."

"Have you seen the Niagara Falls State Park baseball cap I wear at work? I assure you, I don't look good in that."

"But it's good sun protection, which is why your skin is beautiful."

Lauren laughed. "First of all, your skin is beautiful, and secondly, I owe my complexion to sunscreen and that moisturizer Grandma always used that she got me hooked on, too."

"It smelled like roses," Maggie said.

Lauren nodded. "You remember."

Lauren put on the wide-brimmed straw hat with a green polka-dot ribbon. "What do you think?"

"It's perfect for a gardener. And I'm hooked on that rose stuff, too," Maggie said. "Even from a few states away, I think of Grandma every night when I slather on the moisturizer before bed."

"I miss her," Lauren said. "I'm propagating a plant from the yellow rosebush she loved in her garden. I'll plant it this fall at her gravesite."

Maggie gave her a long hug, and Lauren held the hat away from her body so it wouldn't get crushed. Grandma Vera had hoped her letter would be a final gift to Lauren, and the genuine, warm hug from her sister was the fruit of that gift. There was nothing hanging between them now, especially after Maggie apologized for believing Seth and Lauren were in love and then getting engaged to him anyway. Lauren hadn't even realized she was mad at her sister for that, for all these years. It was freeing to admit she'd been mad but had buried that anger under the weight of family obligations. It was also freeing to admit that she'd wanted to clear away all the old angst by apologizing to Seth and wrestling an acceptance out of him, which she now realized was a flawed plan. Apologies and forgiveness have to be freely exchanged.

“What are you going to do about Seth?” Maggie asked.

Lauren shook her head. “You ask that like Seth is a problem I have to solve, like a missing tile in my shower or a houseplant with yellow leaves.”

“You know what I mean,” Maggie said. “Do you think there’s a second chance for you and him?”

“We didn’t exactly have a first chance,” Lauren said. “And we’re adults now. We’re different people. We grew up together, but ten years is a long separation. Plus, even if I wanted to see if there’s something there, Seth may not feel the same way.”

“I think you should give him, and yourself, a chance,” Maggie said. “And not just because it would make me feel better.” She smiled at Lauren. “I’m sorry I accused you of wanting to apologize to Seth for that reason.”

“You don’t have to keep apologizing for everything,” Lauren said, returning her sister’s smile. “Unless it makes you feel better.”

They laughed, and it felt so good to Lauren to laugh with her sister again like they had when they were kids. She had a lot of great memories from childhood, but she was working on keeping them where they belonged. Which was why she’d told her parents earlier that day that they could keep Grandma Vera's house in the family if they wanted to, but Lauren would not be moving into it.

"I'm almost sorry I have to leave after dinner," Maggie said. "You know I've avoided coming home because I was...avoiding a lot. Now that everything is out in the open, I feel like Niagara Falls is my hometown again."

"You could stay longer," Lauren said.

Maggie shook her head. "Mom and Dad have an evening flight, and if I drop them off at the airport, I'm already an hour closer to home. I don't mind making the five-hour drive late in the day, even when it gets dark. There's less traffic that way, and my family is expecting me home soon."

They finished shopping, Maggie picking up little gifts for her kids in the cute downtown boutiques, and then they headed back home across the border and met up with their parents for a last dinner. As they ate, their dad entertained them with stories about their Florida neighbor's battle with the HOA over his rosebushes planted too close to the sidewalk. Lauren took the side of the rosebushes, and she was still smiling after she said her goodbyes at the restaurant and walked back to her apartment to feed Lord Henry.

She had just filled a bowl with ice cream and put her feet on the coffee table, the cat next to her, when Marlin called. Lauren put her on speaker.

"I'm getting married," Marlin announced.

"You mentioned that last week," Lauren said. "Does Darren know yet?"

"I sure hope so. He was the one who asked me."

Lauren put her feet on the floor, her ice cream spoon suspended in air.

"Are you actually serious?"

"The wedding is Friday. Just something really small at the chapel by the falls."

"Sure it is," Lauren said, laughing. "What time?" Now she knew her friend was kidding. Friday was only two days away. She ate a big scoop of chocolate ice cream.

"They're calling me back with a time slot, but I asked for early evening. That way we can take our pictures by the falls at sunset."

The ice cream was a cold block in Lauren's belly. "You really are serious."

"Of course," Marlin said.

"But you've only known Darren a month."

Marlin laughed. "How long do you have to know someone to know you're in love and he's the man for you?"

"I… I don't know," Lauren said.

"That's because lightning hasn't struck you like it struck us. When you know, you know.

We're keeping it small because Darren's family is a train wreck and they'll bring their drama if we invite them, so I'm inviting my parents and just a few friends."

"That sounds really nice," Lauren said. It actually sounded wild and spontaneous and unlike anything she would ever do.

"Will you be my witness? We can call it maid of honor if you want, but then you'd feel obligated to get a new dress, and I don't want anyone to have to fuss just because I went and fell in love. Wear anything, but just come and be there for me, okay?"

"Okay."

"And bring a date if you want. Maybe that hot guy with the cute kid."

"I'll see if the kid is available," Lauren said, smiling despite the shock of her friend's announcement.

"Very funny. See you at work tomorrow," Marlin said. "And will you go shopping with me after work? You don't need to buy a new dress, but I do."

Lauren went back to eating her ice cream when her phone rang again. This time it was her mom saying she was sure they'd left the lights on in the garage, if Lauren could go check on it at her convenience. Knowing the breaker panel was complicated, Lauren wasn't surprised. She finished her ice cream and rode her bike toward her grandmother's house, expecting to be gone only a few minutes and home in plenty of time before dark.

SETH WAS SUPPOSED to be off-duty, but one of the other firefighters called in sick. Teddy was having dinner with the chief's family for the third time that summer, which wasn't a disaster, and Teddy liked Chief Bear's son, Jimmy, and his playhouse in the backyard. But Seth still preferred spending his evenings with his son at home, relishing the time before school and homework and shared custody interfered.

The call over the fire station's loudspeaker came in as a garage fire and Seth listened attentively, already heading to his equipment locker and grabbing gear, mentally preparing for all the hazards associated with that kind of fire. Was it attached to a home? Did it have an electric car with a volatile battery? Were there gas cans stored for a lawn mower?

All those concerns vanished in a flash of pure adrenaline when he heard the dispatcher give the address. Nanna Vera's house. In a terrible repeat of the call over six weeks ago, Seth sped out of the station and headed for the home he knew so well. Chief Bear was next to him in the cab.

"Ask the dispatcher if the residents are out of the house," Seth said.

"That's the house where the old lady—Vera Benedict—lived, right? It's probably empty."

"Her family was in town this week—for Lauren Benedict's award. They could be staying there."

Bear picked up the radio and asked the dispatcher for additional details, including who had called in the fire.

"It was called in by Lauren Benedict and she confirmed there were no people inside," the dispatcher said.

Just hearing Lauren's name made Seth push harder on the accelerator. The Benedict family might be physically safe, but the home of his childhood memories was not. He knew too well how attached garages tended to take the whole house when they caught fire.

When he came into view of the house, black smoke was already rolling off the garage roof. Lauren had a garden hose in one hand, shielding her face from the heat with the other, as she attempted to hose down the neighbor's garage so it wouldn't catch fire. She was alone. Had her parents and sister left town?

"Lauren," Seth yelled when he'd parked the truck by a nearby hydrant. "Get back!" The crew in the truck behind him was already hooking a large hose to the hydrant and Chief Bear was at the pump. Lauren's garden hose was no match for the flames breaking through the closed garage door, and Seth couldn't tolerate any bystander in danger—especially one he loved.

He swallowed. The heat rolled off the burning structure in waves, but he had a moment of cool clarity. Yes, he had loved Lauren in the past. And then he'd lost her love and tried to forget her. But this summer had brought his childhood memories back into focus and Lauren back into his life. The past six weeks had been about rediscovering Lauren and finding out who she was now, but always through the lens of the person he'd known and the question of *what if.*

He didn't care about any of that anymore. All he could think about was a future where he and Lauren could be together. This house should be hers. He had to save it for her.

"Electric," Lauren said over the noise of more approaching sirens. "I think it's electric because Grandma had this sketchy electrical panel from the Dark Ages that she used as basically a light switch. My parents left an hour ago for the airport, and I bet they flipped the wrong thing."

"I'll get the power company on standby in case we need to cut the power," Seth said. He relayed the information to the chief, amazed at himself for having a totally rational conversation at a fire scene with the woman he'd just realized he was deeply in love with.

Lauren gave him a long look and then crossed her arms and stared at the burning garage. Of course she was devastated, but she wasn't crying. She looked stoic. He'd seen it plenty of times, people finding a strange calm within themselves even while facing a fire or car accident or medical emergency. He'd even seen it in Lauren herself after the hornet encounter. Seth knew that, in most cases, the calm was actually shock and people fell apart later.

He wanted to hug her now and be there for her later when the tears came.

But right now he had a job to do. The garage was a loss, but they could save the house that held so many happy memories. Seth and another firefighter opened hoses and doused flames, just as they'd been trained to do and had done dozens of times before. It was his job, but it felt personal.

Another firefighter pointed to the eaves of the house near the garage where smoke curled from under the roof.

"Not good," the chief said. "We need to get in the house and attack from inside or we're just going to drive the flames into the house."

Lauren had retreated to a corner of the yard, but Seth trudged over to her in his heavy fire boots. "Is the front door unlocked?" Of course, they could break it down, something they often had to do, but it would be easier to get inside without doing that, and their goal was to minimize damage to the structure.

Lauren pulled out a key. "Want me to unlock it?"

"No," Seth said. He held out his hand and Lauren put the key to her grandmother's house into his palm.

"Don't risk your life or anyone else's. It's just a house," she said.

Seth curled his fingers around the key. "We have protocols. We'll save the house if we can."

It seemed so sterile, reducing that very special home to the status of a protocol. He meant so much more than just those words. He hesitated only another moment and then stalked over to the chief where they made their plan of attack.

An hour later, the flames were out. The garage was reduced to black, smoldering, wet wood hanging off the house like an ugly shadow. But the rest of the house had been saved. With the garage practically leveled, there was a clear view of the backyard garden, where flowers bloomed despite the devastation. He was glad the garden was untouched.

Lauren had watched from across the street, but Seth was conscious of her standing over there. His department was on cleanup duty, clearing enough debris to make sure the fire was truly out, and then gathering equipment and securing the scene. The power company had shown up and cut the current, and the local police were there blocking street traffic.

Everyone was doing something except Lauren, who just watched. Seth caught Bear's attention and nodded across the street. "Go ahead," the chief said.

Seth took slow steps toward Lauren. He wanted her to see him coming so he didn't blindside her. She'd had enough surprises for one night. It was dark and the evening air was cool all around them. It was too early for stars, but the birds and insects were already making their night sounds.

"Hey," Seth said gently.

Lauren tried to smile at him. "Thanks for doing everything you could."

"I'm sorry."

"Don't be. It wasn't your fault. Grandma should have fixed the electrical years ago, but she was used to it and knew how to navigate it."

Seth reached out and touched her arm.

"I had a lot of time to think about that while I watched you fight the flames," Lauren said.

"The damage to the house is mostly smoke and water and mostly just the mudroom area. It can be repaired if you and the cat want to move in."

She shook her head. "We're not moving in. My parents offered it to me, but I already turned them down. I like my apartment and my life. Grandma is gone, and I can't re-create the past by moving into her house, even though sometimes I wish I could. Parts of it anyway."

"The good parts," Seth agreed.

Lauren nodded. "But even the good parts are in the past."

Seth suspected what was coming next. Lauren was finally ready to move on. From her childhood memories. From her beloved grandmother's house. From him.

He had to do something. He'd let her slip away years ago and had never put up any kind of a fight for himself and what he wanted. He spent all his time helping other people, saving lives and property, but he'd never made an effort to save himself.

"I have to tell you something," he said. "And this may be the wrong time to say it, and I know your day has already been chaos. There may never be a perfect time, but I have to take a chance."

For the first time since he'd rolled up in the fire truck, Lauren's expression looked alive. Interested. Not the faraway shocked look she'd worn as she watched the fire.

It gave him hope.

"Your sister was right. I did love you back then. A lot of time has passed, but even if I'd just met you for the first time at the beginning of this summer, I would have fallen in love with you—with who you are now. I would have fallen in love with the woman who stood her ground on my front lawn even when I was too stubborn to accept her apology. I would have fallen in love with the flower lady who brought joy to my son. I would have fallen in love with the brave woman who battled the hornets and saved someone's life. I would have fallen in love with the person who believed I could plant a garden and keep it alive. That's the person I fell in love with this summer," Seth said.

Lauren had not shed a single tear as she watched her grandmother's home in flames, but tears glistened in her eyes now.

"I love you, Lauren. We'll always have the past, but we can have the present, too. And the future."

He held his breath. Behind him he heard the sound of one fire truck driving away, and the buzz of radio traffic through the open cab of another truck. But all he wanted to hear was one sentence from Lauren.

She reached up and brushed her fingertips over his forehead. She smiled as she showed him the smudged ash she'd swiped away. "I don't know how long it takes someone to fall in love, and I can't separate loving you then from loving you now. And I don't think I have to. I'm in love with the man who planted a garden this summer out of pure love."

Seth thought his heart would burst from happiness. He pulled Lauren close and held her until it occurred to him how smelly and filthy his fire coat was. "Sorry," he said. "You're going to smell like smoke now."

She smiled. "I'll get used to it. It's who you are."

"Confession. I planted that garden out of love for Teddy, yes. But I also couldn't quite resist communicating with you. I was afraid to let even one tiny ray of you into my life at first, but then the crack kept getting wider until I started holding it open for you. I loved your notes and the way you could imagine a garden, picturing something before it even happened. It's part of who you are, and you shared it with me and Teddy."

"I love him, too," Lauren said. "He has all your sweetness and love of the outdoors."

"He adores you," Seth said. He put his hands on both her cheeks, and she put her hands over his, not minding how dirty he was.

Lauren tilted her face up and kissed him, and the kiss was longer and sweeter than the ones they'd shared during the fireworks on Independence Day. Seth didn't care that his boss and coworkers were behind him cleaning up a fire scene. For all he knew, all the neighbors on the street were watching. All he knew was that he loved Lauren Benedict and she loved him.

She broke the kiss and leaned back but smiled at him. She had a smudge of black soot on her nose and Seth wiped it off.

"Now what do we do?" she asked.

"I'm going to make sure you get home safely tonight, even if you have to ride in the fire truck."

"Can I do that?"

He shrugged. "Sometimes we let family members ride in the truck."

She kissed him again and took his hand. "Are you saying I'm your family?"

"You are, and you always have been."

CHAPTER TWENTY-ONE

"We were all set to use the wedding chapel in the hotel because I was afraid to count on the weather at the end of July," Marlin said. "I didn't want an afternoon thunderstorm wrecking our big day, but this weather is actually perfect and I'm really glad we're outside."

Lauren laughed and adjusted the small veil—thrifted along with a dress from a secondhand shop just off downtown—that sat on Marlin's dark hair. "I've seen dozens of weddings at the falls," she said, "but I've never been an official guest."

"Or a maid of honor," Marlin said.

"I thought I was just a witness, only here to make it legal."

Marlin grinned. "I elevated your status now that the weather is perfect."

"I'll take it."

"Plus we're having a slightly bigger wedding than I originally planned, which is why I ended up getting help from a local wedding planner—

Minnie from Falling for You. Do you know her? She took care of all the details."

"She's great. I'm so happy for you," Lauren said, giving her friend a hug.

"Wait until you hear the vows I wrote. I admit I cried a little when I wrote the part about finding my soulmate," Marlin said.

Lauren glanced over at Seth, who had shown up in his firefighter's uniform with Teddy by the hand. Seth caught her eye and came over and gave her a kiss on the temple.

"Sorry I barely got here in time," he said.

"You're perfect," Lauren said. She knelt and pinned a flower on Teddy, who had been persuaded to be the ring bearer at the wedding that now consisted of at least three dozen guests—the bride's parents, the groom's brother and parents—they'd decided to invite his family after all—and coworkers from the state park.

"Sparky wanted to come but Daddy said no," Teddy said.

"Actually, I said I don't know if dogs enjoy weddings," Seth said. "But I do know that dogs enjoy walks, and we'll go get him after the wedding for a walk along the falls."

"With you," Teddy added.

"You are all adorable, but this is my wedding so you need to tone it down," Marlin said. She grinned but then held a hand over her mouth. "I'm suddenly nervous and I feel a little sick."

"Deep breaths," Lauren said. She made waving motions. "Inhale the fresh misty air of Niagara Falls. Remember we're in the honeymoon capital of the world. You can't go wrong getting married in the land of honeymoons and rainbows."

Marlin closed her eyes and breathed deeply. Without opening her eyes, she said, "You're right. I feel better. I'm ready."

Behind them, they overheard Darren talking to his brother. "Wait until you hear the vows I wrote. I sound all gushy, but I swear Marlin is my soulmate."

Marlin put a hand over her heart. "See what I mean?" she said to Lauren.

Lauren laughed. "Go get married so I can play my official role."

Lauren stood next to Seth and Teddy and watched as the bride's father took her hand ceremonially and gave it to Darren. They were all standing at the top of the Bridal Veil Falls. Wildflowers bloomed around them and the falls provided the background music for the short laid-back ceremony.

"Everyone is meeting for dinner later," Lauren said to Seth when the ceremony ended and the bride and groom kissed. "But we have time for that walk with Sparky first."

"Ice cream?" Teddy asked, pointing toward the snack stand.

Seth smiled at his son and ruffled his hair. "Sure, but I want you to order your own while I stay right here with Miss Lauren."

"Can I get anything I want?"

"Anything you order yourself," Seth said. He gave Teddy some cash and said, "We'll be right here where we can see you."

"I'll be right back," Teddy said. He clutched the cash in his fist and practically ran to the vendor, which was close enough to them that Lauren could overhear the other patrons placing their orders.

"He's come a long way this summer," Lauren said. "From hardly talking to ordering his own ice cream."

"It's been a great summer, and we still have one more month until Teddy goes back to school." Seth took her hand. "We've made up for a lot of lost time."

"Don't think of it that way," Lauren said.

"Okay, but I don't want to lose any more time. I want to be with you, Lauren. You, me and Teddy can be a family if you'll only say the word."

She smiled and gave him a quick kiss. "Would the word be *yes*?"

Seth glanced at his son, who was already coming back with a giant ice cream cone leaning precariously to one side.

"We're a package deal," Seth said.

"Does that include Sparky?"

"And Lord Henry."

Lauren smiled. "Then my answer is yes. I believe the five of us will be very happy together."

Seth leaned in for a kiss but made a quick pivot and saved Teddy's ice cream cone from hitting the ground. He parked Teddy on a bench and spread napkins on his lap.

"I've seen a lot of weddings here at the falls," Lauren said. "Big, fancy ones with billowing dresses and veils, orchestras, huge wedding parties, tents, tall cakes. And I've seen plenty of small fun ones, including a picnic-themed one a year ago."

Seth waited, taking her hands in his but also keeping an eye on his son.

"I haven't seen anyone get married in my new rose garden yet, though."

"Then I think it's time," Seth said.

"I just cut a bunch of them back, which means they're going to rebloom even better than before in about two weeks."

Seth kissed her. "I don't want to wait another

day to marry you, but I can wait two weeks if it makes the flower lady happy."

Lauren smiled at her childhood friend who had unexpectedly blossomed into her future husband over the course of a very eventful summer. "It makes me very happy," she said.

* * * * *